D1531093

ALSO BY JUS ACCARDO

Infinity

THE DENAZEN SERIES
Touch
Untouched
Toxic
Faceless
Tremble

THE DARKER AGENCY SERIES
Darker Days
A Darker Past

FOR NEW ADULT READERS
Ruined
Released
Embraced
Rules of Survival

omega

JUS ACCARDO

This book is a work of fiction. Names, characters, places, and incidents are the product of the author's imagination or are used fictitiously. Any resemblance to actual events, locales, or persons, living or dead, is coincidental.

Entangled Publishing, LLC
2614 South Timberline Road
Suite 109
Fort Collins, CO 80525

Entangled Teen is an imprint of Entangled Publishing, LLC.

Visit our website at www.entangledpublishing.com.

Edited by Stacy Abrams
Cover design by LJ Anderson, Mayhem Cover Creations
Interior design by Toni Kerr

ISBN 9781633758254
Ebook ISBN 9781633758247

Manufactured in the United States of America

First Edition August 2017

10 9 8 7 6 5 4 3 2 1

For the readers. All the readers in all the places…
Thank you from the bottom of my heart ♥

Chapter One

Noah

Live your life in vivid color.

That was what Kori's—my sister-from-another-world's-mister—new tattoo said. I didn't disapprove. Personally, I loved ink. Had a few of my own, though nothing quite so lame... No, what pissed me off was the situation it had put us in.

"Get down!" Something tackled me from behind and drove us both into the dirt as a spray of gunfire assaulted the earth at my feet. Dust and debris kicked up, getting into my eyes and mouth. This damn world tasted like sardines.

"Why the hell are they shooting at us, *Noah*?" My best friend Cade rolled off me and shimmied to a safe spot behind a parked van. Glass shattered above us, a million tiny pieces raining down on our heads like New Year's Eve confetti.

"Why are you asking me?" I growled and ducked as another hail of gunfire came. This time it hit the street sign a few feet away, the echoing ping of metal against metal ringing in my ears. "All I did was ask for a goddamned cheeseburger."

Kori's eyes grew wide and her mouth fell open. It was an expression I was becoming annoyingly accustomed to when it came to me. "On a world that *outlawed* meat?"

Okay. Maybe the tattoo wasn't *one hundred percent* to blame for the situation…

"How was I supposed to know that?" The guy had just bandaged her new ink and my stomach growled. Loud and unavoidable. All I'd done was ask where I could get a decent burger. You would have thought I'd requested a pound of toddler tartar with a nice big side of kitten sorbet.

Cade shook the glass from his hair, then reached over and carefully pulled a piece from Kori's. His lips tilted upward and it was like the guy forgot about the chaos raging all around us. Gunfire and imminent danger? *Pssh*. Who cared about that shit? "You need to be more careful." He was talking to me, but he was looking at her.

He was *always* looking at her.

"He was hungry," came Kori's reply. She, like him, was equally lost, grinning like a jackass as bullets bounced off the building to our left and right and shouting voices in the not so distant area called for our heads. "He doesn't think clearly when he's hungry."

Cade rolled his eyes and his grin widened. "When is he not hungry?" He glanced down at his ankle and relief settled over his features. I knew why. I'd felt it, too. The smallest rise in temperature from the cuff—the thing that allowed us to travel between dimensions—that signaled the main cuff had just been activated. We would be pulled along shortly, ready or not. They were linked together. Where it went, we went—which was fine with me.

We had a score to settle with the asshole wearing it.

"Just have to hold out a few minutes more." Cade and I had slapped on the cuffs and willingly left our home behind to chase after his brother, Dylan, after he killed my sister in an attempt to exact revenge on the people he felt had wronged him—Cade and our father included. He'd promised to wipe her away completely. Erase her from existence by killing every single version of Kori Anderson he could find.

At first we failed. Over and over, I helplessly watched girls who walked, talked, and looked like my sister die. They fell like dominos, one after another in baths of bloody carnage…until we found *her*.

"Oh my God. Hurry it up!" Kori tapped her own cuff, the one Dylan snapped around her wrist when he'd found her on her earth, against the side of the van. "Is this thing even on?"

"Yeah. Smart move. Smack it into submission. That's exactly how you treat a highly advanced piece of scientific equipment." Truthfully, though, I'd done the same damn thing a hundred times before. We were so much alike. Cade joked that the universe didn't need two of me, and he was right.

When it came to perfection, obviously two wasn't nearly enough.

With our arrival on her earth, this Kori had learned about the existence of the Infinity Division and inter-dimensional travel, her parents' role in it all, and that she'd had a brother, a Noah of her own, who died before being born. She'd gotten caught up in the whole thing and had been forced to skip with us. She was handling it pretty well, all things considered.

"That's three worlds in a row now." I slid down the side of

the van and settled on the ground beside her as the team of Animal-Ingestion officers—seriously, that's what the idiots called themselves—shouted from the other side of the road. "We've only been here, like, what? Six hours? Not enough time for Dylan to do what he needs to do."

What he needs to do.

Kill Kori to punish Cade and my father, the army general who refused his request to skip off and find his dead girlfriend, Ava, and the three council members, Miles Hann, Penny Bloom, and Odette Ferguson, responsible for locking him away and calling for his head.

And people said *I* had issues.

Footsteps pounded against the pavement, getting closer. A second later, they surrounded us, guns at the ready, and… nothing. The cuff heated through my threadbare sock and I felt slightly dizzy. It didn't last long, though, and when it was all over the men were gone and we were in the middle of a downpour.

"Well that's fantastic," Cade grumbled and waved his hand.

I spread my arms wide and let out a hoot. "Come on, man. This is way better than desert Wells."

"Now what? Should we start looking for—" Kori glanced down at her wrist, frowning. "No way…"

He'd just activated the cuff again.

Cade slicked his hair back and flicked water in every direction. "Maybe he ran into trouble? Wouldn't be the first time we got dumped into a hostile territory."

"No way, man. It's the cuff." We knew there was something wrong with it. Dylan had all but admitted it a few skips ago. "Come on." I took off across the street and wedged myself next to a large stone building with a small overhang. It wouldn't block the rain completely, but it gave us a bit of shelter. Cade and Kori did the same. All we could do now was avoid trouble while we waited to be dragged along to whatever new nightmare was out there.

I gathered the edge of my shirt and twisted, ringing out as much rainwater as I could and trying hard to ignore my best friend and my...sister? Sort-of sister? I had no damn clue what I was supposed to call her. Didn't know what I *wanted* to call her... What I did know was that our relationship was complicated.

I found myself oscillating between keeping her out and wanting to let her in. I'd been close to my biological sister. So close that when I lost her, I lost my bearings in the world. In the universe. She'd been my true north. The voice of reason when Cade and I waded into water too deep. We'd both lost a part of our souls when she died, but the healing had begun, and even though I refused to admit it to them, this Kori had a lot to do with it. She was nothing like my sister in most ways but shared a kind of light and a capacity for love and loyalty that was the very essence of who Kori had been.

Her relationship with Cade was off kilter, too. On again, off again, hot and cold. Icy and volcanic. If only the two idiots could see what I saw. Realize they could have something amazing if they'd just get out of their own damn way. They fit together in a way that my sister and Cade never had, and despite the pain of what I'd lost, I was glad for him. For both of them...

"Jesus Christ. If you two—" With a single blink of my eyes and the slightest churn of my gut, the rain was gone. The sun was out and the sidewalks that seconds ago were dark and deserted, now teemed with late afternoon life.

Kori groaned. "How the hell are we supposed to stop Dylan if he keeps skipping like this?"

"I dunno, but I'm starving. Gonna grab something to eat."

I started in the opposite direction, but only got two steps before Kori jumped out in front of me. "What happens if he skips while we're separated? How will we find you?"

"Kori." Cade came up beside her and took her hand. "We've never stayed glued to each other's side. We'd never be able to track down the Tribunal that way." His jaw tightened. The Tribunal, the three people responsible for handing down his brother's death sentence for trying to misguidedly save his dead girl, were a deeply buried sore spot for Cade. He wanted to save the innocent versions of them, but I knew deep down he was raw over what happened at home. His expression relaxed a little and he smiled. "Plus, all Noah all the time? Even I'm not that big of a saint…"

I flipped him off and fought a grin. We both knew it was total bullshit. Cade was the only one who'd ever been able to take my shit on a daily basis. The guy had the patience of a saint on Prozac. After a four-day bender… "If we ever get separated—during or after a skip—we meet at the Doon."

She didn't look convinced, but Cade tugged her aside so I could pass. Sometimes I just needed some space. He understood that. In those first days after we'd left home, the grief, the anger…it'd been hard on us both. Still was. But we each dealt with it in a different way. Alone time was mine. "If we're still here in a couple of hours, find a place to hunker down for the night. Text me."

I surveyed the streets as I went, looking for the differences. In some worlds it was obvious. Horses instead of cars. Oddly colored pebbles instead of pavement. Other times the differences were less noticeable. Overall diet of the population or the extinction of a species. In one world, cats disappeared somewhere in the eighteenth century and were viewed like unicorns. In another world, business suits were made out of plaid and everyone was required by law to wear their hair cut above the neck. And who the hell could forget meatless world… *shudder.*

A woman passed, giving a friendly nod as she held tight to her kid. So far everything looked normal. Still, the rule was to proceed with caution. Observe before speaking or interacting. We'd learned that the hard way when trying to buy coffee with cash on an entirely cash-free world. Cade ordered a bagel and forked over a twenty. The proprietor nearly shit himself.

I spotted a brightly colored phone booth ahead. Back home they'd been gone since the eighties, but once in a while we saw one. I passed it and kept going, ignoring the tattered phone book peeking out from the small shelf below. I wanted to stop, but fought the urge. We had to get the cuff mess figured out. Usually the first thing we did was look ourselves up; it'd come in handy a few times. The last few skips, though, we hadn't bothered. Since it'd become obvious that things were out of whack, Dylan didn't seem to be going after his normal targets. Lately we just jumped in and kept focused on trying to track *him* down. Well, Cade did. I always found time for a side mission.

Ashlyn Calvert.

A flash of dark eyes and long hair swept through my mind and made my heart beat a little bit faster. The image of a phantom, of a hauntingly beautiful girl with an addictive laugh. She was what Cade called a constant. The bullshit name he'd given to the unrelated people who showed up linked in multiple realities. Cade was one of mine: we had yet to find an earth that we both existed on and weren't friends.

Ash was the other.

When I first saw her, the idea intrigued me. I'd never been lacking in the female attention department, but I'd also never gotten serious with anyone. I tended to sabotage things when they started getting heavy. There was no way any girl out there would put up with me long-term. I was too abrasive. Too rough. I had plans to go to med school and had no interest in tying myself to someone in any kind of monogamous capacity. There was no reason to get invested in something that had no chance and I was fine with that — until I started seeing multiple versions of myself with her.

With each new skip I'd looked for her. Night after night I'd slip away from Cade and search. When she was there, I sought her out even if I only got a quick glimpse of the life she led. It continued for months, becoming almost as much of an obsession as making Dylan pay for what he'd done to my sister. But then I started to wonder what the hell I was doing. What good did finding her, over and over, do? Spying on her like some freaking pervert. One day Cade and I *would* be going home. And Ash Calvert didn't exist there as far as I knew.

The first time I found her in a world I hadn't existed on, I approached her. It was spontaneous — like most of the things I did — and hadn't gone as planned. Also like most of the things I did...

I'd intended to say hello, see what the fuss was about, and be on my way. If I could talk to her, see that she was no big deal, I could stop the insanity and move the hell on with my existence. But the chemistry between us had been explosive and we'd hooked up. It'd been crazy and mind blowing—and I couldn't live with that. Couldn't be tied to that. Naturally, I did what I always did when it came to relationships.

I picked it apart and found all the ways that she was wrong for me.

Whenever I started to waffle, I sought her out. The end result was always the same. Cade was right about that. The universe had designed us with some insane pull toward each other, but it was physical and nothing more. Just some kind of ramped-up freaky pheromone thing. I'd proved that time and time again by walking away.

I stuffed my hands into the pockets of my coat and slowed as a familiar sensation crept up my leg. "You've gotta be kidding me…" The cuff heated—only this time the skip was nearly instant.

I was standing at the edge of the park, same as I'd been a second ago, only now there was a tall wrought-iron fence where the crumbling rock wall had been. Just beyond the fence, movement caught my attention. I stepped up, squinting against the growing darkness. It took a minute for my vision to acclimate, but when it did, I saw *him*. "Bastard…"

I stepped back and leaped at the fence, grabbing hold and wedging my foot into the curling design. Several less than graceful moves and I was over the side and hitting the ground.

Dylan saw me and grinned. With a flip of his finger, he took off toward the woods and disappeared into the foliage.

Feet relentlessly pounding the earth, I raced across the field and darted for the trees. I remember the large branches overhead blotting out what little light remained, and the thunder of my heartbeat echoing inside my head. There was a cocky laugh and a rustle of material, then everything went dark.

Chapter Two

Ash

I tugged my jacket just a bit tighter and pulled the sleeves down over my fingers. The faint scent of the buttery leather was comforting—which was something I needed. There was a very real chance I might vomit.

It was nearing November, and the bitter cold had come early this year. It kind of sucked since I was staying someplace sans electric. If tonight went badly, though, electricity would be the least of my problems.

I crushed the piles of dead leaves beneath my feet to stave off some of the silence. I'd come to the Doon to meet a guy—and not for recreational purposes—but he was late and I was starting to think he wouldn't show.

Crunch. Crunch. Crunch. I stomped my foot until all the leaves beneath me were reduced to crumbles. Next, I started picking at the loose thread at the hem of my shirt. It was stupid. This was one of my last good ones. Since getting booted from my home, and cut off financially from my surrogate family, I was running on fumes. A new wardrobe wasn't in the cards.

Thankfully—or, depending on how you looked at things, unthankfully—just when I was about to give up, the faint crunching of footsteps sliced through the silence.

"Ash?" someone whispered from the darkness. A few moments later, a familiar boy with brown hair and linebacker shoulders stepped into the moonlight. He stopped in the middle of the clearing and spun in a slow circle beside a large rock.

My heart hammered at light speed, and as I stepped out from behind the side of the tree, I had to remind myself to breathe. An insane moment of panic tempted me to step back into the shadows and run away as fast as my feet could carry me. But that wouldn't do me any good. I had to face this thing head on. I had one shot and this was it. "I'm here."

He made a move to come closer, but hesitated. It made sense. I was like a raging forest fire these days. Venture too close and you'd be incinerated. "It was a huge gamble calling me out, ya know?"

"I know, Corey." I swallowed the growing lump of fear that threatened to choke me.

"Why did you even think I'd come?"

"I didn't, but you're here, so…" Honestly, I was beyond surprised he'd come. But, I'd had to try something. My best friend was dead and my life was in shambles. If there was a chance to fix it, albeit minute, I had to try. "Thanks for coming. I know you must hate me—"

"I don't hate you, Ash. I don't really know how to feel about you. Never did. Things with you have always been… weird."

I bit down hard on the inside of my cheek. To keep from crying? Maybe just a little. The Anderson family took me in when I was just ten years old. Cora and Karl had been cold and distant, viewing me as nothing more than a publicity stunt, and their sons? Things got even murkier there. Corey and I had never hit it off. He'd always regarded me as more of an annoyance he had to put up with than an extension of his family. But his brother Noah? We'd clicked from moment one. He'd been my best friend. My rock. The one person who'd always had my back.

And now he was dead, and I felt like the entire world had been yanked out from underneath me. His being gone was bad enough, but the way it happened? The questions surrounding it—those were unbearable.

"Look." He stuffed his hands into his pockets and dropped his gaze to the ground. "I don't know exactly what happened between you and my brother, but whatever it was, no one really believes he'd kill himself over it."

The fact that anyone would ever think that a guy like Noah Anderson would commit suicide was the most ludicrous thing in the world. And over someone like *me*? Sure. Maybe in an alternate universe.

I threw up my hands, a huge weight lifting from my shoulders. "That's what I've been trying to tell everyone."

He lifted his head, his gaze meeting mine. There was sadness there, but also intense anger. "They think he was killed."

Good. *Finally* someone was paying attention. I'd been saying this from day one. The whole thing was suspicious as hell. I'd spoken to him only hours before he was found. We'd arranged to hang out later that night. He'd said he wanted to talk… "There was something going on. He'd been acting weird, said he had something to tell me. Something—"

"They think *you* killed him, Ash."

Everything stilled and the world around me grew silent. The wind ceased and the twitching leaves all stilled. The faint sound of traffic died away and left nothing but dead air in its wake. A new kind of pain throbbed inside my chest.

Noah and I had been…complicated. We'd had this weird push-pull thing going from almost the moment I walked through the Andersons' front door. I was to him the freedom he so desperately wanted from his parents' world, and he was to me the sense of connection, of belonging that I'd never had. We'd had an almost instant bond, but as we grew older, something else began to simmer beneath the surface. We talked about it once. Acknowledged it and agreed that it wasn't something either of us ever wanted to explore. It'd be too weird, and neither one of us wanted to risk damaging the relationship that had become such a vital part of our sanity. But one moment changed all that. I was stupid.

I was selfish…

We'd been up late watching cheesy B-rated horror flicks—our Saturday night tradition. Sprawled out across his bed, popcorn all over the place. Noah's hand resting on my hip…slowly moving up and down. My fingers playing with strands of his hair. I turned to look at him, to point out the stereotypical stupidity of the movie's heroine. Our eyes met and my pulse went wild. I could still feel it sometimes. An erratic thumping that threatened to break me apart. My mouth went dry and every nerve ending turned into a live wire.

It wasn't like I'd never thought about it. A girl would have to be blind not to. But each and every time it crossed my mind, I spent days mentally flogging myself until the fantasy was gone and reality had replaced it. But in that instant I wanted—no, *needed*—to know what he tasted like.

He knew what I was thinking. Begged me not to do it. *Ash, don't...* I'll never forget the small noise of surrender that he made just a second before I pressed my lips to his. It wasn't anything worthy of a porn marathon. A lightweight make-out session that was interrupted when Cora, his mother, walked in.

The next morning was awkward, and we'd both agreed that it would *never* happen again. On the one hand, it made me a little sad. The kiss was great, but I lied. I told him it was weird and clunky and left me feeling all kinds of wrong. Even though I'd never seen him as a brother, he was my best friend. The one person in my life I couldn't bear to lose. I refused to put that in jeopardy for something purely physical. Because that's what it was. When the dust all cleared, I knew that there were no feelings there aside from friendship. It was all I wanted from him—and I refused to destroy it.

"*I* killed him?" I repeated. I tamped down the memories and the horrible ache that came with them and focused on the absurdity of his words. "And why—*how*—exactly could anyone come to that conclusion?"

A week after the kiss, Noah had started acting cagey. He was jumpy and on edge, and I'll admit it, a part of me worried that he was going to ask his parents to make me leave. I was concerned that maybe he didn't agree with the *hands-off* rule, and that my presence in the house was making him uncomfortable now that we'd crossed a line we could never come back from. But when I confronted him, I knew that wasn't the case.

"*I have to talk to you,*" he'd said. "*I found out something— something you need to know... Just give me a few days to get my facts straight.*"

Yeah. Three days later Noah was dead. *Suicide.*

He'd taken a handful of pills that had stopped his heart and left a note. It went into painful detail about his *real feelings* for me and how I'd rejected him. How he couldn't live with it anymore. Cora threw me out—despite my protests that his feelings—and the letter—were pure fabrication. Even if I had rejected him, Noah was too damn stubborn to give up on life over some stupid crush. But she'd *seen* the kiss. That single moment of weakness was all the fuel she'd needed to grant validity to that absurd letter.

"Mom told the police about your relationship. How he tried to end things and you lost it."

My mouth fell open. "What? That's not what happened and you know it! We didn't have a *relationship*. Not the way you're insinuating. He was my best friend." I fought back the tears threatening to spill and focused on the anger over his accusation. I couldn't let him see me fall apart. "What happened between us was a onetime thing—and it wasn't even a *thing*! It was a single freaking kiss."

But Corey didn't hear me. Didn't hear me, or didn't care. "She said he came to his senses. That he finally saw that you were using him."

I stared. Forget about the insanity of the *facts* she was basing this all on, but what on earth could I have used Noah Anderson for? "Using him *how*?"

"You're Bottom Tier, Ash. He was Top Tier. Someone like you will do anything to pull yourself out of the gutter. Your time was almost up and you were desperate."

The Tier system had been started by President Capone in 1934. The Top Tier, the cream of society, was given all the advantages. The best schools, the best education. They were allowed access to the best restaurants and clothing stores. The Mid-Tier were just below them. They were given access to moderate schooling, adequate food and clothing. They were prohibited from entering Top Tier establishments, but they fared well enough with their own.

Then there was the Bottom Tier. People like me were given the leftovers. All the hand-me-downs. All the shit that trickled downward? Yep. That's what we *deserved*. I'd been luckier than most. Each year one Top Tier family takes in a Bottom Tier orphan. They feed them, clothe them, and house them until they turn eighteen. After that they're unceremoniously dumped back into the Bottom Tier trash drawer, but for a few short years, they get to live the good life. Usually it's an infant. Some poor kid lost in the system. But for some reason, the Andersons chose me when I was ten.

"You know damn well that isn't true!" While he had a point—latching onto a Top Tier citizen had, in the past, lifted a Bottom Tier through the ranks—the thought had never occurred to me. "I made a mistake, okay? We kissed *once*. It wasn't like that with us." I couldn't help it. My voice shook.

He shook his head. "Doesn't matter what I think." There was a tremble in his shoulders and a quake in his tone. "You guys played your twisted little game. If you were content to let him use and destroy you, then far be it from me to intervene."

"Use me? Are you insane? It was one—"

"And for the record, I don't think you killed him, Ash. I think he killed himself. I think my brother was a highly disturbed individual with more problems that he could ever get help for."

That much was true, too. Noah Anderson had his demons—mainly when it came to family. He'd been known to dabble in recreational drugs and drank more than he should at times. He could be moody and dark and withdrawn, and he tended to take whatever toxic girl threw herself at him each week. But I'd always been there to drag him from the mire. He knew he could count on me just as I knew I could count on him.

At my side, my fingers twitched. I kept it together, though. Knocking the crap out of him probably wouldn't get me what I wanted. Corey wasn't a bad guy really, but he was blind as all hell. He didn't deal well with conflict. "You know better than that. Something was going on…and I think it had to do with Infinity."

He shifted from foot to foot. He stuffed his hands into his pocket, then a second later, pulled them out and began tapping his thigh. Code for *I'm uncomfortable and am looking for a chance to bail*. He glanced over his shoulder, then back to me. "I know what they do is a little controversial. Look, I have to—"

"Controversial?" Either Corey was knocking back the good drugs—which was actually the popular rumor these days from what I'd heard—or he was delusional. "Governments around the world pay them to skip criminals. They dump the worst of our society on the heads of unsuspecting others! If you ask me, I'd call it inter-dimensional terrorism. You know damn well how Noah felt about it. I think he found something and someone had him killed."

His eyes bulged. "Someone? As in, who? *My parents*? The people who took you in and fed and clothed you? Is that what you're saying?"

Was it? Cora and Karl had never liked me, and they treated their own children with a fair amount of detachment— but would they kill one? Just to preserve company secrets? There was a time I would have said no. Now? I wasn't so sure.

"I've got no idea what they're working on now, and honestly? I don't care. I don't care about your theories. I don't care about Infinity. My brother is dead and I just want to move forward." He sighed. Even if he believed me, he'd never say it. The guy had a notorious reputation for being spineless when it came to his parents. They said jump and he asked exactly how high. "You didn't call me out here to rag on my parents. What did you need?"

I'd come here to get his help looking into Noah's death, but it was obvious that wasn't going to happen. Maybe I could get something, though. "Ask your father to call this whole thing off."

"Whole thing?"

Like he didn't know exactly what I meant.

"This crusade to destroy my life." Losing what little fear I had left, I stalked forward and poked him hard in the chest, then thrust my upturned wrist at him. "Get him to repeal *this*."

They'd kicked me out, and that was fine. Despite living within the walls of their privilege, I'd learned how to fend for myself because I knew it wouldn't last forever. But kicking me out hadn't been enough. They'd demanded that I be *listed*. Listed individuals were outcasts. Branded by a black circle tattoo, we were shunned by society. Ghosts. It happened for many reasons and could only be repealed by a court of law—which would never happen. The Andersons *owned* the law. They were close personal friends of President Gotti and were therefore untouchable. They did what they wanted with whomever they wanted.

People were forbidden to interact with listed in any way, shape, or form. I could set myself on fire and walk into the middle of a crowded church, and because of the Andersons' power and push, no one would lift a finger to help me. The fact that Corey had even shown tonight was a miracle.

"Maybe he wasn't using you. Maybe *you* were using *him*. Maybe you destroyed him. He killed himself because of *you*. Something you said, something you did—who the hell knows." There was venom in his voice, but really, who could blame him? Corey and Noah Anderson were as different as night and day—but they'd been close.

In the days following Noah's death, rumors swirled about drug and alcohol abuse. There was talk about Corey not being able to hold it together. Looking at him now, I could see the change. The shift was heartbreaking. Always dressed to the nines and breaking hearts, but these days, the guy was lucky to shrug into clean clothes. His hair had grown out and, judging by the scruff on his face, he'd given up shaving.

"Listen to yourself." I ground my teeth and took a deep breath, trying hard to remind myself that he was hurting as much as I was. "Do you hear what you're saying? I crushed Noah? Really?" I threw up my hands and started to pace. "Open your eyes! Someone *killed* your brother. Don't you want to know who?"

"Look, it doesn't matter." He took another step back, almost as though he needed to put some distance between us like I was a time bomb waiting to detonate. There was fear in his eyes, and I had a feeling it wasn't because of me. "He's gone. Nothing you do or say—or *prove*—is going to change things. Not for you. Mom tolerated you because it made Infinity look good. Taking you in *humanized* the face of the company. Make no mistake, though. She *hates* you. Always did. I'm sure it was the last straw when she found you sticking your tongue down my brother's throat. If he hadn't died, she would have found a way to get rid of you before your eighteenth birthday."

My face heated and the involuntary sting of tears gathered in the corners of my eyes. I blinked it away and clenched my fists. "You know." I wasn't surprised. Not really. I'd known getting his help was a long shot. "You know your parents had something to do with his death. Am I the only one who loved him enough to see them brought to justice?"

He took another step back and exhaled slowly. "Maybe you could leave. Start over someplace else? Try covering the brand or something. I hear Canada doesn't have a Tier system."

Every step he took back, I matched with one forward. "Cover the brand?" A guy last year did that. When he was caught, they skipped him the next day. And while it might seem like a better alternative for someone like me, the rumor was, the pre-approved skipping worlds were worse than hell itself.

"You—"

"Corey Anderson?"

We both whirled around, surprised.

"That you?" the newcomer prodded. I had no idea who he was, but the guy standing there was taller than both of us by several inches with jet black hair and an almost wicked gleam in his eyes. The way his gaze traveled over Corey gave me the chills and had me taking a subtle step backward. He squinted and came a little closer. "This is damn near hysterical—and a first. You're a dude!"

Corey glanced at me, then back to the stranger. "Um, thank you for noticing? You're not really my type though…"

The guy frowned and stuffed a hand into his pocket. "I gotta be honest, man. That's gonna take some of the joy out of this." He shrugged. "But, we all have to sacrifice, am I right?"

He pulled his hand free and flicked his wrist in our general direction. At first I didn't realize what had happened. I mean, I saw something flash in the rising moonlight and fly toward us, but I thought he'd simply tossed something to Corey.

He hadn't. He'd tossed something *at* him.

Corey clutched his throat, almost like he was choking. The guy laughed. No. *Laughed* was the wrong word. Chortled. He was hacking it up like someone had slipped him a half dozen happy pills and a beer to chase them with. It was almost infectious…

Until I saw the blood.

It was a single trickle at first, slipping past Corey's fingers to trail down his neck. Mesmerized, I watched as it hit the collar of his shirt, soaking in and staining the light blue material. Then came more. So much more. My heart hammered and I opened my mouth to scream, but no sound came. I could only stare, helpless, as he dropped to his knees, hands still wrapped around his neck as the blood flowed like a river. His wide eyes bulged as he looked up at me, lips parted just a bit as he fell to the ground with a gurgling sound that I'd never forget.

I was torn between trying to help him—even though I knew he was far beyond that now—and running like hell. We'd never been close, but I'd watched Corey Anderson grow up. From a pudgy faced boy to a strikingly handsome young man with an unreal talent for art. "Oh my… What did you do?"

The guy shrugged like it was no big thing. Like he hadn't just slit the throat of one of the town's most prominent sons.

"Only what I promised." He focused on me as I took a step back. I couldn't help it. My gaze flickered to Corey, bleeding into the dirt, and I shuddered. "And look at you. Getting all cozy with the wrong brother."

Another step. A part of me wondered if this weirdo wasn't a stranger but rather Corey's dealer. Maybe he hadn't paid up. "Whatever your beef with Corey was, I've got nothing to do with it." I wasn't confident that I could outrun him. "I was never here. You were never here." *Breathe. Focus on getting away.*

My gaze drifted down to Corey's still form one last time. He hadn't hated me like his parents, but he'd never viewed me as an equal, either. To him, I was always and only ever the Bottom Tier girl his parents had forced him to share his home with. It wasn't his fault. It was how he'd been raised.

There was just enough light to see the growing puddle of darkness beneath him, spreading out and soaking into the dirt. Dead. Corey was dead. This guy had killed him. Right in front of me. No one—not a Bottom Tier or Top Tier, as bad as most were—deserved to die like that.

"You know, normally I'd be okay with letting you walk away. It's the general and Cade who burned me, and where I'm from, you're not important. But Noah recently moved up on my shit list. He's not far behind, and something tells me he'll come looking for you... He always does." He snickered again. "Yeah. I think this can work."

I didn't ask what *this* was. Something told me he didn't want to bake me a cake. And what this had to do with Noah, I couldn't even imagine. He had his fair share of enemies— being one of the richest, most sought after guys in town did have some drawbacks. And he did have a tendency to mess around with other guys' girlfriends, but none of that had anything to do with me. As for the general? I had no idea who that was and no intention of asking.

Breathe…

I let my hand fall slack at my side, then slowly reached into my pocket. The cool metal of my keys brushed the tips of my fingers, and with a few careful twitches of my pointer, I found what I was looking for.

"I can make it quick. You won't feel a thing."

"Wish I could say the same thing about you." I whipped my hand from my pocket and pressed the aerosol nozzle on the small bottle of pepper spray Noah had insisted I carry. I might not be an Anderson, but I'd lived with them. There was a small portion of the population who didn't worship the ground they walked on. The same group of people who protested the way our government worked and its policies of law enforcement, the ones who vehemently opposed the Tier system. It didn't matter that I was one of them, or that I agreed with everything they stood for. Nope. I lived with the Andersons so I was just as bad, eating their food and wearing their clothes. Sitting pretty under their arched ceilings and marble trim walls.

The guy cursed and doubled over, clawing at his eyes. As soon as he was down, I brought my knee up as hard as I could and smashed it into his forehead.

As he cursed some more and flailed, I took off. I didn't need to look behind me to know he was already in pursuit, though. The crackling leaves and furious grunts were warning enough. "Hey," I roared. My voice echoed off the trees, a booming sound against the silence of the night. "Anyone! Help!" It was stupid. No one was out in the woods at night. No one except stupid, desperate girls who should have known better.

I came to the boulders at the head of the Doon and made a sharp right, almost toppling over as I went. My heart hammered and despite the chill in the air, I was sweating like a pig. I threw myself down the path that led to the lake. Sometimes some of the older listed camped out. The chances of aid were slim—even among my fellow outcasts—but I'd take my chances.

My pulse was erratic and the blood rushed in my head. I banked hard and pushed forward, pumping my legs as fast as I could. Breath coming in short, uneven gasps, I grabbed the trunk of a thin tree and propelled myself around. I stumbled and went down, my right knee knocking into something solid. Stars exploded behind my eyes and involuntary tears stung the corners.

Body-numbing fear bubbled up in my gut and turned my vision watery. But, despite the near paralyzing terror, I picked myself up and ran.

Chapter Three

Noah

I forced my eyes open and turned my head, getting a mouthful of dirt and a serious case of vertigo for the effort. When it passed and everything stopped swimming, I picked myself up off the ground. I was alone. That bastard had taken me down with a dirty punch—though who was I kidding? If I hadn't charged in like a mindless asshole it never would have happened.

I started walking toward the Doon. Had to find Cade and Kori. This was a new level of bad. The cuff had officially gone ape-shit and I had no idea what that meant for us. An instantaneous skip? That had disaster written all over it. What if it stopped working completely? Would we all be stuck wherever we landed? Would Dylan be able to move on without us? My mind spun with the possibilities, but more than that, with anger. I'd had him in my sights and failed.

Again.

I made it to the clearing where, on our world, a small playground had been erected to honor some dude who'd saved a bunch of people in an apartment complex fire. At least, that was the official story. The truth was he'd been trying to rob one of the apartments and set off the alarm, not realizing the building was burning and the fire detection system was broken. On this earth, instead of a collection of swings and monkey bars, there was a lake.

Walking to the edge, I peered into the water. The moon was full and I barely recognized the guy looking back up at me. He was tired and scruffy for all the wrong reasons. A wave of grief rolled through me. Right now I was supposed to be backpacking across Europe with Cade and Kori. One last hurrah before heading off to med school. We'd had it planned forever, even got the general to promise Cade the time off. Instead I was skipping from one dimension to another hunting down the bastard who gutted my life like the belly of a fish.

I sank down between two bushes, balancing on the heels of my worn boots, and dipped my fingers into the water. It was icy, yet refreshing. It used to drive Kori crazy. She hated the cold, while I thrived in it. "I'll get him," I said to my reflection. "If it takes the rest of my life, he'll pay for what he did to you."

I made a move to stand, but hesitated. Someone was coming. The sun had gone down and the moon was rising. I didn't know what the deal was here, but it seemed unlikely that people were jogging through the woods after dark. Kori and Cade maybe...or Dylan. Still, I had to be careful. I readied myself to pounce as the person—who was running like hell—stampeded closer. Right about the time that I realized it wasn't Kori and Cade, and it wasn't Dylan—the footfalls were all wrong—something crashed into me, jarring my body backward. I tipped and my feet kicked out from under me.

Someone cursed, and something hit me in the head, and then I was in the water.

An impressive string of curses fought to be heard over the sound of splashing. "What the hell are you doing hiding in the bushes on the edge of a lake?"

I hauled myself back onto land and held out my hand to help the girl—yeah, it was a girl—who'd just tried to drown me, out of the water.

She smacked my hand away and climbed onto the shore. "What the hell are you doing skulking in the bushes in the middle of the night?"

"What the hell were *you* doing tearing through—" The moon moved out from behind the clouds and the girl lifted her head. I tried to force the rest of the sentence past my lips, but the inside of my mouth was suddenly like the Sahara. I was the king of cool. Smooth with the ladies. Yet standing here now, with this soaking wet girl, my heart rate spiked to epic proportions. Why? Because it was *her*.

Ash Calvert was standing in front of me.

She was pale and winded—not to mention soaking wet— and had that same haunted look in her eyes I'd seen a dozen times before. I'd never met her in an easy life. It was like there was some dark cloud hanging over every version of her in the universe. This place didn't appear to be any different.

I tore my gaze away from her and scanned the forest. There was no one else out here. "Were you running from something?"

Instead of answering, her eyes went wide and her mouth fell open. She leaned closer, then jerked her entire body back like, well, like she'd seen a damned ghost.

"*Habla anglais*?" I tried again. Something had obviously just gone down. Maybe she was in shock. "*Usar un traje de perro cuando me bano mi abuela.*"

She squinted and tilted her head. A chunk of what looked like multicolored hair—strands of red and purple, it was hard to tell in the dark—fell forward into her face. "You wear a dog suit to bathe your grandmother?"

"Yes—wait—huh?" She took another long step away and glanced over her shoulder. When she looked back, there was an instant of wonder. Almost like she was staring at something out of a fantasy flick. I waved my hand in front of her face.

She pushed a chunk of wet hair from her eyes. Still, she said nothing. Only stared in a way that had me wanting to move in closer. To put my arms around her. Because there was wonder in that stare, but there was also pain. A kind of pain I understood. You tried to hide it but it was always there, always throbbing just beneath the surface.

I raked my hand down my face, then squeezed the bridge of my nose. *Say something.* I had to speak. "Do I have, like, snot on my face? Or are you just struck silent by how hot I am?" I meant it to be funny, but from the look on her face, she wasn't amused.

"Where did you come from?" She frowned, her features hardening a little. God. She was prettier than I remembered. I hadn't seen her in a couple of skips and realized the memory I had didn't do her justice. Then again, the times I had encountered her, we hadn't spent much time gazing at each other... "You're not from here. I know you're not."

"How do you know that?" Not the most pressing question at the moment, but the force behind her words intrigued me. That, and my brain had suddenly stopped functioning. It happened a lot when I was around this girl. That's why she was dangerous. Kryptonite and crack all rolled into one.

Her shoulders sagged and she hitched a thumb in the direction she'd come from. "Obviously you don't know who I am, which is—"

"I know who you are." Shit. Had that come out weird? Too eager? Maybe I sounded like a damn stalker. "You're the crazy chick who just knocked my ass into the water." There. Better.

Her eyes widened, but the surprise only lasted a moment. She recovered and took another step away. "Knowing you, you probably deserved it. You need to stay the hell away from me."

Knowing me? Stay away from her? Had this world's version of me hurt her?

"Look, whatever it is you think—"

"Don't move!" Footsteps thundered all around us.

Wow. Way to be observant, asshole.

I sighed. "Could this turn into more of a clusterfuck?" When I turned, I saw four armed men in what I assumed were this world's version of a police uniform. Dark purple from head to toe with a crest on their chest that had the words *Protect, Serve, and Enforce* in bright white letters. Not exactly a fear-inciting fashion statement. Better than the bright pink uniforms a few worlds back, though. They'd come complete with skinny jeans and bowties. "If I've broken any laws, I'm sorry. I'm new to the—"

The man at the front of the group sprang forward, and before I knew what was happening, I was being thrown against the nearest tree, face first, and my arms were yanked behind my back. A second later there was a soft snap as a strip of cool metal rested against my wrists and my right cheek got an up close and personal introduction to the sharp bark.

Beside me, they were doing the same to Ash. She was cuffed and dragged toward the tree line. But she wasn't moving fast enough for them.

"This isn't a nature hike, sweetheart." One of the cops shoved her and she stumbled, tripping and falling to the dirt. The asshole *nudged* her with his boot. "Get up and move."

I didn't think—which was pretty normal for me—just lunged at him. "Watch it!"

The response I got was a knock to the back of the head with something solid, and another heaping dose of darkness.

The air smelled of sweetness. That kind of fruity crap girls loved to douse themselves in. I forced my eyes open. Everything was blurry for a second, colors bled together and the edges of my vision swam at warp speed. If I'd eaten anything recently, I probably would have puked.

"—to. Need to get—all over." Bits and pieces of broken conversation filled the room. I wasn't able to put together the conversation, but I *could* make out the voice. I'd know it anywhere.

"Ma?" I was dizzy and disoriented, and as soon as the word left my mouth, I felt like an ass. When everything stopped swimming, sure enough, there she was standing in front of me. Cora Anderson.

My mother had always been a soft, understated beauty. She'd never worn make-up, usually pulled her hair back into a simple tail to keep it tamed as she pored over her work. This Cora had her hair meticulously curled and pinned, eyes slathered in black, and lips painted fire engine red. Where my mother was content to wear long cotton skirts on even her dressiest days, this version of her looked like she'd just stepped out of a power suit catalog. Despite the differences, though, I couldn't help the feeling of happiness at seeing her face…

…at least until she gripped a chunk of my hair and yanked back hard. "Tell me what you're doing here! Is it about Omega? Are you trying to sabotage the project?" The venom in her voice was alien. I'd encountered multiple versions of my mother during the time we'd been at this. They'd always been much like my own. Sure, there were subtle differences—hair color, style, speech pattern—but the two things that I'd never seen change was career and disposition. Apparently there was a first for everything.

This Cora Anderson was a raging bitch.

I had no idea what Omega was, and I couldn't give ten rotting rats' asses to find out. I narrowed my eyes and pulled defiantly against her grip. This wasn't my mother. "Screw you."

"You obnoxious little—"

"Come now, Cora," another voice said, this one equally familiar. A moment later, this world's version of Karl Anderson turned the corner and leaned against the doorframe. His hair peeked out from beneath a homburg hat, streaked with gray. He wore a double-breasted, chalk-striped suit and had a walking cane trimmed in silver balanced over his left shoulder. At some point in his life, he'd been in some kind of trouble. A thick scar decorated the left side of his face, trailing up from his neck and skimming his cheek. "He's not our boy but he looks like him. Surely you can't harm him?"

Cora glared at me for a moment more before straightening. She adjusted the front of her deep blue suit jacket and squared her shoulders, taking a step back to stand beside Karl. He wrapped his arm around her waist, pulling her close while at the same time, never taking his eyes off me.

"The girl who was brought there with me, Ash. Where is she?"

Cora nodded to my left. It wasn't easy—my head was pounding—but I managed to twist in my seat just enough to catch a glimpse of Ash, zip tied to a chair like me. She was out cold.

"Look, I know this must seem strange to you. I look like your son, sound like him, but—"

"You're not him." Cora sighed. "We know who you are."

"If you know who I am, then why the hell do you have me tied to a chair? Is that like a *thing* here?"

She didn't respond. Instead she stepped close again, giving me a nice, long—and slightly creepy—look over. When her gaze fell to the slight bulge at my ankle, she snorted. Grabbing my denim-clad leg, she tugged the material up. "A cuff? You're using a cuff? My God, how crude! Your Infinity must be decades behind ours."

"You don't use cuffs?" Despite the situation, my interest was piqued. We'd seen so many variations of the Infinity Division, but they'd all used the cuff.

"We used cuffs the first and second year. After that, we graduated to implants." She crossed the room and rummaged around until she found what she was looking for. A moment later, she returned with a small chip. "Our deposit operatives have them implanted just beneath the skin on the top side of their wrist."

"Deposit operative?" What the hell did that mean?

Karl cleared his throat. "What is it that you're doing here?"

"My fr—my mission is to find and apprehend a criminal, sir." There was no reason to mention Cade and Kori. As long as they were anonymous, then they were safe. No need for all of us to end up in the deep end of the pool.

"Sir?" Karl snickered. He nudged his wife and tapped the cane against his shoulder twice before letting it fall to his side. "That's new."

"I'm military." Another lie. "Where I'm from, my father— *you*—is a general in the U.S. army."

Beside me, Ash groaned. "What—what the hell is going on?"

"I get why you've got me all strapped up." I glanced in her direction. She was fully awake now and instead of being freaked out by the situation, she looked pissed. "Why haul her in? She's got nothing to do with me."

"She's none of your business," Cora snapped. "A happy side effect of finding you. Someone saw you in town and contacted us immediately. You were tracked and brought here."

No reason to tell them I planned to *make* it my business. This whole thing didn't seem on the level. Those were obviously cops who jacked us, yet we were in a basement? Why not the police station? If I'd accidentally stumbled onto a serial killer version of my parents, I was going to be pissed. "I'm here to find a dangerous criminal. Someone you should be concerned about."

Karl snickered. "Oh?" He winked at his wife. "Did you hear that, doll? Someone *we* should be concerned about." Apparently she found it just as amusing because they both started cackling like idiots.

"He's here looking for several people," I continued over the sounds of their snorting. "One of them is Kori—"

"Corey!" All heads swiveled toward Ash. She didn't seem to care about the scrutiny. She was tense, muscles straining against her bonds and eyes wide. She swallowed and let her head fall for a moment before lifting her gaze to meet Cora's. "We were attacked. In the park. He—"

The humor instantly drained from Cora's face and her eyes glazed over. Lips pulled into a feral snarl, she flew at Ash like a demon and grabbed her by the front of the shirt. If she hadn't been holding tight, the entire chair would have gone over. "What the hell were you doing with my son? I made it clear—"

"Son?" I exclaimed, while at the same time, Ash narrowed her eyes and said, "Trying to talk some sense into him since no one else has the guts to listen."

Karl crossed the room and managed to pry Cora away from Ash. You might have thought he was trying to rescue the girl if it hadn't been for his expression. Feral and deadly, like he was barely restraining himself from doing just what his wife had and then some. Clearly, on this world, he was the voice of reason. "Where is my son?"

"Dead," Ash said. It came out as barely a whisper, but somehow seemed to echo off the walls like she'd shouted it through a megaphone. "Someone attacked us. Corey was killed."

Karl stumbled away, shaking his head as Cora sagged against him. The walking cane fell to the floor. He wrapped his arms around her, eyes never leaving Ash. "I am going to take my wife into the other room, and then I am going to find my son. For your sake, I hope this is a sick joke."

She looked like he'd slapped her. "I would never joke about something like that."

"Then my dear...you are in very big trouble."

Chapter Four

Ash

"This is not happening." I pulled against the restraints. The hard plastic straps cut into my skin but didn't budge an inch.

"Is Corey Anderson really dead?"

I twisted so that I was facing him. His expression was stricken. Like someone had stabbed him in the heart and twisted the knife a few times just for fun—I knew exactly how that felt because every time I glanced over at him I got the same sensation. He was definitely Noah Anderson— shaggy hair, steely eyes, and heart-stopping hitch in his upper lip—just not *this* world's Noah Anderson. Still, seeing him alive sent a shiver of happiness through me. Hearing his voice calmed my nerves just a bit. "Who are you?"

"If you answer my damn question, maybe I'll be your fairy godfather."

This guy…there was darkness there. Far more than the Noah I'd known and loved. He'd hid his demons well. Buried them beneath jokes and addictive vices. This one wore them on his sleeve. They flashed in his eyes and radiated around him like some kind of toxic cloud. His gaze, jagged where my Noah's had been smooth, chased the air from my lungs and made me want to shift in my seat. I opened my mouth to answer, but nothing came out.

"Well?" he prodded.

I swallowed and found my voice. "He's dead." Just like I'd be as soon as they found his body.

His expression softened a bit. "And you know the Andersons how?"

Why not? It wasn't like I had anything left to lose at this point. And on the plus side, keeping him talking allowed me to hear Noah's voice again. "I live with them." I let my head fall back. "I mean, I used to live with them. Until they kicked me out."

"They kicked you out?" He seemed almost horrified. It was actually an expression I was accustomed to. That's how my Noah had looked when anything pertaining to his family came up.

"They blame me for your—our Noah's—death."

"I'm dead here, too?" He threw back his head and snorted. Such an un-Noah-like thing to do. "Well, that blows a big one."

"Your turn," I said. His brows lifted in question. "Who are you?"

"You obviously know I'm not the Noah Anderson you knew."

Duh. "You're with Infinity, right? A *different* Infinity."

"You could say that." He tugged against his binds, then wiggled his fingers. "Which I assume dear ole alternate Mom and Dad know—creepy versions of them, by the way. So why the hell are we tied up?"

"I told you why they tied me up. As for you, I assume they believe you're a Skip."

"A skip?"

"It's what we call inter-dimensional terrorists."

He snorted again. "We're here to catch an *inter-dimensional terrorist*."

"We?"

His right eyebrow twitched. He hadn't meant to say that. "I'm willing to bet that the person who attacked you and killed Corey is the same person I'm here to stop—that's not going to happen while I'm strapped to this stupid chair. And about that—what are they going to do to us?"

"Cora and Karl?" I wanted to know who *we* were, but first things first. "Probably kill us."

He rolled his eyes. "Oh. Is that all?"

"Pretty much."

"Well, I don't know about you, but I'm not in the mood to be dead. Stuff to do, people to catch. You know the drill. We need to get out of here. Can you get free?"

I tried—and failed—again. "Not happening." The contents of my pockets, and I assumed Noah's, were piled on a workbench a few feet away. Even if I could get to my cell, though, who would I call? The police wouldn't come running. Even before this all went down. I wasn't big in the *friend* department. I was a Bottom Tier citizen thrust on Top Tier society. Most people I encountered barely glanced in my direction, much less gave me the time of day. They were respectful when they had to be. Living in the Anderson house afforded me *some* perks. But no one went out of their way.

"You lived here, right? Any ideas?"

I scanned the basement. We hardly came down here, but

from what I knew, there wasn't anything useful. Cora kept the boys' old clothing and toys stashed away, along with boxes and boxes of old books and antiques she'd deemed *out of style*. The far corner was used to house some of her old research material, but nothing that might help us. "Can't say anything is coming to mind."

He glanced around the room. His gaze caught on something I couldn't see in the far corner. "Then I have one."

"Okay…" It sounded like there was a *but*. If he was *anything* like my Noah, that could be a bad thing. He had the tendency to act irrationally at times and it always got him into trouble. Then again, that guy could talk himself out of pretty much any situation. I didn't get the impression that this Noah was a talker.

"Fair warning that it might just make things worse."

Yep. Definitely a bad thing… "Doubt that's possible at this point."

"Always possible," he mumbled. He nodded and leaned forward until he was standing, the legs of his chair hovering off the ground at an awkward angle. He was slightly bulkier than my Noah. Harder and more defined. I cursed myself for noticing, but despite the situation, it was impossible not to see how the material of his shirt stretched and moved across the planes of his torso.

Noah cringed, then inhaled. He leaped up and threw himself backward, crashing to the floor. There was a horrible crack and pieces of the chair splintered in every direction.

"Oh my God. What if one of the pieces had splintered and, I dunno, stabbed you?"

"Then it would have saved your foster parents a little time and effort." He grunted and rolled onto his feet, wobbling just a bit. The zip ties remained, but they were no longer attached to anything. He was free. "Didn't know you cared."

Lurching toward the work bench, he grabbed a small pocket knife and went to work sawing the ties off my wrists. Twice his fingertips brushed my skin and I cringed. Not because it was unpleasant. The opposite, actually. The contact sent a ripple of warmth through me, which was confusing, not to mention badly timed. I swallowed against an involuntary shudder and said, "I don't. If you'd gotten yourself killed, though, I would have been stuck down here with your corpse."

First hand free, he moved onto the next. I saw his lip twitch, like he was holding back a grin. "Right."

Once I was free, he dragged one of the unbroken lawn chairs over and positioned it beneath the small window. "Suck it in and squeeze through," he commanded, giving me a shove.

His hand grazed my backside and I whirled on him, an even mix of horrified and angry. "Watch it."

A spark of mischief glinted in his eyes, there and gone in a single beat of my heart before being replaced with steely resignation. "Oh yeah. I got kidnapped and tossed in a mad scientist's basement just so I could have a shot at touching your ass. Get over yourself and move."

I did as I was told, biting down hard on the inside of my cheek to keep from telling him off.

Once I wriggled through, Noah was right behind me. "This was fun. Let's not do it again anytime soon, huh?"

"Gladly. Now if you—"

A black and purple blur flew past me, colliding with Noah and taking him to the ground. One of the Andersons' security detail had him pinned, elbow to his throat, massive body crushing his. "I've got orders not to kill you," the guy said. "But, hey. Accidents happen."

I could have run. Turned on my heel and beat feet just as fast as I possibly could until I was somewhere in the next state—not that it would have changed my situation. Should have, even. And even though this guy wasn't the Noah I loved, he was still *a* Noah. I couldn't leave him—especially not after he'd saved me.

I threw myself forward at them, knocking the guard off balance. He cursed and rolled on top of me, smushing the air from my lungs and nearly crushing me beneath his considerable weight.

Just when I thought I'd suffocate, the corners of my vision growing watery and dark, the weight disappeared and the sounds of melee drifted through the night. A moment later, someone was hauling me to my feet and dragging me across the lawn.

"Second time in less than an hour," Noah shouted. "Saved your ass."

I tripped several times, but it didn't seem to faze him. He didn't slow down. By the time we made it off the Andersons' property and several blocks away, I was sure he'd dislocated my arm and broken my thumb. I cradled it, opening and closing my fingers several times just to be sure everything still worked as it should.

"If I were you, I'd lay low until you push off." I waggled a finger at him. "That face is going to get you into trouble. Knowing the Andersons, they've already notified the news outlets that there is an unauthorized Skip in town."

"Unauthorized?" He tilted his head and I noticed for the first time that his hair was much longer than my Noah's. He had it pulled into a stubby tail that hung just above his neck while the bangs and sides fell free. "How the hell would you go about getting authorized?"

I shrugged. "Don't think you would. The Andersons have this town locked up tight." That should have been the end of it. I should have turned on my heel and walked away. Run, actually. There was still the matter of the Andersons' wrath to deal with. Except I couldn't. Not just yet.

I'd last laid eyes on Noah more than a month ago. It'd been more than thirty days since I'd heard his voice. Now here he was, standing in front of me against all reasonable odds, and I wasn't ready to let that go just yet. "Thank you. For helping me."

His lip hitched. "Yeah, well, I guess I didn't have much of a choice. I mean, it was my fault they nabbed you." He took a step toward me.

"That's true," I said. Like him, I made the smallest move forward. A tiny voice inside my head goaded me to reach out and touch him. A simple brush of my hand against his. Just one small moment to commit the feeling to permanent memory. At my side, my hand twitched, but I managed to keep it to myself. God. Was I insane? "You won't be staying long, right? It's not safe here."

Noah's gaze flickered to my hand, then settled on my face. For an insane moment, it almost seemed like he was focusing just a little too hard, fighting his own silent war. "Just here to do what I came to do. Then I'm out."

"Find this criminal?" Closure, I realized. That was what this was all about. That was the freaky pull I was feeling here. Why I couldn't just up and walk away. Noah and I had been so close for so long. The best of friends. Then, we had that moment, that crazy kiss—and he was gone. Erased from this world and my life. Sure, we'd both agreed it was a mistake, but deep down, I think both of us had needed more closure than that. I'd pushed it and I realized now that I wanted to apologize for that. For possibly wrecking something we both depended so heavily on.

"Yeah." He reached across and pulled something off my shoulder. A leaf. "The guy is crazy. Dangerous as fuck."

They looked alike but were still so different. Observation number one: language. My Noah would never have spoken like that. I cursed, but him? No. He had other vices but I'd never heard him utter a single four-letter word. There was no closure to be had here. Noah was gone and getting to see him one last time was a small gift, but also a dangerous distraction. This Noah had a different vibe. Enticing and oddly magnetic. I had to get moving before I repeated that same mistake. "Then you should probably be careful."

I turned and started in the direction of home, but he grabbed my arm—the good one, thankfully. "Where are you going?"

"Through the woods to grandma's house." I pivoted to face him but didn't pull free from his grip. "Why?"

He faltered for a second, mouth opening and closing like a fish out of water. He glanced down at his hand on my arm and gave the slightest shake of his head before letting go as though my skin were made of poison. For an instant his expression was pained, then it quickly hardened and he took a step back. "Have a nice life." Without another word, he turned and stalked into the night, swallowed a moment later by the dark. As I watched him go, it took every ounce of strength I had not to run after him.

It took me almost twenty minutes to make my way home. I was looking over my shoulder the entire way. What I'd told Noah was the truth. The Andersons were ruthless and controlling and there was no way they'd tolerate a rogue Skip—especially their own son's doppelganger—strolling around town. But it wasn't my problem. I'd pushed it aside and had my own crap to deal with.

By the time I got home, I was beat. It was about five miles from the Andersons to the compound and it'd been a long night. I stopped for a moment and stared at my front door—if you could call it that. Home sweet home was one of two hundred efficiency cottages donated by the Andersons' *supreme generosity*—cough-cough publicity stunt—to the Listed Youth project in 2001. The whole movement was billed as a way to get listed teens off the street. You got to live here, rent free, until you turned eighteen. You had to pay for your own food and utilities, but your roof was covered. After that, you were on your own. No one in the U.S. would—or *could*—hire you except one of the two *houses*. Basically agencies that rented their employees out to a multitude of *service* related jobs that even the Bottom Tier citizens didn't want.

I slipped into the house and closed the door, not bothering to be quiet. I had a couple roommates—Mary and Felice—but they were hardly ever here.

I crossed the small room and pulled open my dresser—a cardboard-like thing that smelled oddly of mothballs even though I'd never had any—and began pulling things out. Corey Anderson was dead and I was the last one—that they knew of—to see him. If I didn't get the hell out of town tonight, this was going to go down one of two ways. The police would come for me. There'd be a trial—doubtfully a fair one—and I would be blamed for Corey's death. The Andersons would get their justice in the end. Or, more likely, they'd simply take it upon themselves to get rid of me.

Getting out of town was my only chance at seeing the sun again. Sure, they'd follow, but the farther I got from Wells, the better my chances. I would have to ditch my plans of proving Noah had been murdered. For now at least. He'd want that, though. He'd want me to be safe...

I filled the bag with the first things my hands touched. Several pairs of jeans, a handful of assorted items from my underwear drawer—a hairbrush. It was mindless and random and chaotic, but it slowed the pounding of my heart beneath my ribs. I'd always found comfort in chaos. The more hectic things were, the more at ease I felt.

I zipped the backpack and swung the duffel over my shoulder. I was about to start for the door when an odd feeling crept across my skin. That eerie tingle that comes from fear. Something clattered outside. I held my breath and listened. There was another noise, this one softer but longer lasting. A sudden banging followed it.

"What the hell?" I set the bags down and crossed to the door. The entire front wall of the house was shaking. Someone was out there, banging against the cottage on either side of the door. I grabbed the handle and twisted. It turned like it was supposed to, but the door didn't open. "Hey! What's going on?"

Whoever was on the other side of the door didn't answer. There was more banging, then footsteps. A moment later I smelled it. Smoke.

"No!" I slammed my hand against the door. When that didn't work, I rammed my shoulder into it. Over and over until my entire arm was numb. It was pointless, though. Whatever they'd braced the door with wasn't budging. I gave up and backed away, then spun in a slow circle. There were no windows in the efficiency cabins. Hell, there were barely four walls and a roof. The mini homes were made from the cheapest materials and every corner was cut.

Thick gray smoke began wafting beneath the gap at the bottom of the door. The smell grew stronger. I threw myself at the door again and started pounding. "You can't do this! Someone, help!"

No one would come, though. Even if someone could hear me, the other listed would look the other way. Everyone in the small compound knew who I was. They all knew who'd put me here. We were no longer accepted members of society, but that didn't stop the Andersons from striking fear into the hearts of the people.

The door heated. I had to back away to keep from getting burned. The structure caught quickly since they hadn't needed to operate within the building codes. The entire place was as flammable as a pile of dead leaves.

Grabbing a shirt from the pile on my bed, I raced across to the small rusted sink and ran it under the water. The pressure sucked and it dribbled out, but I managed to get it saturated. Breathing through wet material helped, right? With smoke inhalation? I was sure I'd heard that somewhere…

I moved back to the center of the room. I could see the flames licking at the door now, the smoke growing darker and thicker. It burned my eyes and throat, and with each passing second, made it harder and harder to catch my breath.

Something crashed against the wall behind me, shaking the entire cabin. For a second I thought it was the same people who'd locked me in here, but there was something different about the sound. Something frantic.

Someone was trying to break through the wall.

Maybe it was possible. The cabins had no solid foundation. The walls were several layers of sheet rock and plywood and not much else. I lunged forward and started kicking at the wall where the sound was coming from. "I'm trapped in here!"

There was no reply, but the banging continued with even more vigor. After a few moments, the wall cracked and split, and a boot rammed through as I fell to my knees. There was no air left in the small space. Only thick, noxious smoke. I was vaguely aware that I was moving, that someone had hefted me up and thrown me over their shoulder.

"Damn it, Ash. Answer me!" my savior commanded, setting me back on the ground. I stayed upright for about a half second before crumbling to the grass. "Are you okay?"

I coughed and wheezed, gasping greedily at the fresh air. "I—yeah." Breathing under control, I rubbed my eyes with the heel of my hand and stared as the cabin came into focus.

What was left of it.

Another moment inside and I wouldn't have made it out. The entire thing was engulfed, flames shooting up through the roof—or, where the roof had been—and sending dark gray smoke curling into the night sky.

"Why the hell hasn't the fire department gotten here yet?" It was Noah. He'd pulled me out. "There's no way your neighbors missed all the smoke."

"I'm sure they didn't," I said, struggling to my feet. I couldn't take my eyes off him. His face was dirt-streaked and the edges of his jacket looked singed. Most of his hair had pulled free from the band, the bulk of it thrashing wildly in the wind. In that moment, he looked taller than he ever had. Like some avenging angel sent not from heaven or hell, but someplace in between. I swallowed the large lump in my throat. "But I doubt anyone here has a phone. And even if someone *did* call, the fire department wouldn't have come. Not here."

"Why the hell not?"

I spread my arms wide. "This is a listed compound. They'd rather set up chairs and scarf popcorn to watch it burn."

"I have no idea what that means." He shook his head, then hitched a thumb over his shoulder. "Don't care, either. We should get out of here, though."

"And go where?" I jabbed a finger at my still-smoldering cabin. "I don't exactly have a backup place."

His expression softened. In that moment, he looked so much like the Noah I'd known. Sweet and caring. Unaffected by money and power. It lasted about three seconds before the scowl set in. "So you plan on, what? Camping out on the grass? Good plan. I'm sure when they come back to drag away your charred corpse and find you waiting here for them they'll apologize and offer you a cookie."

"You're—"

"Look, I'll level with you. I don't think the Andersons are your only problem. I think you're in danger."

"Danger? From what?"

"More like who."

"The guy who killed Corey…" The smell from the fire was starting to get to me.

He nodded and hitched his thumb over his shoulder. "I promise I'll explain it to you, but right now you have to trust me. We need to get gone."

"Fine." I didn't trust him—and I didn't trust *myself* with him. His appearance kept throwing me off. It was making my mind wander to places it shouldn't go. But he *was* right.

It wasn't safe to stay here. The moment I'd admitted to being with Corey tonight, my life had been over. Now that he was dead, it was only a matter of time until I joined him. The fire proved that in spades. Then again, if what he'd said about Cora telling the cops she believed I'd killed Noah, what happened with Corey had only sped things along. The short of it was, if Cora Anderson wanted you dead, you might as well go dig yourself a nice big hole…

I had no intention of buying a shovel.

Chapter Five

Noah

"Is it really smart to be heading back in the same general direction we were caught in the first place?"

"Probably not," I said without looking back. Ash was trailing behind and had been asking questions nonstop. Like the goddamned Energizer Bunny, that girl. "Probably doesn't help that you're stomping through the woods like an elephant and chattering like a monkey, either."

"Are you always this much of a dick?"

"Only on my good days." Granted, I was an asshole, but in this particular instance I was going out of my way to ramp it up. It was the only way I could stay focused. If she was irritated by my attitude, if I pissed her off, then maybe she'd stop looking at me the way she was. Like I'd hung the fucking moon or some lame shit like that. When she looked at me like that, it made me want to… No. This girl was a distraction. The universe's way of trying to throw me off track. I refused to give in. Not this time.

We weren't far from the Doon. The sooner we got there,

the better. I'd spent countless hours scouring different earths for this girl. When I found her, there wasn't usually much conversation. Our chemistry was instant and wild and we caught fire pretty damn quick. I'd convinced myself that she was nothing special and that I could easily live without her, but in the back of my mind, I always walked away from our encounters a little bit raw. Ashlyn Calvert was going to be the death of me some day, but I was determined not to let it be *this* Ashlyn Calvert. It was time I had some damn self-control.

"Well?" she snapped after a few moments of blissful silence.

"Well, what?"

"You said you were going to explain. Danger, remember?" She rushed ahead and jumped out in front of me. "How do I know that it's not you I'm in danger from?" She jabbed her finger in the direction we'd been walking. "Looks to me like we're heading back to the Doon. Back to the place that guy attacked Corey."

"That would be because we are." I sidestepped her and started walking again. She didn't follow.

"I can't go back there."

"So stay here." I slowed my pace but didn't turn around. She'd follow.

"How did you find me? At the cabin? Did you follow me?" Her tone was soft. Hopeful, almost. It made me uncomfortable, while at the same time, had me desperate to tell her the truth. To see how she'd react. Of course I'd followed her. I couldn't *not* follow her. That was the problem.

It was getting brighter. In an hour or so the sun would be up. We must have been in the Andersons' basement for a hell of a lot longer than I'd thought. I had to find Cade and

Kori and figure out what the hell was going on with the cuffs.

I threw up both hands and shrugged. I still couldn't force myself to turn around and face her. "Look, you wanna stay here, then stay. I don't—"

"Noah?" A second later, Kori came bounding out of the woods. She crashed into me, throwing her arms tight around my neck. My arms tightened around her instinctively. "It's been hours. Where have you"—she caught sight of Ash and pulled away—"been?"

Cade came up behind her. He glanced from Ash to me and shook his head. "Really?"

"Obviously this isn't what it looks like," I said—though I didn't have to. There was no way Cade thought I'd blown off checking in with them to go looking for Ash. Except, I had done it in the past. I'd never told him I'd met her before, much less had any kind of *interaction*. Up until this moment, she'd been my dirty little secret. The addiction I couldn't bear to face.

"Um, excuse me?" Ash pushed past me and positioned herself between Kori and me. "And what exactly would they think it looked like? Maybe like some crazy guy was dragging me back into the woods to, I dunno, murder me?"

"Aren't you dramatic." God. Hot and sarcastic. "And just a refresher—since your memory seems to be on the fritz—I saved your ass. *Twice*."

"Saved her?" Kori said.

"Oh. Yeah. Mommy and Daddy dearest are like mobsters or something on this particular rock. Should have seen them. Totally surreal."

Her eyes kind of bugged—I loved saying shit that shocked her—and her mouth fell open. "You've gotta be kidding me! They—"

An irritatingly familiar whistle cut through the chatter and all heads spun toward Cade. The guy could be stiff at times, but he sure knew how to grab the attention of a crowd. "Focusing now." With a nod toward me, he said, "You were about to tell us what happened?"

"Obviously the problem is getting worse. That last skip was almost instantaneous. I caught sight of Dylan and I thought I had him, but he sucker punched me." Admitting this to Cade in private would have been hard enough. Add Kori? Harder. Fessing up in front of Ash? Yeah. I felt like the biggest loser alive. I squared my shoulders. "I went down and—"

"And I ran into him. We went for a swim, then got kidnapped and stashed in the Andersons' basement. It was a lovely evening I can't wait to forget. Will someone please tell me what the hell is going on?"

"Andersons' basement?" Kori took a step toward me, and I could see the hope brewing in her eyes. She'd been with us for several skips now and having lost her own Cora Anderson, was eager to interact with another. She hadn't gotten the chance yet. "As in—"

"Take a breath, Kor. Like I said, Mom and Dad Anderson aren't the friendly type here."

"Mom and dad?" Ash looked from me to Kori. "Kor? Are you—"

"Yeah. Guess I should do introductions. Guys, this is *Ash*. Ash, this is my best friend, Cade Granger, and this is my…this is Kori."

"You're a girl?" Ash almost looked like she wanted to poke Kori to see if she was real.

"Thanks for noticing?"

I rolled my eyes. "Moving on…. It looks like Dylan isn't

skipping from this earth right away. At least, he doesn't seem to be planning to. He's already taken out this world's version of you—a dude, I might add—and is probably already looking for Miles, Odette, and Penny."

"Maybe not," Cade said. "He hasn't gone after them for a few skips now. Like you said, the cuff is getting worse. I know him. If I had to guess, he's going to be looking for a way to fix it."

"But he took out this world's Kori."

"The guy that killed Corey was surprised to find us," Ash said. "If that's who you're talking about, maybe it was by accident?"

Cade nodded. "That would be my guess. Dylan is going to be focused on the cuff right now."

"You're saying he might hit up Infinity?" He was in for a nasty surprise if he did. They hadn't struck me as the helpful type.

"That's what I would do." He glanced at Ash before turning back to me. "What do we know about this world's Infinity?"

I pointed to Ash. "She's the expert. I'll let her fill you in."

All heads swiveled toward her, and Ash's mouth fell open. She even blushed. It was adorable. "I'm not an expert!"

"But you know more than we do," Cade prompted. "How about we go someplace safe and you can fill us in?"

She hesitated for a moment, then nodded. "I'll tell you what I know, but it won't matter where we go. There isn't any place *safe*."

• • •

We rented a room downtown. Ash suggested that Cade take care of it, since she'd never seen him before, which probably meant the Andersons didn't know him. We hadn't had time to look into our doubles here yet so we had to rely on her. Kori was safe, too. Since her double was dead here—and a dude—there was zero chance she'd be recognized. Ash said there was a definite resemblance, but not something you'd put together unless you knew the connection.

"I can't believe they deal with crime like that." Kori set down the crust from her pizza—made with cottage cheese on this world instead of mozzarella—and shook her head. She looked as horrified as I felt about the abomination we were eating.

Apparently on this world, the government didn't run the Infinity Division like it did on both our home worlds. Here, it was a corporation that sold its services to the law by ridding their world of undesirables. Yeah. And the term *undesirables*? That was a little different, too. We'd stumbled onto some kind of Mob-like society. There was a Gotti in the White House, and the most prominent people in America were crime families—like the Andersons.

Ash frowned. "Anything above a level two offense will get you skipped. There's a trial, of course, but if found guilty, the ruling is final. They got rid of the appeal process a year ago."

"I'll probably hate myself for asking, but what kinds of things are we talking?" While we didn't know the exact use for Infinity on our world, I was pretty damn sure we weren't using it to dump killers and rapists on unsuspecting societies.

"Things like minor traffic infractions would be considered a level one. Level twos are your domestic disputes and squabbles with authority figures. Level three and above is everything from petty theft to murder. Of the right person, that is."

"Right person?" Kori asked. Her expression soured even more. I wasn't sure if it was the pizza or Ash's description. Probably both. "What's that supposed to mean?"

"It means," Ash said with a frown, "that if someone like, we'll say me, was robbed or murdered in front of, oh, I dunno, a crowd of two hundred, that person would walk free. Really, the severity of the punishment depends on the Tier of the victim."

"Tier?" Cade shifted in his seat, utterly enthralled. We did this for a specific reason—to catch a criminal—but that didn't stop him from being fascinated by the different *cultures* we'd discovered.

"President Al Capone implemented the—"

"President Al Capone?" Kori said with a squeal. Ash regarded her quizzically.

"On my world, and I guess Kori's, Capone was a high-profile criminal," I said.

"Sorry." Kori waved her hand. She looked almost as star struck as Cade did. "Please, continue."

"We have a tier system. The Andersons are Top Tier citizens. You cross one of those, consider yourself skipped—if they don't kill you for it first. They can pretty much do whatever they want to whoever they want, but if you so much as give them the side-eye, it's all over. The Mid Tiers are a little more structured. Things like petty crime and violence will get them skipped—especially if committed against a Top Tier. And as far as the Bottom Tiers go, it's open season. We get skipped the most. Some committing crimes out of desperation or anger, others having simply pissed off the wrong people."

"Whoa." Cade leaned back in his chair. "That's the harshest judicial system we've seen so far."

"And the most unfair," Kori said. "There are some harsh, unlivable worlds out there. What's to say they aren't shipping them off to a death sentence for stealing a pack of gum from some elitist snob? And what about the good ones? What happens when someone truly horrific gets dumped on innocent lives?"

"They've done *research*." Ash's tone was bitter. "Some of the public had the same concerns when the program started. Felt it could be a bit much, bordering on inhumane. But Karl Anderson is smooth. He insisted that they have a pool of seven other skip locations that they choose from — depending on the crime — and that each has been thoroughly researched."

"Doesn't sound like you buy into that." The look on her face said it all. She wasn't a fan of Infinity.

"There's no real proof that they don't, but Noah didn't believe the research ever happened. He was convinced they skip them at random. Doesn't matter where they land."

"Either way, that's barbaric."

"He was looking into it." She paused to take a shaky breath. "Who knows? Maybe that's the something that started all this."

"Something?" Cade said.

"My — *our* — Noah is dead. A little less than a month now. I think his death had to do with Infinity. He was poking around, said there was something he had to tell me, but before he got the chance, he committed *suicide*."

"And you don't think he did," Cade said.

"I *know* he didn't." I had no idea what the deal between

her and this world's version of me was, but I was suddenly jealous. The ferocity in her voice left no room for argument. She squared her shoulders and certainty flashed in her eyes. "Noah would never do that. I think he was killed because of what he found out."

Kori's expression fell. "That would mean—"

"That Cora and Karl had something to do with it," I finished for her. "Yeah. Trust me, it's not a stretch from what I've seen. What about Omega? Could that have something to do with it?"

Ash frowned. "Omega?"

"Cora mentioned it back at the house. You were still unconscious, I guess. She asked me if I was here to sabotage it. They've—"

A loud wail filled the room. Everyone but Ash jumped and covered their ears, and Cade leaped to his feet, instantly on guard. "What is that?"

Unconcerned, Ash slid off the edge of the bed and hit the power button on the television mounted to the far wall. She pointed to the speakers by the door. "The alert system. Means there's a special news broadcast. Everyone is required to tune in."

The picture flickered to life and a tall man with a snow-white beard took front and center behind a stainless steel desk. "Good morning, people of Wells. We're about to go live to a press conference at the Infinity Center. Please stand by…"

There were a few moments of static and some feedback, and when the picture came back into focus, Karl Anderson was standing at a podium, Cora on one side, and a tall man in a dark suit on the other.

"As most of you know, our son, Noah Emeal, was found

dead not long ago."

There was a soft whisper through the crowd as Cora gripped his arm and held tight. I got the impression it was for show.

"As the news reported, he took his own life and left a note. Kindly, they did not disclose the contents of that note, and neither my wife nor I had any plans to do so. However, things have changed."

The camera panned out to capture the crowd's surprise and a growing feeling of dread seeped into the room. A few feet from the TV, Ash had gone pale. Her mouth was open and at her sides, her fists were balled tight.

"Noah's note claimed that he was unable to live after being so cruelly toyed with for years, then discarded, by someone he cared deeply for."

She shook her head and took a step away from the television. "No…"

"Ashlyn Calvert, the young Bottom Tier orphan girl we took into our home, the girl we fed and clothed. Unknown to us, she carried on with my son for years. My wife witnessed the sick affair with her own eyes! This girl seduced him, made him care for her—only to play with his affections. Information has come to light that now leads us to believe that the note left by Noah was, in fact, a fake forged by the girl. A source has informed us that Noah tried several times to cut the ties of their sick relationship and that Ashlyn refused. She intended to use her relationship with him to boost her tier level, knowing that in just a few short months she would turn eighteen and be returned to where she *belonged*."

"Sonofabitch," I cursed. I'd kill them. I'd fucking kill them…

"Last night…" Cora stepped forward. "My other son, Corey, was found dead in the woods. The last message on his phone was from Ashlyn Calvert, who confessed to me personally that she was meeting with him despite my pleas for her to leave my family be. We believe that when her efforts failed with Noah, she turned to a devastated and emotionally vulnerable Corey in hopes that a tryst would evolve."

"This is not happening," Ash said, backing away from the screen. "How could they do this?"

"We believe that she is working with a Skip," Karl said. He slammed his hand down on the podium. The microphone rattled and crackled. "Another world's version of Noah. We believe he is here to sabotage the Infinity Division, having allied himself to Miss Calvert who has vowed to make us pay for having her listed."

She looked crushed and furious at the same time, and for some damn reason, all I wanted to do was wrap my arms around her and tell her it was all going to be fine. "Ash…"

She snorted and ran a shaking hand through her hair. "Well, they got that part right. I *did* promise they'd pay…"

"These people are insane," Cade said. He slid from the bed and began to pace. "Now not only do we have to worry about the cuffs malfunctioning, we have a target on our heads."

"Technically the target is on *Ash's* head. Mine, too, since they're not thrilled to have me walking around with their son's mug and all," I said. He was right, though. This was going to make things ten times harder. I turned back to Ash. "And you're sure no one will help you? Law enforcement? Friends?"

She frowned and sank onto the edge of the other bed. "Do you have listed on your Earth?"

I shook my head and she held up her hand and rolled her sleeve. On the inside of her wrist, there was what looked like a small black circle tattoo.

"See this mark? It means that I'm one of the listed. Basically invisible. No one is allowed to speak to or help me in any way."

Now it made sense. "That's why no one came for the fire."

"Fire?" Kori said.

"Yep." Ash pulled her sleeve down over the mark. "Because I'm under eighteen, they're required to keep a roof over my head. The Andersons couldn't stop them from giving me a spot at the compound. When I turn eighteen in six months, though, I'm out."

"That's barbaric." Kori was always horrified over something on every Earth, only this time I agreed with her. This system was twisted and wrong. "If no one can speak to you, then how will you work? Feed yourself?"

"Once I turn eighteen I have the option of being employed by one of two companies—neither of which is pleasant." She glanced back at the television, eyes narrowing to thin slits. "Hundreds of people are listed every day, some whose biggest crime was simply refusing to sleep with someone in a higher Tier than them. Hundreds of people, yet there are only about a thousand worldwide. There's a good reason for that. The suicide rate in this country is the highest in the world."

"How did you end up listed?"

Ash shifted from foot to foot. "The Andersons. Cora never liked me. She always hated how close Noah and I were. If they did really have something to do with his death then this is a perfect way to support that *suicide* note. Grief-stricken parents banish the girl who broke their son's heart?

Classic. They told the court I stole from them. It wasn't hard to get it approved with their rank and power. I doubt anyone even looked at the paperwork before it was pushed through."

"Maybe we can help each other." Cade stopped pacing. "That guy who attacked you? The one who killed your Corey? We're here to stop him."

"Except the device we use to go from one Earth to another is on the fritz," Kori added. "His movements have been erratic."

Cade nodded. "He killed Corey, but there's a good chance he's not finished yet. There are three other people that might be in danger. We need to find them before he does, but we also need to see if there's some way of fixing our cuffs. If you could help us find someone at Infinity who could give us some information, then maybe we can help you figure out exactly what happened to your Noah. Clear your name."

"I'm not sure how much help I can be to you. In case you misunderstood, not only am I listed, but I'm also now a murder suspect. Most people at Infinity know who I am. I doubt any of them would talk to me."

"Please," Kori prodded. "There has to be someone. Anyone?"

Ash thought about it for a minute before sighing. "I know someone inside Infinity who *might* talk to you."

"Cade and Dylan don't seem to have been born here," Kori said. "We did a little digging while we were waiting for you. And no one will recognize me."

I nodded. "Then you and Cade work on tracking down Penny, Miles, and Odette. Ash and I will see if we can make contact with her friend."

There was a murmur of agreement, but I didn't miss the way Ash cringed when I'd said *friend,* which worried me.

Chapter Six

Ash

How could they do this? I knew the Andersons had never liked me, but murder? They knew damn well I hadn't hurt Noah. They knew because *they'd* had something to do with it. I couldn't let them get away with it. If I could somehow manage to prove they were responsible, then maybe I could get the courts to take another look at the theft charges. Maybe I could have my listed status revoked. Helping this Noah and his friends might actually be the key to my freedom.

I pulled the hood of my borrowed sweatshirt just a bit tighter. Kori had loaned it to me since mine smelled like smoke. We'd parted ways with Cade and her—I still had a hard time getting right with a female version of Corey—and were off to try and get some information on Infinity. Noah had been quiet and it was starting to drive me insane. "So what's the deal with this Dylan guy?"

Noah kept walking, eyes remaining front and center. He was going out of his way not to look at me and I was dying to know why. Had he known me where he'd come from? If not for the way I caught him looking at me sometimes, with a mix of desperation and greed, I would have thought he had—and hated me. As it was, I had no idea what was going through his mind. My Noah had been so easy to read. This one was a locked box. I was desperate to ask, but I had a feeling he wouldn't tell me. "He's a bad guy."

"I got that. Why is he a bad guy?"

"Because he kills people. In most societies, that's earmarked as *bad*. Unless of course you're talking about here, where apparently it's a privilege for some."

Comparison number two: not a great conversationalist. My Noah had been a smooth talker. Smart and witty, he could charm the nun right out of her habit with a single conversation. He loved to talk—sometimes a little too much. Obviously this one hadn't learned the skill. "You're just a load full of sunshine, aren't you?"

He sighed. For a brief moment it almost seemed like he was going to apologize—something else my Noah would never do—but instead, he said, "Who is it that we're trying to see?"

"His name is Phil. He was one of Noah's best friends."

That got his attention. He stopped and turned, eyes wide. There was a shimmer of excitement there. "Rabbit?"

"No... Phil is a *person*."

"Rabbit is a nickname..." The spark died and he grumbled something under his breath before saying, "Never mind," and starting forward again. "So Phil. He's your *friend*?"

I hadn't spoken to Phil in several months. While he'd never disliked me in the same ways Cora and Karl did, he wasn't my biggest fan, as he was a huge supporter of the Tier system. You couldn't blame him—or half the people our age.

We were raised in the system. It was a way of life. He always insisted that Noah was crazy to treat me as an equal. I was beneath him. He could do better. I was holding him back, playing with his head, keeping him emotionally unavailable, the whole thing was sick and twisted—the list went on for days. Never mind that Noah and I, until that one stupid night, had never been anything other than friends. Forget that I would never have risked our friendship in that way.

Except I had, hadn't I?

God. Why had I done it? In hindsight, it was probably one of the stupider moments of my life. A milestone mark of idiocy.

"Not really," I said, pushing the heavy feelings of guilt aside.

We reached the bridge under the Seventh Street overpass and I slowed, remembering the last time I'd been here. It was with Noah. Just like I was now, he'd been here to leave a message for Phil. On the way home we'd gotten ice cream. Half my cone ended up smeared to the side of his face—an ice cream duel gone bad—and when we walked back through the door at home, we were still laughing about it. That was what I missed most about him. There were so many things, but his ability to make me laugh, to brighten my mood in even the darkest situation, was like a black hole in the pit of my soul.

"So then why are we going to him? If you're blacklisted, then why not go to someone you consider a friend?"

Phil was a little on the weird side. Okay, scratch that. He was a lot weird. Probably the weirdest person I'd ever met. He didn't own a house phone or a car, and refused to tell anyone where he lived. The rumor was, even Cora and Karl didn't know—not that they would care. Scoring

Phil for Infinity had been big news and a huge win for the company. The guy was a genius, and from what Noah had told me, hadn't come cheap.

"I don't have any friends." The bitterness in my tone was unmistakable. I'd tried. With Corey, with the people at their posh school, but it'd been no use. I was an outsider. Someone who didn't—and would never—belong. "And neither does Phil. Other than his mother, who he's close with, Noah was the only one he'd really talk to. That's why I'm going to him. Because if anyone will help me, he will. For Noah."

For some reason, Noah was really the only one he trusted—and even that had its limits. He still refused to tell him where he lived, insisting on this strange method of communication whenever Noah wanted to talk to him. Something that had happened increasingly often in the days prior to his death.

"This is where we're meeting your contact?" Noah snorted and gestured to the bridge. Moss grew in huge clumps along the rim of the ceiling, and every once in a while something in the distance dripped loudly. "Is he a troll?"

"No, this isn't where we're meeting him—if he meets with us. And he's not *my* contact. He was a friend of yours." Heat flamed to life in my cheeks as his brow lifted. Crap! I couldn't even believe I'd slipped. This Noah was nothing like mine. Not that he'd been *mine*. "Of *his*."

I turned away quickly and hustled to the middle of the underpass, where there was a loose brick. Digging in my fingers, I wiggled it back and forth until there was enough room for me to grab the stone. Once it was off, I dipped my hand into the small hollow space and pulled out a cell phone.

I powered it on and opened the camera app, then hit record. "Phil, I need to talk to you. It's important. Meet me in two hours. The same spot you met Noah last Christmas Eve." I hit stop, replaced the phone and brick, then turned back to Noah.

He blinked several times, looking from me to the brick, then back again. "Now what? That was it? That's how you contact Rabbit? A regular phone call is just too easy?"

"His name is—"

"Phil—whatever the hell he calls himself here. What's up with the *Mission Impossible* crap?"

"Phil is crazy paranoid."

"I got that." He looked like there was more he wanted to say on the subject, but sighed instead. "And how do we even know he'll get it before two hours pass?"

I pointed upward, to the tiny camera mounted in the corner. "He already knows I left him a message." I waved to the camera and started walking back the way we'd come. Staying in one place too long was bound to be bad for my health.

Noah caught up and fell in step beside me. "Where to now? Because if you didn't have a preference, I'm starving."

"You're—" A purple police car rounded the corner and headed right at us. "Crap!" I whirled and grabbed the front of Noah's shirt, then swung him around and propelled us into the small cluster of trees at the edge of the underpass.

There was only a tiny space that wasn't visible from the road. A small crevice within the trees. In order for us both to fit, I'd had to cram myself up against him, and damn me to hell if it didn't send a healthy and embarrassing rush of heat to my cheeks—and parts beyond—despite the situation. This Noah was nothing like mine. He was brash and jagged and darkness, and a part of me found that fascinating. I'd always been secretly attracted to my Noah, but until that one night, I'd never felt truly compelled to act on it. Ever since meeting this Noah, though, I'd found myself having to focus harder than I should have on the situation at hand rather than reaching out to graze his skin, or staring just a moment too long.

Noah obviously hadn't seen the car. He snickered and let his arms fall slack at his sides. "This is how we say hello on my world, too. Only with more lips—and a lot more tongue."

It was something my Noah would have said. That flirty, sometimes-crossed-the-line quipping that girls of every age found so damn appealing. Everyone had loved him. Beautiful, rich, super-smart...but there'd been so much more than that. Few people had really *known* him. Sometimes I wasn't sure *I* had known him.

The car slowed, but finally passed without incident. Once it was out of sight, I stomped my foot down on Noah's and backed away. "Jackass."

"What?" He threw his hands into the air, a mock show of surrender that my Noah had mimicked a million times over. Comparison number three: Some of the same mannerisms. While I found it a bit comforting, it also reminded me just how much I missed him.

I sighed. "We should get moving."

"Where, though?"

"To meet Phil."

We started walking, keeping to the darker parts of town. As we went, Noah watched the scenery, and every few minutes he'd kind of cringe. "What's up with all the people sitting on the sidewalk?"

"They're Bottom Tier."

"Okay...so why are they just sitting there?"

"Some of them are hoping for work. Occasionally

someone from a higher tier will venture down to this part of town looking for an employee for a few hours. Some live here."

He stopped walking. "Live here? Like, right on the damn street?"

"Pretty much."

"Your society is pretty fucked up. You know that?" He snorted and glared at a tall man talking to one of the women sitting up against the building. He was grinning. Laughing and animated, but she wasn't as interested in the conversation as he seemed to be.

When she didn't respond the way he wanted, he grew angry. "Stupid Bottom Tier trash." He brought his leg back and let loose, kicking the poor woman hard enough to knock her over.

There was no hesitation on Noah's part. He cursed and threw himself at the man. It was over in several swings, the man scampering to his feet and tripping all over himself to get away.

Noah sank to the ground and balanced on his heels, then helped the woman sit up. Tears streaked her face, and I couldn't hear what she was saying, but he nodded and spoke back to her, voice low. When he was finished, he stood and the woman flashed him a grateful smile.

When he reached me again I found that I was speechless and unable to tear my eyes away from him. His stance stiffened and his demeanor slipped back into the same surly exterior it'd been a few moments ago. "What?" he snapped.

"Nothing," I said, hiding a smile.

Maybe there was more to this version of Noah Anderson than his looks.

...

*M*eeting Phil someplace run of the mill wasn't going to happen for two reasons. One, the obvious, Noah and I were both wanted. Knowing the Andersons, there were cops pulling triple time patrolling every corner of the city looking for us. Two, Phil would never go for it.

It was a rare occasion that he left the lab. Noah and I once argued if it was his choice to stay locked away — or Cora's. He was a treasure that other companies had tried stealing away multiple times. On special events when he did venture out, he couldn't deal with crowds. Small get-togethers — usually him, Noah, Corey, and I — were about as much as the guy could handle without a meltdown.

Last Christmas eve, Noah convinced him to leave the lab, begging for him to come to the family's party. He usually spent the holidays with his mom — they were crazy close — but she'd been called out of town on business at the last minute. Of course Phil refused, suggesting an alternate location instead. A small cabin on top of Hollow Hill Mountain.

Noah once admitted to me that night had been one of the best Christmas Eves in his life. It was just me, him, Corey, and Phil. All the beer we could drink and a truckload of fast food from every joint in town. Even though it was less than a year ago, it felt like another lifetime.

"We're early." I pulled back the mat to find the dirty silver key right where we'd left it last holiday. "Let's get inside and warm up."

I stepped through the door, Noah on my heels, and shook off the cold. The furniture was covered in old sheets. All of it except the small coffee table in the center of the room. That was covered in dusty beer bottles and yellowing paper bags. Phil had gotten a call early the next morning from the lab and had to rush off. He said to leave everything and he'd be back to clean up. Apparently he'd never returned.

"This looks cozy." Noah shut the door and yanked off the sheet on the nearest piece of furniture. Plopping down, he kicked his feet onto the small table, sending some of the bottles onto the floor. They crashed to the hardwood, two of them shattering, sending small bits of glass skipping across the room.

"Make yourself comfy," I mumbled.

"Always do," he shot back. "So tell me about your Rabb—Phil. What's he like?"

"He's quiet and a total mamma's boy. Wicked smart. Likes cheese..."

Noah snorted. "They all do. Mine had an entire wall in his room devoted to cheese posters. And the smell... It was kind of freaky."

"So you knew him, too?" I pulled off the sheet over the rocking chair and settled in. A part of me wanted to keep him talking. If I could pretend, even just for a little while, that he was my Noah, that I hadn't lost him, then maybe this whole thing would be bearable. "Why do they call him Rabbit?"

"Nickname. Not sure how he got it. Never said. Honestly, yours is the first one I've come across that goes by *Phil*. I intend to give him shit about it when I get home."

I'd never been good at small talk—which drove my Noah insane since he was a talker. Besides that, being back here made my heart hurt. My life had never been perfect. I knew my foster parents didn't love me, much less care about me. Everything they gave me, every opportunity I got, was a circus. They used it as publicity. *Look what we're doing for this poor, pathetic bottom tier orphan we took in.* It made me sick, but I'd vowed to use it to make a better life for myself. To thrive and find someplace I truly belonged. Noah had always looked out for me. I knew that no matter how bad things were, at the end of the day, someone cared.

Now all that had been taken away. Even if we somehow managed to prove that the Andersons were involved in Noah's death and got my listed status revoked, what kind of future did I have? I was broke, homeless, and would always be a Bottom Tier citizen.

Noah wasn't as content with the silence as I was. He shifted uncomfortably, pulling his feet off the table, wiggling in the chair, then kicking them back up—knocking more of the bottles to the floor. "So what was the deal between you and the other me?"

Acid boiled up in the pit of my stomach. "Kind of a personal question."

He shrugged. "No such thing."

I believed him, too. My Noah had been sort of the same. Not as intrusive or brash as this one, but his boundaries left a lot to be desired. Comparison number four: Tact. The difference between them was that mine went about it in a more tactful manner. A slow, steady approach instead of steamrolling full speed ahead.

"We were close." There. Short, sweet, and simple.

I should have known he'd never be satisfied with it.

"How close?" He made a circle with his right pointer and thumb, then poked his left pointer through the hole. With a waggle of his brows, he said, "We talking *close* close?"

"God. Are you always this much of an asshole?"

"I recall you already asking that. I answered, too." He kicked his feet off the table again and stood. "Besides, it was a legitimate question."

I stood as well, stalking forward until I was standing directly in front of him. "How the hell is my relationship with him a legitimate question?"

He pushed a little further, eyes narrowing to thin slits. The humor in his expression had drained away, replaced by something darker. "Um, 'cause technically he's *me*?"

"You?" I let out a stream of near-hysterical snorts. "*You?* He was as far from you as physically, mentally, and geologically possible!"

He opened his mouth, but I clamped my hand down across it.

"No. Stop. Don't say another word. Did it ever occur to you that talking about this hurts? That seeing you—hearing you speak—*hurts*?" I removed my hand and took a step back. "You are loud and rude and the most insensitive person I have ever met." Maybe I'd been wrong on the street. Maybe there was nothing more to this Noah Anderson than anger and aggression. Maybe I'd been looking too hard, desperate to find something redeeming to cling to.

"Yeah?" he snapped, matching my step away with one forward.

"Yeah," I fired back. "My Noah might have been a bit rough around the edges, but you...you're like a rusty chainsaw. You don't know when to close your mouth, you dress like a reject from the listed compound, and..."

Every step I took he matched until I had backed myself against the wall.

"Well?" he said. "Don't let me stop you. Keep going. What other ways do I suck? I mean, this other version of me was obviously perfection, right?"

"He wasn't perfect, but he was a good guy beneath it all." He was. Noah had loved me. I'd loved him. And now I was stuck here with this…this pale substitute?

"Sounds like a prize." He tilted his head to the side, his grin going from ear to ear. "So when was the wedding? He was your soul mate, right? Prince Charming?"

"It wasn't like that," I shouted. Every word out of this guy's mouth made me angrier. How the hell could one person push all my buttons at the same time? "He was my best friend. The one person I knew I could count on no matter what."

He tried to hide a smirk—and failed. "There's only one reason you'd be getting so worked up over this. It was like, what, a live-in friends-with-benefits thing? You guys were dancing the horizontal jig?"

"You're disgusting!" My voice rattled a little and I swallowed back the lump forming in my throat.

"So you *weren't* sleeping with him?" He shook his head, expression softening just a bit. There was something in his eyes I couldn't quite name. Anger? Jealousy? Whatever it was, it made me hesitate.

"I—" The rest of the excuse died on my tongue. I realized that I was ashamed of what had happened between Noah and me. It wasn't until that moment, prodded by this Noah's not-so-subtle ribbing, that I recognized where my own anger was coming from. *Guilt.* I'd acknowledged that the kiss had been a mistake, but it hadn't sunk in just how guilty I'd felt about it until right then. "We were just friends—and he was ten times the person you are."

He kept his hands at his sides despite the fact that he looked like he wanted to clock me just as much as I wanted to him, and stepped forward, effectively pushing me back. "That so? And what do you think you know about me?"

"I know you're a jackass."

"Obviously." He lifted his hands and began flicking his fingers, one by one. "But you forgot rude, stubborn, loyal as fuck, hot as hell—"

"Do you ever shut up?"

"Wanna know what I think?"

"I don't even want to be in the same room as you, so safe to say that, no, I don't want to know what you think."

He wasn't deterred. "I think there was more going on than just *friends*. I think something happened—"

I'd never been the violent type. I'd gotten into my fair share of verbal spars. A fistfight, though? No way. But in that moment, my limbs acted of their own accord. My right fist balled tight and zoomed through the air, right at Noah's head. It didn't make contact. At least not with its intended target.

He caught the swing inches from his face, smirking like I'd just whispered all the dirty, dark secrets I had in his ear. "Hit a nerve, did I? Maybe you *like* rude. Maybe jackass is your kink." He let go of my fist and leaned a little closer. "Go ahead. Tell me I'm not even the tiniest bit right. Tell me—"

I let out a howl and launched myself at him, but instead of stopping me, this time he allowed me to collide with him, full force. When I pulled away to smack him, he held tight and let out a sound that stirred something white-hot in the pit of my stomach. Secured tight, pressed up against his annoyingly perfect body, I felt him laugh. "See, I'm getting the impression that you like the chainsaw version of me."

And then he kissed me.

Chapter Seven

Noah

*I*t's wasn't like I planned it. I didn't walk into that dust-infested shack and think, *Hmm. How can I manipulate the situation to get a taste of those teasingly perfect lips…?*

Nope. This was all business and the fact that she was nice to look at was just some kind of pleasant side effect. Then she went and got all feisty and raw, and holy shit I couldn't help myself. Stoic Ash was a looker. Angry Ash was irresistible in a melt-your-dick-off kind of way.

It was a side of her I hadn't come across yet—and I liked it. A little too much.

The kiss was brief, but it was impossible not to notice that she didn't push me away. In fact, she kind of threw her all into it—making me even more curious about what had gone down between her and this world's version of me. We probably could have steamed up the windows, too—if Rabbit hadn't walked through the door, stepping on a squeaky floorboard.

He was standing in the doorway, looking from Ash to

me with a hint of confusion and just a little bit of irritation. He might have even opened his mouth to say something, but he never got the chance.

I burst out laughing.

"What's so funny?" He closed the door behind him and came farther into the room. Even circled me, staring like I had several heads and glowing eyes. "And who are you, exactly?"

Once I got my breathing under control, I let out a whistle and gave him a nice long once-over. He wore Dockers and a crisp, white button-down shirt with black shoes I probably could have seen my reflection in if I got close enough. His hair was slicked back, cut super short and au natural in color, and his normally bushy eyebrows were plucked to precise perfection. "What the hell are you wearing, man?"

The question took him by surprise and he glanced down at himself. For a second he actually looked like the Rabbit I knew. It didn't last. His jaw tightened and his eyes narrowed. "One more time, *man*. Who are you? Why are you in my house and why are you with *her*?"

Ash took a noticeably large step away from me and cleared her throat. Yeah. Because that didn't make her look guilty? "This is Noah. He's from—"

"Another Earth. Duh, Ash. I helped invent the tech, remember? What I want to know is why he's *here*."

"He needs your help—and so do I."

Rabbit snorted. "What makes you think I'd help him?" His eyes traveled over Ash in a way that pissed me off. Not leering, but with disgust. Like he was looking down on her. "Or *you* for that matter."

"Because it's what Noah would have wanted," she snapped.

That seemed to shut him up, so I decided it was my turn. "Look, I just need some answers and then I'm gone. I'll do what I came here to do and be on my merry little way."

"And what did you *come here* to do?"

Ash thrust her hands into her pockets. "They came here after a dangerous skip."

The moment she said it, Ash realized her mistake. I could see it in her eyes.

Rabbit saw it, too. "They? They who?" He turned to me.

I threw up my hands. "Whoa, man. I know I'm not your Noah—"

"Damn right." His disgusted gaze traveled me from tip to toe and he snorted. "The Noah of this earth would never be caught dead in Bottom-Tier clothes."

Clearly this world's Rabbit was a snob. "Well, your Noah's shitty fashion sense aside, where I come from, we're tight. In fact, dear Rabbit," I rushed on before he could argue, "we're tight in most realities."

His face paled. "What did you call me?"

Ha. Nailed it. "So then you *do* go by Rabbit here."

"No one's called me that in years. How did you—"

"Because whatever the reason you got that nickname was, it seems to be a constant."

"Constant?"

I shrugged. "Something that's the same in a majority of universes. Whatever the hell you wanna call it, though, we're close. You've always had my back."

He stepped back and sank into the chair Ash had uncovered. With a sigh, he ran a hand through his over-gelled hair. I got the impression he was bugged by what I'd said. His eyes darted around the room, between me, Ash, and the door, and he was looking a little pale. After a few minutes, he said, "I'm not making you any promises, but tell me what you're looking for."

Ash was still standing beside me. So close that all I would need to do is extend a finger and I could poke her. But after that kiss, I wanted to do a hell of a lot more than poking. Instead, I lifted the leg of my jeans to reveal the cuff I'd been wearing going on a year now. "There's something wrong with our cuffs."

He leaned forward, studying my ankle for a moment before sliding off the chair and getting down on the floor. "Wow. Haven't seen cuffs in ages. The Division still new where you come from?"

"It was in the early stages when I left. That was almost twelve months ago."

He stood. "Twelve months, huh? So you've, what? Been skipping from place to place for almost a year doing…?"

"Chasing," Ash supplied. Rabbit stiffened and grimaced. It was almost as though he'd forgotten she was here. "I told you, he came here looking for a skip. A dangerous one."

"I dunno how it works here, but my cuff is linked to a main—the one this *skip* is wearing. For the last month or so, it's been…malfunctioning. It seems to be getting worse."

With one last glare in Ash's direction, he turned back to me. "Malfunctioning how?"

"The guy we're following has a certain…agenda. Lately though, his movements have been erratic. The timing has been off. He's not doing what he came to in most places."

Rabbit snorted, then flung himself up and backward into the chair. "You're basing this whole thing off a guess?" He jabbed his pointer finger into the arm of the chair. "Couldn't this guy you're following just have decided to skip randomly? What's his agenda? Maybe it's changed. If he knows you're on his tail, then maybe he's trying to keep you guessing."

"It hasn't changed." Simply talking about this made my insides boil. Just thinking about Dylan and the damage he'd done was enough to make me lose my shit. "He's skipping with a single purpose. Revenge. Against those who sentenced him to death, and against my father—by killing Kori. Every single Kori he can find."

He was on his feet and had his cell whipped out in a half second. "Has anyone told Cora? Did Karl—"

Obviously he'd been out of the loop for the last twenty-four hours. I grabbed the phone as he started to dial. "The Andersons know," I said with a glance in Ash's direction.

She cringed, visibly swallowing. "Phil, it's too late. This guy killed Corey last night."

His eyes rounded, skin lightening to an almost translucent color. He stared at her, lip hitched and fingers digging into the arm of the chair so hard that I was sure his nails would pierce the leather.

"It's true," I said, handing him back his cell. I even managed to sound soothing—which was something Cade told me I needed to work on. I didn't understand why. He was the one who sugarcoated shit. To me, there was no point. The world was what it was and pretending anything else only led to heartache and disappointment. "Now that your Corey is gone, he'll probably be going after three others—unless the cuff malfunctions and he has to leave. Or, a worst-case scenario—has to stay. Trust me, you don't want this asshole stuck on your little slice of heaven."

Rabbit recovered and slouched back in his seat. You could see he was rattled, but, still Rabbit at his core, he was able to pull his crap together and work on the bigger picture.

"You think the cuff is forcing him to skip, therefore dragging you—and whoever else you're with—right along with him? Now you're worried it's stopped working all together?"

"That's the concern." There was no point in saying *me* anymore. The cat was out of the bag—but at least it hadn't been given a name yet. Cade and Kori were out there but their identities were still safe. "The timing is also out of whack. There's usually a delay, but this last skip, the one that brought us here, was almost instantaneous. Whatever is wrong with it is definitely getting worse."

"Sounds to me like the core might be going bad. We had a similar problem early on. That's the main reason we switched to the chip system. Prolonged use wears out the cuff's structure, which fries the insides. How often do you normally skip?"

"Normal time frame used to be once every six days or so. Sometimes longer, but that was the majority."

His mouth fell open. "Once every six days using a cuff? *For almost a year? Are you insane?*"

"Is that a trick question?" Ash said with a roll of her eyes. "Because he's—"

"Is it something you might be able to fix or not?" I said.

He didn't answer me right away. Instead, his gaze turned in Ash's direction. "What about you? Why are *you* here?"

She jabbed a thumb in my direction. "I told Noah I would help him."

Rabbit's eyes narrowed and he clenched his jaw, grinding his teeth for a moment before saying, "Like you *helped* our Noah?"

Ash looked like he'd slapped her, and a little voice inside my head goaded me to stalk across the room and wipe the walls with his face—which was bullshit. Why the hell did I care how he talked to her? "What are you babbling about?"

"She didn't tell you?" He jabbed a finger at her. "She might not have killed him, but she's still partially responsible for his death."

I'd met some impressive girls during this crazy ride. Self-reliant, independent and fierce, and ready to kick ass and take names. None of them compared to Ash in that moment. She flew across the room and grabbed Rabbit by the front of his shirt, hauling him off the seat. "Noah did not kill himself because of me!"

If he was stunned by the outburst and force that came with it, it didn't show. He simply removed her hands and took a step back. "Anyone who believes that a guy like Noah Anderson killed himself over a girl like you is smoking the good stuff and crapping out unicorns."

"So you believe me? That he was murdered?" The hope in her voice made me twitchy. I'd sounded like that once. When we'd first started all this. Even though I knew *my* sister was lost, I'd hoped I could save the others.

"I'm sure of it," Phil confirmed, voice barely above a whisper. "Just as much as I'm sure that I'm equally to blame for it."

Chapter Eight

Ash

I opened my mouth but no words came. Phil was still looking at me the same way. With tightly controlled tolerance and barely disguised disgust. Except now in addition to that there was something else. The shadow of guilt gleamed in his eyes. He wasn't the only one who'd changed.

Noah stood stiffer. He moved to stand beside me, almost protective in a way that made my chest ache. How many times had my Noah stood beside me as Cora raged? Everything from my behavior in public to a bad grade in school. He'd defended me through the worst of her tirades, even getting between us the one and only time she attempted to strike me. "What did you do?"

Phil looked from him to me and sighed. "He's always been on the fence about the things that went on at the lab, but last year when you pushed him—"

No one anywhere had ever *pushed* Noah Anderson to do anything. "Pushed him? What are you talking about?"

"You encouraged him to keep digging." His voice hardened and his entire body went rigid. "You said something wasn't right and if anyone could find out what was going on, it was him."

I remember the exact day I'd said it. Infinity had just won the lawsuit against Miriam Wagner, the reporter who claimed to have proof that they'd been skipping criminals to un-researched worlds. Noah had always questioned the work his parents did—probably because he knew what kind of people they were. When Wagner wrote an article claiming she had proof that Infinity had be dumping the worst of our society on random worlds—innocent worlds—for some reason, it made him really sit up and take notice.

"All I said was that someone should find out what kind of *proof* she had. He believed the reporter despite the fact that she retracted the entire article and resigned from the paper, assuming his parents had bullied or bribed her into it." And maybe Phil was right. Maybe I had pushed him. Maybe he would have continued to simply be ashamed of his parents' work instead of hell-bent on proving their wrongdoing if I hadn't suggested he could do something about it.

Maybe he'd still be alive.

"Doesn't matter *what* you said. He started digging into everything he could get his hands on, and when he came to me and asked that I keep an eye open, like an idiot I agreed. For the longest time I didn't see or hear anything. Then, a few months ago, I got wind of something called Omega."

Omega. That word…there was something familiar about it. "What's Omega?" It was the thing Noah had asked me about. Something Cora had said to him while I was out cold in the basement.

"All I know for sure is that it's a project Cora has been

working on for years. From what I gathered, the project even predates Infinity's contract with law enforcement." Phil let his gaze drop to the floor and shuffled from foot to foot. "I think that's why he's dead. I told him what I'd heard, the whispers about Omega, and he ran with it. I think he found a lot more than he bargained for."

"You—I..." Once again, no words would come. But feelings? Oh. Yeah. Those were coming with the force of a tsunami. I slapped him. The sound of it echoed through the eerily silent room, the force behind the blow sending warm pins and needles up my arm. "As cliché as this is gonna sound, how dare you? You knew damn well that note was bullshit and you said nothing? How could you sit there, silent, while Cora tells everyone he killed himself?"

He looked up. "Say something? To who? Cora and Karl Anderson own this town. Hell, they probably own parts of the government. If I'd opened my mouth, then I'd be just as dead as Noah. No one butts heads with the Andersons. You of all people should know that." Expression darkening, he added, "I can't stand you, Ash. I *never* liked you. I put up with you for Noah, but that's it. That note might have been pure fabrication, but the content hit a little close to home, don't you think?"

I knew we'd never be best friends, but his words were like a knife to the gut. Heat flamed to life in my cheeks.

"Yeah," he said. "Noah told me what you did. How you went and messed with his head."

"That's not what I meant to do." Knowing Noah was standing here, witnessing—hearing—all this made it ten times worse. We'd agreed the kiss was a bad idea and that had been that. But Noah had told Phil? That meant he hadn't been okay with it in the end. I *had* screwed things up...

An all-over rush of heat exploded inside me, followed
by an icy chill. I held my breath, choosing fury at his words
over devastation, because down in the deepest bits of my
soul, I knew some small part of what he was saying was true.
It was true and I was ashamed.

"He told you—he asked you not to! I don't believe for
one second that you didn't see how he struggled with your
whole twisted relationship. You're just a Bottom Tier tramp
who was looking for a way—"

"Whoa…" Noah held up his hands and stepped between
us. He grabbed the front of Phil's shirt, and for a second
I was sure he was going to toss the guy across the room.
Instead, though, he shoved him hard. Phil stumbled but
recovered, glaring at me with more hatred than I'd ever seen.
"Whatever went on between them seems like it should be
their business. And honestly? I don't really have time for
the high school drama. Omega? You were saying?"

Phil hesitated. With one last death-glare in my direction,
he refocused on Noah. "I think he found something about
Omega. He had something to tell me."

"Okay…"

He closed his eyes for a moment, and when he opened
them, there was an all too familiar glint there. "Except I kept
blowing him off. I know who Cora and Karl Anderson are.
Probably better than he did, and I was afraid…"

"So you thought putting it off would what, make it all
go away?" Noah was glaring at him like he wanted to slug
him. "Sounds like you were a great *friend*."

"I made a mistake. One I can never take back…" Phil
squared his shoulders and stood a little straighter, but I
didn't miss the way he flinched. With a sigh, he said, "I need
to know what he found about Omega. I want out from under

Cora's thumb. The only way I get to walk away from Infinity is if it doesn't exist anymore. At least not under Cora and Karl's rule. If you find out what it was he uncovered, if you give me a way to take them down, I'll fix your cuffs."

Noah regarded him silently for a moment before shaking his head. "There's little chance I could get my hands on the main cuff. Is that going to be a problem when it comes to fixing them?"

He shook his head. "I need the main cuff to make any type of alterations. You get me the information I need *and* that cuff—" he glanced at me, frowning— "Which should give you enough ammo to have your listed status reversed— and I will fix your little problem. Hell, I'll make them even better. Side note, though. You're on the clock. If I don't get the core out within fifty hours or so of it ceasing to function, it will fry the entire cuff. You'll be stranded."

It was a great idea, yanno, except for a few small problems. "How on earth are we supposed to—"

The sound of gravel out front and a flash of lights had us all frozen.

Noah darted for the window and tugged back the thick drapes with a curse. "Who knew you were coming up here?"

Phil shook his head. "No one. I hardly ever leave the lab, and when I do, I don't leave an itinerary."

"Well, someone followed you." He grabbed my arm and dragged me across the floor toward the back door. "We gotta go. We'll be in touch."

Noah had me pushed over the threshold and running for the tree line before I could even blink. As we went, I could see the glare of several additional sets of headlights as they pulled up the long gravel driveway. Hushed voices drifted toward us, followed by several shouts, one of which bellowed the word *woods*.

"Faster, faster," Noah snapped. He grabbed my wrist and pulled harder, making me stumble. I tried to catch myself, but the momentum was too much. I hit the ground with a grunt. His grip was so tight that I dragged him right along with me.

We'd ventured into the woods far enough that the thick trees overhead had blocked out what little light there was. Aside from a thin beam here and there, I couldn't really see much. Navigation was an issue and seeing obstacles—say, a tall man with a gun standing a few feet in our path—was challenging.

Noah let go of me and jumped to his feet. As the man swung out, he ducked. The action took him away from the path of the blow but disrupted his balance. He wobbled to the right, giving our attacker a chance to land a solid, well placed jab.

But this Noah, like mine, was no pushover. He took the hit like a champ, then fired back with two of his own. He struck the enemy first in the jaw, then again in the neck, just below his Adam's apple. He staggered back, choking, and Noah took the opportunity to bring his knee up, catching the guy in the gut. He crumbled to the ground.

"We need to get gone. Know someplace safe? At the risk of sounding like Cade, we need a plan."

"I know a place."

He hauled me upright in a single, graceful sweep, and we took off into the night.

...

I didn't remember my parents. I had no memory of them dying or the circumstances that landed me in a shambled Bottom Tier orphanage. The day I turned fourteen, Cora had given me an envelope with all my family information and not-so-subtly suggested I try finding a blood relative. Of course, I had—which had led me here.

"What is this place?"

I'd brought us to the outer limits of town, to a barely standing home at the back of an abandoned cul-de-sac. With every year that passed, more houses—hell, entire communities—were turning into this. Families skipped for the stupidest things, their properties left in limbo, sometimes for decades.

I ran my finger along the edge of the rotting deck. "My mom used to live here. She was the maid. Records show that the owner, a guy named Rickard Musa, was skipped just after I was born."

"Skipped? Why?"

I pushed through the door. I'd come here once a week for the first month after I'd found it. It was dirty and falling down, but it made me feel closer to the mother I'd never really known. This wasn't her home, but she'd lived here. Worked here. I had to believe there were pieces of her, regardless of how small, lingering in this place. Those unseen ghosts had brought me comfort on my darkest days. "Something about a debt dispute. I don't have the whole story. He was a Mid-Tier citizen. Treated my mom pretty good from what I found. After he was skipped she moved on. Not much information after that."

Noah closed the door behind him and followed me farther into the house. "Is this really the safest place to come? If this belonged to someone connected to your mother, then won't they come looking?"

"Nah. Cora has no idea I found it. She probably doesn't even know about it herself. I had to dig for almost a year to find it. I don't think we should stay for days, but we should be safe until we figure out exactly what to do. Catch our breath, ya know?"

"Speaking of…" He glanced at the couch. It was filthy and caved in on the right side, and I couldn't tell if the smell was coming from it or the house in general. In the end, Noah decided to settle on the floor in front of it. "Any ideas? They're out there looking for us. That guy back there was packing—but he didn't use it. Cora wants us alive for some reason. I don't wanna drag this whole mess back to Cade and Kori…"

"I know—" A sharp pain thrummed through my chest as I settled on the ground across from him. "I *knew* how Noah's mind worked. He was one of the smartest people I've ever known. If he'd really found something, he'd make a backup plan. Set something up for Phil or me to find in case something happened to him."

He drew his knees up and rested an arm atop them. How he could manage to look so casual, so comfortable, despite the situation and surroundings made me a little jealous. "What Rabbit said about you and him—"

"*Phil* doesn't know what he's talking about," I snapped. I hadn't meant it to come out so sharp, but he was starting to get to me. His face, his voice, the way that kiss caused my skin to heat each time I thought about it… It had tripped me up in a way that kissing my Noah hadn't. That had been a bad judgment call on my part. A mistake made from selfish curiosity. But this one was something else entirely… I shook off the confusion swirling inside my head and refocused on Noah.

Instead of returning the snip, he leaned back against the good side of the couch. He held his hands up in surrender. "Moving on."

I sighed. I could do this. I could play nice. So what if he looked and sounded like my best friend? He wasn't. Every moment I spent with him made that more and more apparent. "I think the first place to start would be his room at the house."

"Which I'm going to assume isn't someplace we can get to by waltzing in through the front door."

"We can't," I agreed. "But it won't be too hard to get in. The estate is massive and the boys always had a way in and out without being caught." I couldn't help snickering. "The Anderson boys were notorious troublemakers."

He smiled and my heart rate spiked a notch. "Yeah. I can see that."

"You sure this is safe?" Noah followed behind as I wove my way through the trees that bordered the Anderson estate. There was a small tunnel that led into the basement, the opening marked by a large bolder on which Corey had spray painted a caricature of his parents during one of his more rebellious stages. I hadn't been in this way in a couple of years, and while I was sure the paint had chipped and faded, I was hoping there was still enough left to mark the spot.

"Yes." We'd waited until noon, then headed back into town. I might have been booted from their lives, but Cora and Karl were notoriously habitual. "Every Tuesday they have a meeting with the heads of the science department at the Infinity building. They'll be out of the house for at least three hours."

"Is that gonna be enough time?"

Would it? Noah hadn't been known for his organizational skills. I often joked that his room was like a black hole. Still… If he'd left something, he'd make sure I'd be able to find it somehow. I hoped. "I'm not sure."

"That doesn't sound encouraging." Noah had called his friends to touch base. They were still looking for three people, plus some girl named Ava, and from what I could glean from the conversation I'd overheard, weren't having any luck. "So, uh, tell me something about me. I mean, him. What was he like?"

The question surprised me. "Oh. Well, he was nice."

Noah snorted. "Nice? Please. If all you can say about the guy is that he was nice, then he must have been boring as all hell."

"He wasn't boring," I said, defensive. He was anything but. Sometimes, I'd almost wished he was a little boring.

"So then tell me something interesting about him. *Please.* Save me from thinking I was a dud on this world."

"He was a hit with the ladies." I didn't know why, but something told me this Noah would appreciate that. "Like, I'm talking all ages. He spoke and every single one just fell in line." I couldn't help snickering. "It got so bad, at one point, he started using the cheesiest pick-up lines he could find to see if he could fail."

"Yeah? Like what?"

"We were out at a club one night. This girl had been eyeing him from the moment we walked in. Batting her eyes, flicking her hair—you know. I knew all he'd have to do was waltz over, flash her a smile, and she'd be his. So I bet him he couldn't turn her off. He walked over and asked her if she regularly sat in sugar because she had the sweetest ass he'd ever seen."

He let out a hoot. "Classic! Did it work?"

"No way. She fell for it and nearly threw him down on the bar right then and there."

"Nice." He laughed. "What about you? What lines have guys used on you?"

"Me?" Heat rushed to my cheeks for several different reasons. The first being him. What would I have done if the Noah standing in front of me had tried that sugar line on me? Truthfully? I probably would have decked him. Secretly? I would have found him adorable as hell. Second, how pathetic was my answer going to be? "I wasn't really in a position to be the target of pickup lines."

He glanced at me from the corner of his eye, past a strand of hair that had fallen loose from his band. "How so?"

"To the other boys in my tier, I was off limits while staying in a Top Tier home. If anyone was ever interested, he never came forward."

He laughed again, this time louder. "Right. You're going to try to get me to believe that a girl who looks like you never had any male attention?"

The heat in my cheeks burned brighter—first from his comment and then because of the truth. "I never said that. I had attention—more than I would have liked sometimes. It's just that the kind of attention I got didn't require the effort of pickup lines, if you know what I mean."

He stopped walking for a second, his expression a mix of horror and rage before wiping it blank and starting forward again. "Did it ever bother you? Seeing him with other girls?"

"I told you, it wasn't like that with us. I was never jealous of him with other girls."

"Well, the boys on this world are morons. I don't care what tier you were. I would have used every line in the book on you."

"Oh yeah?"

He held a hand to his heart and flashed me a smile. "Of all the beautiful curves of your body, your smile is my favorite."

"Pretty tame," I said, while on the inside I swooned just a little.

"On a scale of one to ten, you're a nine. I'm the one you need."

I rolled my eyes and faked a yawn, but I was fighting a grin.

He waggled his brow. Challenge accepted. "You're so damn hot, you'd make the devil himself sweat," he said. "Is your car battery dead? Because I'd like to jump you."

I snickered. "Better, but still…"

He stopped walking and took my hand. I tried to ignore the tingles it sent up and down my arm. Kneeling down in front of me, he waved his free hand and announced, "My attraction to you is like diarrhea—I just can't hold it in."

I burst out laughing—which, from the look on his face, was exactly what he'd been aiming for. He stood and laughed with me, but only for a moment before turning serious. He didn't say anything, but seemed to stand just a bit closer than before. I was about to match the move—even though every cell in my body screamed for me to move away, but then I caught sight of the rock.

"There!" I dashed ahead and circled the thing, amazed at how much of the original picture was still there. The elements hadn't ravaged it quite as much as I'd expected, and a part of me ached, knowing that eventually it would fade. It was one of the few, rare bits of an amazing talent the world would never get to experience. Corey had been a breathtaking artist, but Cora had forbidden him to pursue it. I'd overheard them fighting about it one night. One of the few times Corey had stood up to her. He begged and pleaded and threatened to leave if she wouldn't let him attend school. In the end, though, he caved. He always did. Noah might have had the strength to walk away from the family's money and privilege. Corey never would have.

I reached the boulder and spun in a slow circle, looking for the small grate. It took a moment, but I finally spotted it a few feet away, covered in overgrowth and flora.

"Watch out." Noah shouldered me aside, shrugged out of his leather jacket, and wrapped his fingers around the rusted bars as he went to work. It took several tries—and a whole lot of cursing—but he finally managed to pry the thing loose. I didn't miss the way his muscles flexed beneath the thin black T-shirt, or the way the sleeves rode up to reveal a series of dark black lines peeking out from beneath the material.

"Thanks," I said as he stepped aside to let me pass. As I went, our hands brushed, skin on skin, and a jolt like static zapped me. It left pins and needles in its wake. I bit down on the inside of my cheek and started down the long opening.

The narrow tunnel was dark and smelled of mildew. We walked for a few minutes in silence before Noah cleared his throat. "So are we just avoiding the whole thing?"

"Whole thing?" I was thankful for the dark because I knew exactly what he was talking about and felt my cheeks flame. I was fairly pale skinned, so the smallest hint of reaction and my face lit up like a traffic light. "Oh. Yeah. You win. Your lines are way cheesier than his were." It wasn't what he meant and we both knew it.

"That kiss back at Rabbit's was pretty intense."

What was I supposed to say here? That the kiss had basically almost stopped my heart? That it curled my toes and made me itch in ways I never imagined? Out of the blue and totally fierce, it'd been like he couldn't *not* kiss me. It made me think back to the night I'd kissed my Noah with an even mix of guilt and longing. It'd been a great kiss, but this one? This one had been cosmic.

Comparison number five: This Noah was a *better* kisser. "Of course it was. You assaulted me."

He grabbed my arm and spun me around to face him. "I don't remember you pushing me away."

I jerked free and narrowed my eyes. "Really? We're doing this now?"

He spread his arms. "Just trying to get the elephant out of the room—err, tunnel. That's all."

I rolled my eyes and started moving forward again. "Wasn't aware there was one." But he was right. Ever since Phil busted in, I'd felt it. This heaviness in the air between us. I kept sneaking glances at him, and I'd caught him looking at me, too. The conversation outside had been a nice detour, but it hadn't lasted.

"I'm sorry. Am I making you uncomfortable?" There was a hint of sarcasm in his voice. It was achingly familiar. He was right behind me. I felt his breath on my neck. "How about you just answer one question, then I'll let it drop."

If it would get him to leave it alone, I would have flashed him. I stopped and whirled around. "Fine."

"How did it feel?"

"Feel?" I stared at him. "This is about stroking your ego? Rest easy, then. It wasn't a bad kiss."

"Not what I mean," he said, then grinned. "And no shit. I know it wasn't a bad kiss. I don't *give* bad kisses."

"Another thing you have in common," I mumbled. "Inflated ego."

"Do you feel like you want to do it again?"

I stopped again, this time refusing to turn around. Did I want to do it again? *Yes, please*! Would I? *Hell no*! This was Noah's look-alike. His double. This guy was a poor substitution for the loyal rock I'd known nearly my entire life. So what if the kiss had nearly singed my nerve endings? Big deal if I felt the need to do it again.

"If you're trying to ask if I felt some kind of cosmic connection with you, then the answer is no. The kiss was just a kiss—and not even a great one. My Noah was far better at it than you are." There. That sounded convincing, right?

"Far better?" His face contorted, eyes scrunching and lips twisting. "Far—"

"Hit a nerve, did I?" I said, mimicking his earlier statement. I should have let it go. We weren't down here for a nice evening stroll, but his expression goaded me. That, and a healthy dose of guilt. I'd kissed my Noah, but we weren't a thing. We were never going to be a *thing*. It was just me losing a grip on the weird connection we'd always had. Still, a small part of me felt like I'd betrayed him when I didn't push this Noah away back at Phil's cabin. "Don't feel bad. Like I said, it was a decent kiss. You've obviously had a little practice. Your hand? Maybe on an orange or some other kind of fruit?"

"I've kissed more girls than you," he snapped.

I threw up my hands. "I sure hope so. I've never kissed another girl."

The light in here was horrible, but I was pretty sure his face was turning a funky shade of scarlet. We were on a time crunch, but this was just too damn fun. My Noah hadn't been even tempered by any stretch of the imagination. But he tended to keep his cool when people tried to rattle him. Seeing him like this, so torqued and ready to pop, was pure entertainment.

"You—I—" he stammered.

"Maybe you used to be better at it?" I prodded. "I mean, you probably don't get a lot of time to date while skipping all over creation, right? Maybe you're just out of practice?"

"I'm not out of practice." He seethed.

"It's okay! It's nothing to be ashamed of—" For the second time since we'd met, he assaulted me.

One second I was having the time of my life pushing his buttons—ridiculously easy to do—the next I was against the wall, Noah's body covering mine. His lips moved furiously, scorchingly hot and with a level of passion I'd never felt before. His tongue slipped between my lips and despite having told other guys that I hated that, I melted, reveling in the millions of electrical tingles the action sent shooting through my body. His hands gripped my head on either side. No roaming, no exploration. Somehow it made the whole thing hotter. Like he couldn't bear to release me in fear that I'd move. That I'd get away and he'd have to stop. And *stop*? No. That was a dirty word. A softly whispered sin in the darkest corners of the earth. Stopping this would be a crime of the highest caliber.

Except he did. Stop, that was.

He pulled away just far enough to look me in the eye,

not yet letting go of my head. With an extremely satisfied tilt of his lip, he said, "Decent my ass." Then he let go and took a long step back, gesturing with a flourish in the direction we'd been walking. "We should probably get moving."

I nodded and pushed off the wall, unable to speak. Hell, I was barely able to walk, terrified that I wobbled as I went. If the kiss with my Noah had gone like that, things would have turned out a hell of a lot differently.

Chapter Nine

Noah

We reached the end of the tunnel, then slipped through the basement and up the stairs. I followed behind, mentally kicking my own ass for allowing her to poke me like that, but smug as hell for proving her wrong.

Holy shit did I prove her wrong…

When we got to the top of the steps, Ash poked her head around the corner. "Follow me. His room is upstairs."

We crept up the stairs and moved quietly down to the end of a long hallway decorated with gaudy knickknacks and obnoxious gold foil trim. Everything in the house was done in shades of tacky. My mother would die if she could see this. Her style was what she liked to call farmhouse chic. Nothing fancy or overdone. Just simple rustic accents against neutral colors. This place was giving me a damn headache.

"Here." Ash stopped outside the last room on the right. She slipped inside and gently closed the door behind us—just as something creaked downstairs. She froze, paling. "Someone's here!"

Keys jingled and a door creaked from downstairs. I pressed myself against the door, dangerously close to her. I felt the shift of her body as she inhaled sharply, the action creating just enough friction to be distracting. Twice now I'd kissed her. Twice now I'd been unable to control myself. "Great. This is just what I need right now." I wasn't sure if I meant the person who'd just entered the house—or my inability to keep my lips off Ash.

Ash's face turned a sickly shade of yellow and her mouth fell open. "No one is supposed to—"

I clamped a hand across her mouth and pressed an ear to the door. I even managed to ignore the feel of her warm, soft lips pressed against the inside of my palm. Yep. Definitely someone here. Multiple someones.

"What are we doing here, exactly?" a man's voice said. He didn't sound thrilled to be here.

"Anderson wants us to watch the place. He thinks the Calvert girl might try breaking in," another said.

Wonderful. I turned to Ash, who was staring at the door. "Well?" I whispered. "Can we do this quietly or not?"

"Should be able to. The house is huge. They'll probably set up in the sitting room. There's no reason for them to come up here."

I was sure this was a bad idea, but nodded. Whatever information this world's Noah had, I needed it to get Rabbit to fix the cuffs. "Where do we start?"

The panicked look in her eyes faded and she squared her shoulders. With a nod toward the desk, she said, "You try over there. I'll take the closet."

We set to work, moving as quietly as we could—which wasn't as easy as one might think. Like me, this world's Noah was not only a pack-rat, but a slob. Cade would have a meltdown if he could see this place.

I checked each drawer, pulling everything out and sifting through all the papers. Receipts, ticket stubs, lots of junk. By the time I was done, the most telling thing I'd found was a day planner. It was mostly unused, with only several notes made this month—all benign things.

"Anything?" Ash had moved onto the dresser after clearing the closet, nightstand, and under the bed. She looked like she'd had just as much luck as I had.

She sank to the floor and sighed. "Nothing." Bracing her elbows against her knees, she let her head fall forward into her hands. "Maybe there's nothing here. Maybe we were just wrong. Maybe what Phil said about feeling—"

"Do you think you were wrong?" I crossed the room and settled in front of her. "Do *you* believe he killed himself?"

She lifted her head and our eyes met, and something stirred deep inside. Something I'd been refusing to acknowledge. A beast that I'd buried beneath layers and layers of snark and sarcasm. When I'd seen the first few versions of us together, I'd scoffed. I'd laughed and made fun of Cade when he told me she was my constant. The idea that there was someone out there—a single, perfect person who complimented me in every way—I'd thought it absurd. Fate? Destiny? Love at first sight? What crap. That shit was for losers. I set out to prove, if anything, it was attraction at first sight and nothing more—and I did. Every Ash who hadn't been with a version of me already had sparked and ignited. Then I found this one. This annoying, impossible, twisted-up-in-knots version. One that actually set all the alarms ringing and made me twitch for all the wrong—and right—reasons.

The first kiss had been me falling into old habits. See an Ash, kiss the crap out of her, prove how easy it was to walk away. Boom. Done. The second kiss had been all about proving *her* wrong. She'd gotten under my skin, coaxed out my inner competitive asshole. I did it to teach her a lesson. And I had. It was equal parts passion, pride, spite, and anger. She'd pissed me off and I'd showed her how hot it could have been between us and what she'd have to be going without. That kiss had left one hell of an impression. The problem was, it'd backfired. I was hyper aware of her now. Where she went, my gaze followed. I found myself leaning forward, just to be closer to her.

"No," she whispered, leaning just a bit closer as well. Her lips parted, just enough for a tiny pink tongue to dart out and skate across their surface. That stupid, simple little action was enthralling to watch. Mesmerizing in a way that had the potential to hold me captive, to keep me chained. She was in the zone, too, but before either of us could do something stupid, she froze. "What's that?"

My pulse was doing triple-time and it was a struggle to keep my breathing even. "Hmm?"

The warmth from her nearness dissipated as she scrambled away from me. When I turned, I saw that she'd picked up the day planner I'd found on other-me's desk.

"This is Noah's planner."

"So?" I wasn't sure if I was relieved by the interruption or pissed. Obviously a gropefest in the middle of a potentially life-threatening situation was a bad idea. Bad in a way that even I wasn't normally into. But, holy shit. This girl made my head spin. She made all common sense and logic pack the hell up and shuffle off. She'd managed to get under my skin without even trying. "Doesn't look like he really used it. Didn't see anything useful."

She ignored me and flipped through, skimming the

pages with a renewed sense of hope. "This is weird…"

"What?" I shifted—mainly because the slowly receding tightness in my pants was starting to become uncomfortable—and moved to sit in front of her. She set the book down on the floor between us and jabbed a finger at one of the small squares. It was today's date with the notation *I. G. CP. Cleaver*. In small, almost illegible print, beneath that, it read *doing the Duchess – 11 p.m.*

"IGCP." She thought about it for a moment. "That has to be the Infinity Gala Costume Party."

"Okay…?" I still wasn't seeing the big deal. "And Cleaver?"

She thought about it for a minute. "Only thing that comes to mind is one of the graphic novels Noah loved, *Dark Tide Ridge*. Cleaver is one of the main characters."

"So, maybe he was going to this shindig as Cleaver? Maybe he had a hot date at 11 with some duchess?"

"They throw this thing every year. Cora and Karl guilt Corey into going, but never Noah. He hates this stuff."

"Still not seeing the big deal."

She shook her head. "This is it. This is the clue I was looking for."

"You think he left you a clue by telling you he was going to his parents' costume party dressed as a character from a graphic novel, then planned to screw some duchess at eleven?" I closed the book and pushed it away. "I think you're reaching here."

"Obviously it can't be that simple." She slumped back. "I don't get the duchess thing…"

"Maybe he just had a date, Ash."

"He wasn't dating anyone." Her reply came too fast and with far too much insistence. "And he'd never pencil it in his book. I mean, seriously? If you were going on a date, would you write it down as *doing the duchess*? Even you're not that big an asshole."

Ouch. "And if he was, would you be jealous?" Because as monumentally insane as it was, the idea that she'd be jealous made *me* jealous.

"I told you it wasn't like that. We weren't a couple so why would I be—"

"—just gonna do a round." One of the voices from downstairs grew louder. "Then we'll head out."

"That's our cue." I jumped up and dragged her with me as the footsteps on the stairs grew closer. Shoving her toward the window, I raced back to lock the door. A second later, I was hauling myself over the sill, onto the small balcony right behind Ash.

We raced across the property and didn't stop until we'd made it almost back to the house we'd been squatting in. I was all for getting off the street, but Ash had stopped, watching me with an odd expression.

"What?" I said. "What'd I do now?"

"Tell me," she said, voice barely above a whisper. "I can see the way you look at me—even when you're being an asshole. There's never been anyone who looked at me like you do. Not even, well, you... Tell me what we were to each other where you come from."

Of everything I'd expected, that hadn't been on the list. What the hell was I supposed to say here? "We were nothing," I said. There was no way to disguise the disappointment in my tone. I'd told myself that I was writing this off. Giving up on the idea of the perfect Ash and moving on with my damn life. I was getting the feeling I wouldn't be able to follow through.

"That isn't true." She moved a little closer, now just

inches away. I could smell her shampoo. Coconut mixed with some kind of mint.

"It is. You don't exist where I come from. Or, if you do, we hadn't met." The confession stung more than it should have. "I've seen you before, though."

"Seen me on other earths, you mean?"

"A lot of them." What I felt wasn't love. We'd just met, for fuck's sake. But it wasn't simply infatuation, either. It wasn't just physical—despite the fact that she was hot as hell and the spark between us could burn down an entire country.

"A lot?"

"Most of them." My fingers itched to touch her. I knew I shouldn't. My motives were selfish. I wanted to feel her skin against mine again. I wanted another taste.

"And we were...?"

Silence.

I was intrigued by her. Curious about her past. I found myself wanting to ask questions, to learn what kind of animals she liked and the foods she found disgusting. The answers wouldn't be textbook. Nope. Not with a girl like this. Kittens and corn dogs need not apply. For the first time, I'd met a girl I found *interesting*.

"What were we, Noah?"

Fuck it.

"We were together." My brain was telling me to pull back, but everything else—my heart, my body—shit, even my muscles—were telling me to stay right where I was. "You and me. We were a thing."

"A thing," she repeated. She still hadn't moved, either. "As in—"

"Cade thinks you're my constant."

"Like, we're fated or something?"

"I don't believe in that shit." Reality was starting to seep back in. She was beautiful, standing there with her kiss-me lips and those stormy gray eyes, but she was still just *an Ash*. Another version of the same girl I'd messed around with over and over. And sure, this one was a little different than the others, but what did that mean? Nothing. It *had* to mean nothing. "Do you?"

She gave a soft laugh but still didn't pull away. In fact, I was pretty sure she leaned a little closer. "Not even a little bit. But that kiss was…" She closed the small distance between us, stopping a fraction of an inch from my skin. Without touching me, she moved up my neck and across my cheek, her warm breath sending an involuntary shudder through me that was right up there with Pompeii—and just like that chunk of rock, if she didn't back off, I was going to explode.

I gripped her arms, meaning to push her away, but my muscles refused to obey. "Not the time or place for this." Yeah. Even I wasn't convinced.

"Look at our lives. You run from one version of this town to another to catch a killer, and I've been branded a killer—"

"Then it looks like it's a good thing I found you." I couldn't help it.

She smiled. I could tell she was trying not to, to be all serious and shit, but she failed—and I was glad she did. "There's never going to be a time for *this*," she said. "Right now? This time? It's all we have. It's all we might ever have…"

And without further argument from me, she rose onto her toes and kissed me. Unlike the previous smackers, though, this one was slow. It was more than hormones and lust. It was connection.

And in that moment, I was glad for it.

Chapter Ten

Ash

I'd never really been comfortable around other girls. I'd tried. When I first came to live with the Andersons and they'd placed me in school, my attempts to make friends had been honest but fruitless. Even at that young age, the kids had been programmed to look down on me. I was the girl matriculating well above her stature, the unwanted charity case they all couldn't wait to be rid of. The boys ignored me for the most part, but the girls…the girls had been downright cruel.

Then, as we all got older, the animosity changed. The whole thing shifted. It went from disgust to jealousy. The Anderson boys were the endgame of every Top Tier girl in town. Even a few of the ambitious Mid Tiers thought they'd get a shot. The fact that I had an in with them, sometimes even coming across as having Noah wrapped around my finger, made me public enemy number one. I ignored it for the most part, never bringing attention to it, but now, sitting in the room alone with Kori, I found myself feeling that familiar need to squirm in my seat. She'd been nothing but sweet to me, but old habits died hard.

"How are you doing with all this?" she asked. Probably couldn't stand the silence, either. After I finally screwed up the guts to break that kiss—that amazingly perfect right-in-a-way-that-made-angels-sing kiss—Noah and I had met his friend and sister back at the hotel. Not even five minutes inside the door and Cade was dragging him off to *deal with something*.

I shrugged and pulled my feet onto the bed, tucking them beneath me. "I, uh, guess it's easier for me than it was for you." When she quirked her brows, I added, "Noah told me you had no idea about Infinity. That it was a secret?"

"Oh. Yeah. Where I come from, Infinity is a government project run by my dad. Inter-dimensional travel? That was just for books and movies as far as I knew. Then I found out the truth…"

"Your dad…Karl Anderson, you mean."

"Yes. He's your stepfather here, right?"

"Foster."

She looked uncomfortable. "Right. Foster. And he's… You don't get along?"

"He and Cora never liked me. They only took me in to gain attention. Noah tells me they're not the standard representation. Most others he's encountered have been different." In the beginning I'd tried to win Cora over. I'd worn the pretty dresses with the over-the-top frill in assorted shades of pink and red. I'd happily allowed her to parade me around town, shopping and eating ice cream in an attempt to showcase our new found mother-daughter bond. I'd even scrambled to catch up in school, studying day and night to pull ahead of the others for the chance to make her proud.

Each attempt was met with the same disconnected scowl, then, in later years, flat-out hatred.

She offered a small smile. "They really are."

A few moments of awkward silence ticked by. I had a thousand questions, and while I swore to myself I'd let it go after that—whatever the hell it had been back at the house with Noah—I found myself more and more curious. "Can I ask you something?"

Her lip twitched with an oddly knowing grin. "Is it about Noah?"

"Sort of."

She shifted until she was facing me fully, then nodded. "I'll answer what I can, but remember that I haven't known him that long."

"He said that your boyfriend—"

"Boyfriend?"

"Oh. I thought the other guy, Cade, isn't he—"

She snickered. "I wouldn't call Cade my *boyfriend*. It's so much more complicated than that."

The way Noah had made it sound… "But you guys like each other, right?"

There was a slight blush to her cheeks. "Oh yeah. We like each other *a lot*. I'm just not sure what label I'd slap on us just yet."

"Noah said he's your constant?"

"Seems that way. He's been to multiple realities where we were together. We were together where he came from, too."

"But she died." My heart hurt for Noah. The haunted look in his eyes when he spoke about his biological sister was raw and tormented.

"She did," Kori confirmed. There was a twinge of sadness

in her voice. "Which is just one of the things that complicates things between me and Cade. There's definitely something there. Something I want to chase. We're just being careful, ya know? One day at a time."

I couldn't imagine having to compete with another version of myself. "Noah told me Cade thinks that your brother is my constant."

Her smile faded, replaced by a thoughtful tilt of her lip and the slight lift of her brow. "It looks that way, yeah."

"But I had a Noah. We weren't—it wasn't—" God. I'd never had trouble describing our relationship before. Of course, that was before I went and screwed it all up...

She sighed. "On Cade's world, he and I had been together since, like, grade school I think. Everyone expected them to end up together. He was all for it. He was nuts about her—but she wasn't nuts about him. At least not in the same way. Long story short, he met me and eventually realized that what they had wasn't what he really thought it was. He's got a theory about the whole thing." Pride sparked in her eyes, and it was so obvious when she spoke about him that *she* was nuts about him. "He has a lot of theories."

"I think I'd like to hear this theory."

"Cade believes all the Koris and Cades out there are meant to be." She laughed and the flush in her cheeks got a little bit brighter. "Stupid, huh? That whole destiny thing used to make me want to puke. But I've seen it firsthand now. It's kind of insane."

"But you said his Kori—"

"Just wasn't the *right* Kori for him."

"That's hard to swallow." And even though I spoke the words out loud, a part of me wanted so badly to believe them. I'd always been captivated by Noah Anderson. The physical attraction I'd felt was nothing short of electric and had, at times, scared me a little. That night I'd kissed him, it'd made me stupid. But when this new Noah showed up, all those old feelings flared back to life and intensified. And when *we* kissed…I thought for sure we'd burn the entire town to the ground. But he rubbed me in a way my Noah hadn't. Made me itch and twitch. He said the stupidest things and made me so angry, yet at the same time, made me want to figure out what made him tick. He was confusing and complicated and I found that utterly enthralling.

"Did something happen between you and my brother?"

I didn't miss how she called him her brother, and I wondered how Noah would feel about that. He'd never once referred to her as his sister, but I got the feeling that he felt the same way.

"Let me guess," she said. The humor drained from her expression, replaced by what I could only describe as concern. "You feel this insane attraction to him?"

The plan was to answer simply. One word. Maybe two. I didn't need to give this girl, this stranger, my life story. But the guilt was starting to crush me now, and I felt like the pressure was getting heavier and heavier. "We always had this weird push and pull, me and my Noah. Sometimes when he looked at me I could see the fight in his eyes. The war between staying firmly in the safe zone, and crossing a line we'd both agreed never to venture over."

Her brows drew together, lips tilted in a frown. Not with judgment, but compassion. "And did you? Cross that line?"

"I kissed him. He asked me not to." A small snort escaped my lips. "Begged me. But I was selfish. So caught up in the moment, in what I wanted, that I risked destroying one of the few good things in my life."

"Ash…" Kori stood and crossed to my bed, then settled down beside me. She slipped her arm around my shoulder. It was awkward and stiff, but I still found it comforting in an odd way. "Obviously I don't have a ton of experience with this kind of thing." She leaned away and spread her arms wide. "Other dimensions? That's still kinda new to me. But I do understand complicated. And it sounds like what happened is just that. Complicated. It was just a kiss. One I'm betting he wanted just as much as you did."

She was right. I'd felt it in the way he'd responded. There was no hesitation. But what I felt for this new Noah was so much more intense than anything I'd ever experienced with him. It was more complex—and that scared me. "Noah—the one that came with you… We kissed, too." I felt the heat in my cheeks. "A few times, actually."

There was a sparkle of mischief in her eyes. "And?"

"And… It was nothing like the kiss with my Noah." I found that I was smiling. Grinning, actually. There was a good chance my cheeks were bright red, too, but in that moment I didn't care. Just thinking about that kiss made me feel warm all over. "It was…I've got no words for what it was—which makes zero sense."

She gave a knowing nod. "I think it's the universe's way of telling us to sit up and take notice, ya know? It's saying, pay attention because I just dropped this fairly perfect match right in your lap."

"Perfect match?" I laughed. "It was an amazing kiss, but—"

"He affects you in a way your Noah didn't, right?"

Did he? It was more than that kiss, wasn't it?

"You've affected him, too," she said quietly. "We haven't been here long, and I'm still getting to know him, but I can see it."

I both loved and hated the sentiment. The rational part of me wanted to dismiss it. Who in their right mind bought into this kind of thing?

On the other hand, the idea that there was this perfect complement to me walking around out there was as insane as it was amazing. The thought that there might be someone who both needed and wanted me—for reasons other than to use me for whatever reason—made my heart beat faster.

"Just..." She hesitated, then sighed. "Noah is a complicated guy. Like I said, I'm still getting to know him, but from what Cade's said, after his sister died, he kind of spiraled. I don't get the impression he was ever Mr. Straight and Narrow, but his behavior got a little self-destructive."

I could see that. He was abrasive and could be cruel, but there was something beneath it all that screamed of pain. This Noah Anderson was hurting.

"Everything okay?" Cade asked suddenly. I had been so lost in thought, I hadn't even heard the door open and Cade and Noah slip inside, both carrying several bags of take-out food.

Kori slid off the edge of my bed and crossed the room to where Cade was setting a handful of shopping bags down on the small table. "Yep. You?"

"Didn't have any problems—and we found Odette."

"Alive?"

"Alive," Noah confirmed. "And if I had to guess, I'd say Miles and Penny are alive and well also." He dug into one of the bags, then pulled out a small bag of chips. "Our original theory was right. Doesn't seem like Dylan is looking for them."

"But he went after this world's me?" Kori turned and pointed in my direction. "He tried to kill Ash."

"I think that was more a coincidence than anything else," Cade said. He put his arm around Kori, and the way she leaned into him, taking obvious comfort in his touch, made me a little jealous. They might not have defined the thing between them, but she was his and he was hers. They belonged to each other.

"We think he's focusing on trying to find Ava and fix the cuffs. If they stop working, then he's stuck here." Noah opened one of the bags and pulled out a fry.

"So then how do we find him?"

"We don't," he said. He settled on the bed across from me, demolishing the single fry and tearing open the rest of the bag. He proceeded to dump out its contents—four burgers and two packages of fries—and start shoveling things into his mouth. "At least not this second."

"You think we should focus on getting information on Infinity?" Cade didn't look happy, but he seemed to agree. He dug into one of his bags and pulled out a burger from McDogal's, then passed it to Kori.

"If we get this world's Rabbit the information he needs to take down Cora and Karl, then we can figure out a way to get Dylan—and the main cuff—so he can fix whatever's wrong." She took a burger, then passed the bag to me.

"He'll try to fix it," I corrected. There were three burgers left inside the bag, but I wasn't hungry. Between everything going on with Cora, and Kori pretty much confirming that this thing I felt—whatever it was—for her Noah went both ways, my stomach was in knots.

Besides, I wanted to find that information as much as Phil did. It was the only chance I had at clearing my name. But I didn't want any of them entering into this under false pretenses. Their Cora and Karl were apparently kittens compared to my foster parents. God only knew how this would all turn out.

"Whatever," Noah said with a roll of his eyes. He dumped the remaining contents of the first package of fries into his open mouth, then wadded it up and tossed it into the trash. He missed and the foil bag hit the floor. "Point is, we're in the same boat Dylan is. I, for one, don't want to get stuck in a world where my parents are murderers."

"There's a good possibility that the information Phil— Rabbit—is looking for is something my Noah had. We think we have a lead on Omega, a project Infinity has been working on."

"Then let's move on it." Cade crumbled the wrapper from his burger and tossed it at the trash bin. Unlike Noah's, his went in. "What's the lead?"

I could tell Noah still wasn't convinced the party was anything valid. He sighed and said, "Some party Cora and Karl are throwing tonight. A costume gig."

"That'll make it easier for you two to blend in," Kori said. She'd taken a few bites of her burger, but didn't seem thrilled with it. It had to be weird, going from place to place. I couldn't imagine the kinds of differences they saw in the dietary department. Our burgers were made with 100 percent goat meat. Who knew what they were like where she was from.

"All we know for sure is that he marked it on a calendar, along with what we think is his costume choice and some note about doing some duchess at eleven."

"*Doing* a duchess?" Kori cocked her head to the side, and with the slight tilt of her head, long hair falling down across her cheeks, I was struck by how much she resembled Noah. She actually looked more like him than my world's

Corey had. "Does that mean what I think—"

Noah threw up his hands. "No clue."

"We're not sure exactly what it means," I rushed on before Noah could scoff some more. While it wasn't the rock-solid lead I would have liked, I knew in my gut this was something. "I think maybe he was meeting someone at the party. Possibly a source or something on Omega."

"Do we know anything else about this Omega thing?" Cade glanced at Noah.

"Rabbit said he gave the other me a heads-up about some project Infinity was involved in called Omega. Didn't know what it was, but apparently other me ran with it in hopes of finding enough ammo to bring Mommy and Daddy down."

Kori nodded. "And you think he was going to the party to get information about the project?"

It was more a stab in the dark than anything else, but what more did I have? "That would be my guess."

"Well, then she wouldn't be there, would she? This 'duchess'? Noah is dead. Everyone knows it. If he was meeting someone, she wouldn't still show."

He had a point. An annoying, depressing point. "I'm betting it was someone who was going to be at the party already. To have the information he needed, it has to be someone inside Infinity, so good odds that she'll still attend."

"And we're supposed to find her how?" Noah leaned forward. "Go around and ask who the duchess he was planning to do at eleven is?"

"We'll just have to scope things out. See if anyone—or anything—stands out." Would it be harder? Yes. But what other choice did I have? This was my only way out. Cora and Karl needed to pay. For what they'd done to me, to

Noah…all of it. This was my chance to not only get off the list, but to be free of the Anderson family once and for all.

Cade nodded. He was quiet for a moment before a slow smile spread across his face. He reached into the bag at his feet and pulled out another burger. Jabbing it at Noah, he said, "Up for some partying?"

Noah matched his grin with one of his own—a smile so devastating that it should have been illegal. "Haven't been to a good party in a long time."

Chapter Eleven

Noah

We spent the rest of the day hunting down the things I'd need to become Cleaver. And by *we*, I meant Cade and Kori. It was one thing for Cade and me to skulk around to track down Penny Mills— but mall hopping? Yeah. I was benched, but I wasn't alone.

I still hadn't decided if that was a good thing or not.

Ash had settled on the far side of the room, which was fine with me. The one time she'd crossed to my side, her hand innocently brushing mine as she grabbed the television remote, I thought we'd both explode. She'd been going over the possibilities, making a list and reciting about a trillion variations of the phrase *doing a duchess*—names, places, landmarks—out loud.

I was close to losing it.

"That's getting annoying."

She kept her head down, focusing on the slip of paper in front of her. "Why? Because you want to kiss me again?"

"Meh." I kicked my feet onto the table and leaned back

in the chair. "There are worse ways to kill time." I shouldn't even be joking about it, though. Just the thought had me ready to leap from the chair and pounce on her like some kind of freaking animal.

I'd never had this much of a reaction to her before. Sure, the chemistry had been off the charts the times we'd met. Wham, bam, meet you in heaven then scram. But this Ash, she was different from the others.

I didn't want her to be different... I *needed* her not to be different.

She set the pen down and squared her shoulders. Without a word, she pushed away from the small table and stood. Turning, she crossed the room, stopping a foot or so away from me. "Okay."

"Okay...what?"

"Let's do it." She kicked off her sneakers. "Let's satisfy your curiosity. That's what you want, right? A chance to see what all the fuss is about?" Her eyes narrowed.

"I—"

"You're hot for me. I'm hot for you. Let's just get it over with."

My mouth fell open. "You're saying—"

"We should sleep together. Yeah. I mean, it's not like I haven't fantasized about it before, and like you said, we have time to kill."

"What Rabbit said..." *Noah told me what you did. How you went and messed with his head...* She kept insisting he was her friend, but there was more to it than that. Something had gone down between them. Something had changed right before his death. Something she was having a hard time living with. "What really happened between you and me?"

"If any part of what Phil said was true, it wouldn't be a shock to anyone here." She was directly in front of me now, looking down on me. There was passion in her movements, but also anger. Rage so tightly controlled that it reminded me of me. "Maybe I *was* messing with his head. Maybe I didn't even know I was doing it. What other explanation could I have for doing such a stupid thing?"

"What did you do, Ash?"

She leveled her gaze at me and laughed. She laughed so hard that for a second, I was sure she'd topple over. When she regained control of herself, she took a shaky breath and said, "I kissed him. I kissed him even though I knew it was wrong on so many different levels. Even though he didn't want me to."

I stood and took a single step toward her. Her eyes were wild and her entire body rigid. She was hurting, and even though I knew in my gut that her Noah probably *had* wanted her to kiss him, telling her that now wouldn't make her feel better. If I were in her shoes, it would probably just piss me the hell off. "It was a kiss. An innocent—"

"*Innocent*? You don't understand how this place works, but a Bottom Tier will do *anything* to claw their way out of the slum."

Was that how she really saw herself? As some desperate girl unable to stand on her own?

"It was anything but innocent. I was attracted to him. I didn't love him—not like *that*—but I still wanted him. Deep down, I think I always did." She played with the hem of her T-shirt for a moment, then pressed herself against me. She leaned in and trailed her lips up the side of my neck, to my ear. "Tell me you're not curious. That you don't want to kiss me again…"

I held my breath, willing my hands to stay motionless at my sides.

Of course I *wanted* to. Other than the obvious—hello, I was a guy—this was my go-to cure for the Ash-related sickness. Find her, get her out of my system, move the fuck on. So far it'd worked like a charm, and if ever there was a call for it, it was now—with this girl. Cade told me once that when I found Ash, the *right Ash*, there'd be no way I could walk away. So far, I was 4 for 0. I was determined to prove to Cade that there was no such thing as a constant. If she wanted to make it 5-0, then that was okay with me.

Instead of answering, I wrapped my hands around her waist and pulled her closer. She tangled her fingers through my hair, wrapping them around the longer strands and tugging while at the same time, she captured my mouth and shifted against me.

I let out a groan and my fingers gave an involuntary twitch, digging into the soft skin of her back. She hissed but seemed into it, deepening the kiss. The sensation was intense. I felt like a live wire, yet at the same time, had the most unreal sense of peace. Peace, and guilt.

She was hurting. This was an emotional response to her own guilt. To her grief. From the sound of things, she hadn't had time to process everything that had happened before the Andersons ripped the rug out from under her. The part of my brain that remembered my mother raised me to be a good man, an *honorable* man, screamed for me to put an end to this. That was who I was. At my center, at my core. Under all my own grief and acting out over the loss of my sister, that was the person I was.

But I was also selfish. Greedy in a way that had me taking after my father.

I let go of her waist and reached up, grabbing each of her wrists and bringing them behind her back. My large right hand secured them easily, while I brought my left up, just beneath her chin. I let my fingers linger there, reveling in the softness of her skin before tipping her head back to expose her neck. The taste of her was euphoric and overrode all the protests that had been banging around inside my head. The sensation of her skin beneath my fingers, of her scent all around me. It was like I'd slipped into a drug-induced haze, content to ride the wave straight on into oblivion.

She made a sound. A thrilling cross between a contented sigh and an eager moan. She shifted again, the friction the move created threatening to incinerate me. It nearly drove me over the edge. This Ash was more jagged than the others. Life had tried so damn hard to break her down, yet she was still standing. Still fighting.

No. *No, no, no.* This might feel right, but it was wrong. Letting it happen *like this* was wrong.

She'd instigated this whole thing, but in a single moment of clarity I wasn't so sure it was a good idea—for either of us. Was I selfish? Yep. I'd be the first to admit it. Was I *this* selfish? Could I use her like I had the others?

I'd gone to four different versions of her with the *use and lose* mentality. I made it clear up front that it was never more than a one-hit wonder. Screw the fact that every time she'd agreed, just as eager as me. Here with this Ash, right now, the full realization of what I'd done made me hate myself even more than I hated Dylan. I'd told myself that what I was doing was so that I could keep moving forward, so I could clear my mind, but the ugly truth was, I was just some low-life bastard using his grief as an excuse.

I broke the kiss and let go of her wrists. "As much as

I'd love to do this—God I can't believe I'm actually saying this—we should stop."

"Stop?"

I straightened my shirt and stood, trying hard to swallow what felt like ten pounds of sawdust in my throat. "You had this weird...thing with your Noah. I'm kinda feeling like I'd be taking advantage of that."

She blinked, her lips parting slightly. She backed away several steps. There was a flush in her cheeks. "You don't want to take advantage of me? That's what you're saying?"

Why the fuck did she sound so surprised? "What the hell kind of guy do you think I am? Of course I don't want to take advantage of you."

She stood a little straighter, eyes gleaming with challenge. "But I offered. Free and clear." She spread her arms wide, causing the material of her shirt to shift in the most tantalizing way. "No strings."

"Yeah." I swallowed and focused on the desk just behind her. "You did—but there were strings. I still don't believe that kiss between you and *him* was anything that could have destroyed the friendship you had, but you need to deal with it. You need to get right with what happened and see that for yourself. Right now, you're damaged. Damaged in a way that I have no desire to add to."

I didn't like the way she was looking at me. Like she was seeing me for the first time. Like she was seeing something *good*. "Everyone is damaged."

"They are. Look at me. I'm about as broken as they come." I was haunted. By Kori, by the future I would never have, by the relationships I couldn't—*wouldn't*—hold on to. "And maybe this would have added to my damage, too."

She thought about it for a moment, then stepped forward

and rose onto her toes. A second later, she brushed the softest kiss across my forehead. It was the simplest, purest action, yet it stole the air from my lungs in a way that made me feel both dead and alive in the same moment.

She turned and started for the bathroom. When she reached the door, without turning back, she said, "I'm sorry that I called you selfish."

"Don't be. I am."

She shook her head, shoulders rising and falling with a deep breath. "Maybe, but I think you're far less selfish than you want people to believe."

*W*e spent the remaining time on opposite sides of the room. When Cade and Kori returned, bags in hand, no one said a word as we got ready for the party. They'd managed to put the Cleaver costume together thanks to Ash's impeccable description, not that it'd been very hard. The character was known for worn black jeans, a black T-shirt and motorcycle jacket, and black beanie. Other than the mask, I was pretty much born to play this guy.

They found Ash a simple costume that kept her face hidden, while going for less disguising ones for themselves. They were still anonymous in this world, so moving around was easier for them. Once we were ready, we made our way to the Antiquity Grand Hotel where the gala was to take place.

"That was easier than I expected it to be," Kori whispered once we'd made it through the check-in. She wasn't kidding. For people who believed their son's killer was out and about and determined to cause trouble, the security certainly was lax. Then again, if this world's Cora and Karl were really as bad as Ash said, then maybe they'd never dream she'd have the guts to try waltzing in through the front door. Hell. Maybe they thought she was miles away by now, hiding under some rock.

They didn't know her very well…

"We're in. Now what?" I still felt like this was a waste of time. Ash hadn't had any luck figuring out who Noah had plans to meet. But it seemed important to her so I'd gone along with it. Who knew? Maybe we'd get lucky.

"I guess the best thing we can do is wander around. Look for anything that seems out of place. Maybe something will hit me." Kori had gotten her a sleek black, floor length dress and a mask. Some sparkly white thing with feathers and shining stones glued to the front in an intricate design. The dress wasn't anything revealing. Black satin with a high neckline and long, draping sleeves. But it hugged every curve like a second skin, and when she moved, I couldn't help wondering what it would feel like to slip my hands along the fabric—and underneath.

Cade snapped his fingers. "You okay, man?"

I jumped, guilty. "Yeah. Great. Move around. Standing here looks suspicious."

Kori tried to hide a snicker and Cade gave a knowing grin as he led her away. The crowd swallowed them. I took Ash's hand and started around the outskirts of the room, moving slowly to give her enough time to take it all in. Judging from the way she kept gnawing on her bottom lip, we were still coming up with zero. I could tell it was stressing her out. She was trying so hard to prove there was something here. The thing was, the harder you tried sometimes, the harder it was to get your brain to where it needed to be. While I'd been studying for my MCATs I'd been so focused that I had a hard time retaining the information. My father sat me down and explained that sometimes a little distraction can go a long way toward getting you where you wanted to go.

"So what did you mean earlier? When you said I was less damaged than he was." We sidestepped a small group talking and made our way for the garden. Through the glass doors ahead, I could see large groups of people there, dancing under the stars to the muted sounds of a live band.

The question seemed to take her by surprise. She stiffened and tried to pull her hand from mine, but I held tight. She continued scanning the room and I was sure she wouldn't answer, but after a moment she said, "You say you're selfish." Her voice was low. "You say you only care about a small sphere of people."

"I am who I am." I pushed through the door and into the cool night air.

"That's who he was. You may share some of his personality traits, but in reality, you're nothing like him. Granted, you're more of a dick than he was, but you're also... *more*. I always used to look past it because, well, because he was all I had. But the truth is, my Noah had a cruel streak. He was always good to me, but sometimes..." She shook her head. "There's no trace of that in you. You're—"

A shrill whistle sounded above the music, followed by an annoying hoot. "I'd know that ass anywhere."

Ash stiffened and picked up the pace, heading to the far end of the crowd. We crossed the dance floor and had almost made it to the row of empty tables when the guy spoke again. "Aww, come on. Don't be like that. I'm not gonna tattle or anything."

We kept going, past the tables and along the small gravel path. It was lit with white string lights and led to a small gazebo a few yards away. The guy behind us followed — and kept making comments — and at one point I stiffened, poised to turn around, but she clutched my hand and silently shook her head.

Finally tired of being ignored, the guy rushed ahead and jumped out in front of us. "I just wanna talk, okay?"

"What do you want, Freddy?"

"You are looking *fine*, baby. Haven't heard from you in a while." Freddy looked her up and down, then cast a sideways glance in my direction. "Who're you?"

"Someone whose time you're wasting," I snarled.

"Oh… Getting a head start, huh Ash? I gotta say, I'm surprised. After that speech you gave at the beginning of the year, I thought for sure you'd avoid that house." He looked from Ash to me, grinning. "When you're done, do you mind?"

"Do I mind *what*?" The way he was leering at her, like she was some kind of sugary dessert, pissed me off.

"Sending her my way?" He puffed out his chest a little and had the nerve to wink at her. "We have a history."

"Freddy," Ash warned. There was a tremble in her voice.

"But, I mean, you probably have a history with half the guys at this party, am I right?"

"Excuse me?" I balled my fists tight, fingers itching to choke the shit out of this guy.

He threw up his hands. "No offense or anything. Not like you banged your way around town or whatever. But, come on. We both know you've got some miles." He nudged me with his elbow. *"A lot."*

I could have kept my mouth shut. Should have, really.

But one of my—many if you ask Kori—flaws was self-restraint. Act first, think later—if at all. I stepped up to the guy and made a move to lift my mask, but Ash grabbed my arm.

"Sorry, Freddy. I'm not here on house business, nor am I joining either house when I turn eighteen." Her voice was frigid. "Tonight is strictly a night out with a friend. The past is the past and that's how it stays. I'd appreciate if you didn't tell anyone you saw me here."

He gave a disappointed snort. "It's cool. I'm actually here with Cora's new intern anyway. Have you seen her? Kita Ducesa. She is *hot*." Leaning a little closer, he added, "Between us, did you really off Noah? It would be totally understandable considering—"

"I didn't kill him," she responded icily.

He almost looked sad. Without another word, he turned and left. Ash waited until he was lost to the crowd, then started forward without a word. I followed, more sure than ever that this world's version of Ash was the most damaged yet.

Chapter Twelve

Ash

No. I kept my expression neutral, yet the word echoed a thousand times inside my head. *No. No. No.* That had not just happened. The fact that someone had recognized me should have been more of a concern, but it was the exchange between Freddy and me, the things he'd said—that he'd implied—that made me want to march into the house and present myself to Cora wearing a big, fat bow.

How was I supposed to explain? How could I make Noah understand that the mistakes I'd made—wait… "Kita Ducesa." I stopped short, causing Noah to walk into me.

"Huh?"

Wow. How had I not realized it the moment Freddy opened his mouth? "Kita. Cora's new intern. That's who he was meeting."

"Why do you think that?"

"A few months ago Noah started learning Romanian. He said it had to do with some girl he was hot for… Anyway,

Ducesa is Romanian for duchess. She's our girl."

"Okay." He spun in a slow circle. "See her anywhere?"

"There." I nodded discreetly to the punch bowl on the other side of the dance floor. Freddy must have made a pit stop on his way back to her because Kita was alone, nursing a drink. Before I realized what was happening, Noah was crossing the dance floor. "Crap."

I ran after him as discreetly as possible, catching up just as he reached her. "Hey Kita."

"Hey," she said in an uncertain tone. Dressed in a poufy dress with an uncomfortable looking corset, her blond hair hung in tight ringlets and bounced as she nodded. "Crazy party, right? Leave it to the Andersons to go for the gold."

"Yeah." He took her by the arm and began leading her away from the crowd. "Crazy. Can we talk for a sec?"

She stumbled after him. "Um…"

I came up beside them and pried Kita's arm from his grasp. "Will you cool it?"

She looked around, frowning. "What's going on? Who are you guys?"

I turned my back on the crowd and lifted my mask just long enough for her to gasp and take a step back. Or, at least she tried. Noah had positioned himself behind her so she couldn't run. But she could still scream—and that would land us in a boatload of crap.

"Please. Just hear me out before you freak, okay?"

"What are you doing here?" All the color drained from her face. "I can't be seen talking to you."

"You won't be," Noah said. "She's wearing a mask."

"You're not just listed anymore. You're wanted for murder." There was challenge in her tone. "If they find you—"

"You could scream," I said, heart kicking into overdrive. If she alerted security and I was caught, it was all over. Listed didn't get trials. If they were suspected of a crime, it was the death penalty. "But I'm asking—*begging*—you not to."

"Why?"

"Because I know you were meeting Noah here tonight."

"That's crazy. Why would I—"

"Don't try to hide it." Noah lifted his own mask for a moment. "What do you have to tell me?"

Her mouth fell open and her eyes widened. "You're the skip!"

"No," he said with a sharp shake of his head. He fixed his mask, then subtly scanned the area to make sure no one was looking. "I'm not. My parents knew I was onto them. They staged my death, then said I was another me, here as a skip to cause trouble."

Wow. He was good. I ran with it. "Cora and Karl are horrible people, but even they couldn't get rid of their own son."

He nodded. "Yep. So they made up the story so the law would do it for them."

Her eyes narrowed. She wasn't buying it just yet. "Why didn't you contact me? Give me a heads-up? It's dangerous for you to be here. How did you even know I'd still come?"

"I chanced it. You're my mom's intern. I figured you'd still show. What my parents are doing at Infinity is dangerous. They need to be stopped."

I cringed as Kita's jaw clenched. Crap. This world's Noah never referred to Cora as his *mom* or the two of them as his *parents*. He'd been using their first names since he was in grade school. At first I was sure she'd catch the mistake, but after a moment, she sighed. "I can't tell you much. Like I said on the phone, I don't know exactly what Omega is, but I know that they had some hiccups when they got it off the ground."

"What kind of hiccups?"

"Again, not sure." She glanced around nervously, voice dropping to barely a whisper. "All I know is that they've been working on this one for a long time. There were several test subjects, a few under lock and key in the most secure parts of the facility. The first trials for the project and it didn't go quite as planned."

I frowned. "That's not much to go on."

"Sorry. That's all I know." She shifted, trying to move away. "Whatever the project is, though, they're being very careful to hide it. If the whispers are right, they were not given clearance from President Gotti to proceed."

"The president? Does this have to do with the Guardian program?"

"I don't think so. Whatever it is, the story is, it predates Gotti. His predecessor told Cora to shut it down before it even really got started. That it was too controversial. When Gotti came into office, he agreed."

"Oh, wow." This was huge. The president had to sign off on all business ventures operating within the United States. If he vetoed it, the business wasn't permitted to operate on U.S. soil. It didn't happen often—he got a 10 percent cut from any profits brought in from the first five years and knew the Andersons personally—so it *had* to be bad. Gotti wasn't normally one to shy away from controversy. "Is there anything else? Even the name of someone who might be involved in the project?"

"Cora is heading it. I know that for sure. But there have

been whispers that Markus Brewster is involved, too."

"Brewster... Why do I know that name? Something to do with pharmaceuticals?"

"Yes. He made the news a few years back when his company tested a drug meant to replace tubal ligation surgery."

"I remember that. Every one of the test subjects died."

"Slow and horrible," she said. There was a bitterness in her tone that suggested she'd been personally affected by Brewster's mistakes. "If the rumors are true, he's working his magic for Cora these days."

"What need would Infinity have for a hack like that? They deal in tech, not drugs."

"No idea, but the word is, he's not happy there." She shrugged and stood a little straighter. "Can I go now?"

She turned to leave, but Noah still blocked her path. "And you're in a hurry to...?"

"Get back to my date, Freddy." She cast a scowl in my direction. "*You* know Freddy, right, Ash?" Her voice had returned to normal levels and I cringed at the mention of my name.

I was sure my face had turned a pretty unflattering shade of red. I grabbed Noah's arm and gently pulled him toward me. Kita snorted and stalked back toward the party. "Guess we got what we came for."

He was quiet for a moment. "If you're worried that I'll judge you based on the things I've—"

"I'm not."

"Good. Because I don't have the whole story."

"You don't," I agreed.

"And even if I did, trust me when I tell you, I'm the last one who should be judging anyone for anything."

"I don't *know* every guy here." My reputation was highly inflated. I had been with Freddy and one other guy. It ended badly when he made it clear he'd used me because he'd heard he could. That drove me into the arms of one other guy—who made it clear what kind of a relationship he was looking for before things went on too long. I'd been sixteen at the time. Stupid and heartbroken and utterly alone in the world. Searching for something to hold on to. After that, my brain finally kicked in and I realized I didn't need them to feel whole. I didn't need anyone.

"I didn't think you did." His voice was low and his tone gentle. The way he was looking at me was something so completely foreign. Not with pity or greed or lust, but with… respect?

"I've made mistakes." I wanted to shut my mouth, but the words kept coming. Like violent, verbal diarrhea. "Done things that, in the moment, felt like they were my only choices. Not life and death, but—"

"I've fucked things up more times than I can count."

He had. It wasn't just lip service. I could see it in his eyes and in the way that he spoke. He'd seen things. Done things… This Noah Anderson was just as damaged as I was. He'd made stupid choices and probably hadn't learned from them as quickly as he should have. On top of everything else that seemed to spark and fizz between us, this realization just made me like him even more. He was something relatable now. Someone I could understand a little more.

"Sometimes *in the moment* is all you have, Ash." He glanced around, then refocused on me. "Sometimes those mistakes are the only thing that makes you feel real. *Alive*. It's okay to live there for a while if it's what you need to get through to the other side."

"What if there is no getting through?"

He smiled. It was something I'd seen my Noah do a thousand times, and though it'd always been a beautiful sight, now...now it was so much more than that. "There's always a way through—even if we don't see it right away."

"You really believe that?"

"I didn't used to. I think I do now." He slipped his arm me around and let his hand rest against the small of my back. "Let's find Cade and Kori and see if we can't track down this Brewster guy. Sound good?"

I nodded and, without thinking, leaned into him just a bit. "Sounds good."

Chapter Thirteen

Noah

Everyone had been oddly quiet on the walk back to our hotel. Cade was lost in thought—probably trying to come up with a plan, a backup plan, and a backup-backup plan. Kori was worried. I could always tell by the way she kept wringing her hands and looking over her shoulder. And Ash… Ash's quiet was the worst. She'd nearly shit elephants over what that Freddy asshole said. I could tell she was still freaked about it, and even though I wanted to know what he meant, I didn't dare ask.

When we arrived back at the hotel, Kori grabbed me as I was about to head in. "We, uh, got some information about Miles. Hang back and I can fill you in?"

Cade hovered in the doorway, shooting Kori a weird look. One I knew too damn well. Whatever it was she had to tell me, he didn't want her to spill. "Yeah. Sure." I flipped him off, then followed her back onto the sidewalk. We'd gotten a corner room at the farthest end of the lot. Thankfully the place was empty.

"This place is *horrible*," she said when Cade finally closed the hotel room door.

I rolled my eyes, but the truth was, I agreed—and I didn't even know much about it. "What is it this time?"

"This world is more technologically advanced than mine was, but when it comes to human rights, they're about a century behind."

"Huh?"

"Those people that end up listed? They're basically sold into slavery."

"What?" She has to have the wrong information. "Where did you hear this crap?"

"Just listening to the people at that party talk was more than enough." Her expression contorted, nose scrunching and lips pulling back in disgust. "That tattoo Ash has on her wrist? A bunch of the service people had them, so I started poking around. Overheard some things. There are two companies—they call them houses. They basically rent people out."

"*Rent* people?"

"When a person is listed, or in the case of a minor being listed—which is rare—when they turn eighteen, they have the choice to join one of the two houses."

"Yeah. Ash mentioned something about that."

"Did she also mention that in exchange for food, shelter, and clothing—all of which are deplorable in condition— these houses will rent them out to society?"

"Rent them out to what?" A sick feeling bubbled in my gut, but more than that, anger. Who the fuck thought it was okay to *rent* a person?

She hesitated. "Depends on the house. A lot of the service people at the party were listed. Rented for the night to be the waitstaff. From what I gathered, they were used to fill in the holes left by several sick bottom tier staff members."

This place made me sick. "The houses? You said there were two?"

"There's a general labor house." She gestured to the building. "Waitstaff, house cleaners—anything demeaning and menial that a person of higher standing would find degrading. And then there's the entertainment house."

"Entertainment, meaning..."

"Meaning, well, anything entertainment wise..."

She was being vague, and for some reason, it scared the shit out of me. "You're talking about actors?"

"I'm not sure. I doubt it, though."

"Then, what? Birthday party clowns?"

"Maybe." She paused, then inhaled sharply. "I think mainly, though, it's more for adult entertainment..."

"You're saying—"

"Prostitution is legal here. Encouraged, actually. The people in that house are rented as escorts. Strippers, companionship." She scrunched up her nose again. "I even heard the words 'fantasy fulfillment.'"

"Jesus."

Kori cringed. "That's where Ash was heading. I overheard Cora talking. She and Karl had it arranged. She wasn't getting a choice. The day she turned eighteen, they were going to show up on her doorstep to cart her away— like it or not."

She wasn't mine. There was nothing between us but an amazing spark. But the idea of some stranger putting his hands all over her—on anyone, really—because she'd been *rented out* enraged me. "Like hell—"

"Relax, Noah. It's a moot point. She's wanted for murder. She can't go to the house."

Because that was so much better?

"And we'll fix that. We'll get what we need to clear her name when Rabbit fixes the cuffs. She won't be wanted for murder and we'll get her off the listed roster."

Damn right we would. I had no intention of leaving Ash to play the starring role in some sicko's fantasy scene.

I waited for Kori to go back inside—I needed some air to try and calm down—but she stayed where she was, watching me expectantly. "What?"

"You okay?"

I shrugged. "Why wouldn't I be?"

"Because this is Ash. *Ash*, Noah." She stepped around and came to stand in front of me. Arms folded, chin thrust out in defiance. She was also blocking my escape. Smart girl. "You might keep it from Cade, but you can't hide it from me. We're too much alike. I can see right through you."

I hated it, but she was right. My biological sister had been the polar opposite of me. Sweet where I was sour. Smooth where I was jagged. She'd been love and light, while I lived more on the darker side of things. This Kori, while not as entrenched in that darkness, understood it. She was harder than mine. In many ways, more capable and far more observant.

"You don't have to pretend that seeing her means nothing to you," she said when I didn't answer. "How do you think I feel when I imagine seeing my mom again?"

There was barely anything I couldn't tell Cade. He was, and always had been, my brother. But when it came to Ash, I just couldn't do it. Maybe it was because in the beginning, when I first found her, Cade was still alone. We hadn't found this Kori yet. Talking to him about my dream girl when he'd just lost his seemed like a dick thing to do.

"You lost your mother, Kor. I didn't lose Ash. I never had her." I nudged her aside and started walking. I knew she'd follow. We'd fallen into this weird but comfortable routine.

She fell in step beside me. "Just say that you like her."

I shrugged again and pinned her with a pointed glare. "She's not the most *annoying* girl I know."

This was what we did. That back-and-forth, love-and-hate shtick. It was easier for me this way. The thought of embracing her openly as my sister—even as another sister—still felt like I was betraying mine in some small way. At least this way, there was the guise of annoyance. Though she saw right through it. Always did.

Kori fought a grin but failed. "What's really bothering you? The fact that you didn't meet her on your world—or the fact that you've met her and are afraid to lose her?"

I stopped walking, my defense mechanisms instantly jumping to the surface. "You've been with me for, what? Like, two and a half minutes? Suddenly you know the inner workings of my mind?"

But she was used to it. Shrugged it off and soldiered on—her words, not mine. "So, I'm right then?"

I sighed. "Maybe." We walked a few more feet and I stopped. I didn't want to venture too far from the motel. "The whole thing is asinine. Why the hell does it even bother me? Why do I care where she ends up?"

Kori smiled, then rose onto her toes and kissed my cheek. "You don't need me to tell you why. You already know." Without another word, she turned and walked back to the motel. I waited until I saw that she was safely inside before sliding down the nearest tree trunk to think.

...

*C*ade talked us all into getting a good night's sleep before striking out to search for Markus Brewster. My argument was that if we'd been able to find out about him, so would Dylan. But Cade, always the logical one, insisted on getting some rest. His plan was further backed by Ash, who explained that we'd be more noticeable traveling at night. I didn't get the logic, but what did I know. I was just a visitor—thank God.

By the time morning rolled around and we'd found ourselves a ride—an old Chevy belonging to a man Ash said had been skipped several months ago when he was caught sleeping with his brother's wife—I was ready to rip something apart.

"What do we do when we find him?" I asked. Cade and I had taken the front, and Ash and Kori the back. She'd attempted to claim shotgun, probably her way of pushing Ash and me together, but I'd been too fast. The closer I was to Ash, the more I felt the need to touch her. A simple brush of the hand...or something more.

"I've never met him," Ash said, leaning between the two front seats. "But from what I've heard of Brewster, he's not a very loyal person. The only reason he got out of jail is because he sold out his own father and sister, pinning the blame for the trial test disaster on them. He's only got his own interests in mind."

"But where does that leave us?" Cade pushed down harder on the gas to pass the car in front of us, still making sure to keep our speed within the legal limit. "I imagine Cora and Karl are paying him *very well*. We don't have anything to offer him."

"We don't," she agreed. "But Noah's source from the party said he wasn't happy with the Andersons. We might be able to work with that."

"How?" I couldn't imagine what the hell we could offer him. Three of us weren't even from around here, and Ash was on the run. We had no money—not that he'd need it from the sound of things.

"Better figure it out fast," Cade said as he killed the engine. "Because we're here."

Brewster's place was a huge farm just outside of town. We'd parked at the end of a long dirt driveway, in front of a red barn that annoyingly matched the charming farmhouse a few yards away.

"Not exactly what I'd expected," Ash said as she closed her door.

She started toward the house, but Cade jumped out in front of her. Grabbing her arm, he said, "Where are you going?"

She looked from him to me, then back again. "Is that a trick question?"

Kori dislodged Cade's grip on Ash and smiled. "I think what he's asking is, won't Brewster recognize you?" She inclined her head toward me. "Both of you?"

"This is it." Ash shrugged. "It's not going to matter if he sees us or not. You go in there asking about Omega and he's going to know why. Whatever this thing is, it's big. You're going to be just as wanted as we are." She shook her head. "No. We all go in and make the best play we can. Whatever happens, happens."

Cade thought about it for a minute, then stepped back and gestured for her to take the lead. Ash squared her shoulders and marched up the walk, determination oozing from every pore. God. She was amazing. Plenty of other people would have fallen apart under the circumstances she'd had to deal with. Maybe they would have crumbled, or maybe they would have run and hid. Tucked themselves away under some rock and hoped for the best. Not this girl. This girl was a fighter. She was determined to give it all she had. You had to admire the hell out of that.

She knocked, and it wasn't long before an older guy, probably in his fifties, appeared in the doorway. "Miss Calvert. Mr. Anderson. I was wondering how long it would be before you darkened my doorstep. I trust that you've not been followed?"

"No one knows we're here," Ash said. She stood a little straighter. If his greeting surprised her, it didn't show.

He pushed the door open and stepped aside. "Well, in that case, come in."

She didn't hesitate, stepping over the threshold and into the house like she owned the place. The rest of us followed, more cautious.

"You don't seem shocked to see us," I said, peering around the corner. For all we knew, Cora had learned of our plans somehow and had an ambush waiting in this guy's living room.

"Not much surprises me these days, Mr. Anderson." He led us to a large sitting room and gestured to the two wraparound couches in either corner. No ambush, but that didn't mean shit. "Please. Make yourselves comfortable. Something to eat? Drink?"

"I'm sure you'll understand if we want to make this quick." Ash was all business. Serious and stoic. I didn't normally go for this kind of thing, but watching her take charge was pretty damn hot.

Brewster settled in the armchair on the other side of the room. "I suppose that would be for the best. Please. Tell me what I can do for you."

Ash pointed to me. "Obviously you know this isn't Cora and Karl's son."

"Technically, he *is* Cora and Karl's son—just not our earth's Cora and Karl."

"Well, the Noah of this earth *didn't* kill himself."

"I've no doubt about that. The boy was poking his head where he shouldn't have been. It was only a matter of time."

"You knew the Andersons had something to do with the death of their own son and you said nothing?" Ash said.

He leaned back in the chair and folded his hands in his lap. The expression on his face, while not smug, was indifferent. "He was their son. Their problem to deal with. It wasn't my business."

Ash opened her mouth, then closed it, recovering. "Well, it's my business now."

The old man's lips tilted upward. "Ah. Yes. I heard you killed the boy. A *lover's quarrel*?"

Ash's fingers tightened. She was having just as much of a hard time keeping her shit together as I was. "I need a way to prove I didn't have anything to do with his death. To do that, I need to prove the Andersons did."

"So?"

"I need to take them down. You must be able to give me something—anything—that would prove they're dirty."

He let out a short laugh, cleared his throat, and fixed Ash with a genuinely perplexed expression. "Dear girl, I would love nothing more than to help you—simply because I shouldn't. You're listed. A no-no in polite society. Nothing would give me greater pleasure than to hand you the keys to the kingdom, so to speak. But…" He adjusted his shirt and winked. "I don't do something for nothing. Not ever."

"A trade," I said, standing. From the look on her face, I didn't know how long Ash would be able to keep it together. "There must be something you want. You give us what we need to get Ash off that list and prove the Andersons are murdering freaks, and we'll…what? What do you want?"

He thought about it for a moment, gaze going to each one of us in turn. When it landed on Ash, there was a twinge of something evil in his eyes. Whatever it was he knew, it was big. "I have something that will not only prove the Andersons got rid of their own son, but that they have been hiding their research—research the president ordered a cease and desist on—for years."

"And in exchange you want…?" We needed to get this show on the road. Time was ticking.

"I want to leave."

"Leave?" Cade asked, about as confused as I was. "Leave and go where?"

"To another earth, of course." Brewster glared at Ash for a moment longer before turning his attention to me. "You get me a ride off this rock, and I'll give you what you need."

Chapter Fourteen

Ash

"I don't understand." I sank back onto the couch, between Kori and Cade. The way he kept looking at me was creepy, but considering the source, I wasn't that freaked out. "You want to skip?"

Mr. Brewster nodded. "I do."

"Why?" Noah's eyes narrowed. He didn't trust the guy. Then again, neither did I. He had one hell of a reputation. And even though coming here had been a necessary risk, I wasn't an idiot. "Don't you have this place wired? Money, power, pull? That kind of thing?"

"I'm quite certain my time with Infinity is coming to a close. They've gotten what they need from me." He tapped the side of his head. "I've got knowledge that could unravel things. I imagine they're trying to decide how best to deal with me as we speak. They're playing in a sandbox they were told not to and I've been around far longer than anybody else. I've seen it all. Any loose ends will need to be tied up nice and tight."

"And what was it they needed?" I'd been curious since Kita told us he was involved. I couldn't imagine what use Cora could have for a guy like Markus Brewster. "What did you do for Cora?"

"They needed a drug that would safely wipe someone's memory. More specifically, certain parts of the memory."

Everyone in the room was quiet.

Brewster must have realized it wasn't what we'd been expecting, because he said, "They'd tried using a surgical procedure. It kept failing. Since my company had a somewhat"—he waved a hand in the air with a flourish and shrugged—"jaded reputation when it came to moral gray areas, Cora contacted me."

"Why did they want to wipe people's memories?"

Brewster shrugged again. "I wasn't told. I simply know they were blowing through test subjects left and right—subjects who had been hard to come by—and needed a quick fix."

Noah slammed a hand down against the small end table beside the couch. "You're saying that you helped them lobotomize people and you didn't even know why you were doing it? What the hell is wrong with you?"

"We weren't lobotomizing anyone. That's why they needed me. They needed a clean pharmaceutical wipe that left everything else intact and functioning. They were looking to get rid of certain parts of the memory, while leaving others—basic functions and information—untouched."

I wondered if Noah had gotten this far. Surely if he'd spoken to Brewster, he would have blown the whistle on the whole thing. "And did you?"

"Eventually, yes—which is why I'm sure they're looking for a way to tie up this old loose end. Whatever it is they're doing with Omega, it's huge. Even the smallest bit of knowledge is dangerous. Five people associated with the project in ways much smaller than I was have had, shall we say, unfortunate accidents. I've been around for the better part of fifteen years. It's time—"

"Fifteen years?"

He offered a small smile. "Oh yes. Omega has been in the works for quite some time now. I've been around since just before its actual conception."

"Why the hell did you help them in the first place?" Noah snapped.

"Had I known how this would all turn out, I wouldn't have." He laughed. "Or, maybe I would have. They offered me *a lot* of money."

"What if we could find you a chip?" Noah said. "If we got you a way to skip, then would you give us the proof we need?"

"That sounds like a fair deal."

It was a good idea in theory, but it had some issues. First, we'd need to get a chip. It wasn't going to be as easy as waltzing back into the Anderson estate and picking a few safe locks. They kept those in the tightest security areas inside of the Infinity Division. Our only shot at a chip would be Phil—which I'm sure Noah knew. The problem was, he didn't know the guy like I did. There was no way he'd give us something for nothing. "I can get you a chip," I confirmed— even though I still wasn't 100 percent sure. "But it's not going to come for free."

"Of course not," Brewster said. "As I said. I'll—"

"We'll need something, a show of good faith, if you will."

"Such as?"

"You're a businessman. You know everything in this

world is push and pull. I can get you the chip, but I'll need something to *buy* it with. Information." This had been Noah's element. Talking people into—and out of—things. The guy could have charmed the candy right from a chocoholic's mouth. I just hoped I'd learned enough from watching him. "Cora has someone stashed away in the basement of Infinity. Who is it and why is this person being held?"

Brewster waggled a finger at me and clucked his tongue. "If I tell you that, then it renders me obsolete. I can tell you why, though. My first trial of the drug was successful. The subject wiped perfectly. Unfortunately it started—and ended—with that subject. Attempts after that one were unsuccessful. Some of the patients died, while others were mentally altered in ways that made them unviable. Some were wholly unaffected."

"So they're keeping one of the failed test subjects?" Noah asked. Comparison number six: same irritated tone when losing his patience.

"Oh, well, I imagine they have several test subjects locked away down there. Omega isn't the only project Cora has brewing in the sandbox."

"But why keep them?" Kori had been quiet until now. "If they're willing to kill their own son, why wouldn't they just get rid of them?"

"The failure wasn't with my drug but with the subjects themselves. Certain individuals seemed to be immune to the drug, while others were affected in different, unpleasant ways. I imagine that they've kept people to try and identify what the resistance is and how to combat it." He leaned forward and winked at me. "But these are just guesses."

"I won't be able to get that chip without something to trade for it."

He sighed and stood, making his way across the room to a cabinet. "Very well." Pulling out a set of keys, he unlocked the door and shuffled around for a moment before pulling out a thin blue notebook. "Here you go."

I crossed the room and took the thing, flipping it open to find only three sheets left. The pages were covered in names, all scrawled out in barely legible scratch. Some were highlighted, while others had lines through the center. "What is this supposed to do?"

"It's a list of names."

Because that was supposed to tell me everything I needed to know?

"Names of who?" Cade stood and took the book from me. "And where's the rest of it?"

"Don't know, and don't know," was Brewster's reply. "I stole it from Cora's office a few weeks ago. Her intern was in the process of shredding the pages, but left *suddenly*. I procured the book and scampered off."

"Phil might be able to make something out of this," Cade said. He was skimming the pages. From the look on his face, it made as much sense to him as it did me. "If it's all we have…?"

"It's all you have," Mr. Brewster confirmed. "While I'm sure it's not enough to have Cora convicted and Infinity dismantled, I do know that it was being destroyed. It must have some value."

"We'll be in touch." Cade stood and handed me the notebook. I folded it in half, length-wise, and stuffed it into my back pocket, then headed for the door. Kori followed without question, but Noah looked annoyed.

He looked like he was going to say something, so I gently grabbed his arm and steered him toward the hall. There were a million things I wanted to say to Brewster, but we couldn't afford to piss him off. If what he told us was true, he'd stooped to a new low by helping Cora do…whatever Omega was. But we needed him and he could still screw us over. I bit my tongue, and hard.

Once we were outside, we started for the car. We'd almost made it when the sound of a car pulling up the driveway stopped everyone cold. "Could just be someone Brewster knows," Cade said. He didn't believe that, though. He stood rigid and was gripping the keys so hard that his knuckles had turned white.

"Not worth taking the chance." Noah nodded toward the barn. "Hurry."

"But the car?" Kori yelled over her shoulder as Cade dragged her into motion.

"Don't worry about it."

We managed to get ourselves into the barn and close the door as two dark-colored SUVs pulled up in front of the main house. "Who is it?" Kori peered around Cade to try and get a peek outside.

I didn't need to see their badges or trademark red ties to know. "They work for Infinity. For Cora…" The tallest one, Yancy, had been to the house multiple times over the years. If there was something she wanted done behind the scenes, someone she needed persuaded or *nudged* in a certain direction, Yancy was called in. "This isn't good."

Mr. Brewster answered the door after a few moments, then swung it open to let the men inside. "Bad idea, Markus," I whispered. As they disappeared, I held my breath. There was only one reason for Yancy to pay a visit to someone. In a matter of minutes, Markus Brewster would no longer be an option for helping us get what we wanted. "We have to go."

"Why? What's—"

Two shots rang out and Kori jumped. She punched Cade hard in the arm. "Car's something to worry about *now*, huh?"

A moment later, the men stepped from the house and sure enough, one of them pointed to our borrowed ride. Cade cursed and spun in a slow circle, a slightly panicked look in his eyes. "Gonna have to bolt and hope for the best."

Noah snorted. "There's three of them and four of us…"

"So you're packing?"

Noah groaned. "Run it is."

We rushed for the small door on the far side of the barn and managed to get it open just as the main barn doors flung open at the front. Cade slammed the door closed behind us in an attempt to slow them down, but they busted through, the barrier useless.

The sound was like firecrackers, only the feeling that came with it was a cold chill rather than excitement. One shot landed on the ground between Noah and me, dangerously close, and made the hairs on my arms jump to attention.

He grabbed my arm and tried to get to Cade, who'd run the other way in an attempt to avoid the shots, but another round fired in his path prevented it. One of the men tackled him to the ground, which seemed to instantly ensure Kori's surrender. She had her hands up as the second man kept his gun trained on her.

Noah's face paled and he immediately tried to get to her. "Kori!"

I grabbed him and held tight with everything I had. "No! Getting caught ensures we *all* end up dead."

"Shit." He hesitated for a moment longer, raking a hand through his messy hair before letting out a low growl. "We gotta go."

Chapter Fifteen

Noah

Leaving Cade and Kori behind was like holding a blowtorch to my skin. The fact that I hadn't gone after them—what the hell had I been thinking?

The answer was simple. I hadn't been.

For the third time since we'd arrived, I jumped up and started for the door.

Ash, quick little thing that she was, jumped in front of me. Again. "Noah, no. We talked about this. Storming off in a huff is not the way to do this. All you'll do is give Cora exactly what she wants."

We'd run through the woods behind Brewster's place until the air had left our lungs and both our legs refused to work anymore. When we'd come out the other end, we tucked ourselves away in the first vacant house we could find. The place was empty. It'd been looted long ago and every inch of every surface was covered in graffiti—and not the good kind. Kori would have been horrified.

I elbowed Ash aside and reached for the handle. But

instead of storming out, I closed my eyes and held my breath, counting to five.

"I understand how you must feel."

"No you don't." I opened my eyes and blew out slowly. It pissed me off that she was standing in the way of me getting to my friends. To my family. It infuriated me that she even had that much power over me. And the look in her eyes? That pitying stare? That almost sent me into a rage-filled tailspin. "Someone like you can't possibly understand."

The words horrified me, and yet I couldn't stop the verbal spewage. It was fueled by my fury for Dylan, over everything that had happened, and fear. For Cade, for Kori— for Ash. I'd lost enough in this world already. My sister, my parents—my life and home. After finding Kori again, I swore that was it. I hadn't meant to feel anything other than relief over the fact that we'd saved her, then ended up viewing her as an extension of myself, of my blood. She was family—whether I liked it or not, whether I refused to admit it or not. And Cade... I would do anything for him. He was my brother not by blood, but by choice. The one person who would stand with me no matter what. Right, wrong, ugly crimes, or pathetic mistakes—he would always have my back.

But Ash? I was incensed by the strong need to...what? Protect her? Care? If it'd been anyone else in that room with me, I would have stormed out and not looked back. But her? By just telling me not to leave, I found myself paralyzed. In that moment, with all the shit weighing down on me, all I could think about was the promise I'd made to myself. The promise to give her up. To blow the whole thing off and not let anyone else inside. The fact that I hadn't been able to shake her like I had the others made me twitchy and raw.

It made me an asshole.

"You've got no one, right? No family, no friends. There's no one for you to miss, to lose."

"Wow." She folded her arms and stood there, an attempt to look casual that she didn't quite pull off. Underneath the mask was horror. I'd struck and landed my blow with precision accuracy.

"You cannot possibly understand what it's like to lose someone."

She gritted her teeth but held her ground. "I've lost people. I lost Noah."

The cut was deep, but I wanted more. In that moment, I wanted her to hate me as much as I hated myself. "You lost a *friend*. It happens to all of us."

"He was more than a friend."

"Oh. Yeah, right. He was a friend you made out with."

"Asshole," she spat, lunging forward. I caught her fist before it connected, kind of impressed by the force behind the blow, then pushed her backward. I should have let her hit me—God knew I deserved it—but it only added insult to the injury to stop the attack.

"Damn right I am. Probably a good thing you don't forget that." Without another word, I yanked open the door and stormed out.

This version of Wells was slightly different. The buildings were taller with more of a gaudy spin, and the foliage was more colorful, but the layout was mostly the same. Navigating my way through town wasn't hard, and after wandering around in the darker corners of the city to find a safe path, I finally made it back to the bridge where we'd come to contact Rabbit.

I worked the stone free, pulled out the cell, and turned it on. The battery was almost dead, but there was just enough for me to leave a message letting him know we'd found something—not that I was sure we had. The notebook was just a collection of names, but I was hoping he could sort it out.

Going back to his cabin was probably a bad idea, so I gave him the address of the vacant house we were in, then replaced the whole thing. Cora wouldn't risk hurting Cade and Kori until she had me—at least, I hoped. The idea of having me waltzing around town, wearing her son's face, would be too much. That, and I got the impression she was bat-shit crazy. Like it or not, Rabbit was going to help me get them back, and then he was going to fix the damn cuffs.

Making my way back to the house took almost as long as getting to the bridge despite all the detours and unfortunately gave me time to think. I'd been an ass to Ash—which, at the time, had been the point. But now that I'd cooled and could view things in hindsight—a nasty habit according to, well, everyone who knew me—I realized just how far over the line I'd stepped. I'd been angry. At her, at the situation—at myself. The way she'd been looking at me, like I was someone worthy of her pity, of her kindness, had sent me over the edge. Maybe that was the real reason I kept talking myself out of any kind of future with her. Deep down, I knew I didn't deserve it. I didn't deserve her—not any version. Especially not this one.

From the time she could walk, I'd always been Kori's protector. My sister had been fragile. Sweet and full of light and life, yet oddly vulnerable. From the moment I laid eyes on her, I knew it was my job to keep her safe. A job that, with Cade's help, I excelled at. No one messed with Kori Anderson. That day when we found her in the basement, bleeding out right in front of our eyes, I failed. Me, a pre-med student who couldn't save one of the most important people in his life. That moment had changed me. It'd changed my outlook on life and on medicine. If I had to admit it—which I never would—it had shaken me. Dislodged my center and screwed with my confidence in twisted ways.

There was no way to change who I was. I couldn't push away the feelings of self-hatred and guilt that had been festering since that day. But I didn't have to take it out on Ash. Not anymore. I pushed through the door, half expecting her not to be there anymore. The place was quiet and dark, the electricity off and the sun going down. I stopped in the middle of the room and listened. Nothing. "Ash? You here?"

A few moments passed before a soft sigh drifted through the room. "Here."

Her voice sounded like it'd come from the far corner, and when I rounded the couch, I found her sitting on the floor against the wall. "Listen, I—"

She held up a familiar thin black thing. "You left your phone. When you stormed off like a child? You left your phone behind."

"Um, okay." I leaned over and took it from her. "Thanks?"

"It rang."

"Someone called?" I looked down at the phone and pulled up the call log. Normally the only number there was Cade's. Sometimes it'd go weeks without ringing. We'd found our phones worked in most places—which still kind of blew our minds—but in some it didn't. Now, in addition to Cade's number, there was one I'd never seen.

"That guy called. The one you came here after."

"Dylan?" Every muscle in my body was instantly on alert. This wasn't good. "What did he say? What did—"

"You said yourself he knew the cuff wasn't working right. That he'd go looking for a way to fix it? Well, he did. He went looking for a *person* to fix it."

It only took me a few seconds to figure it out. There were only two people who could fix the cuff. It would have either been Cora—which probably would have had Ash dancing in the streets—or... "Rabbit." I groaned. "He went after Rabbit..."

She nodded and stood. "He says Phil is unharmed and that if you want it to stay that way, you and Cade will meet with him to discuss terms."

"He's gonna have to settle for just me."

"And me."

"Doesn't Rabbit hate you?" Not exactly eloquent, considering the circumstances and the shit that went down between us earlier, but as usual, I opened my mouth and shit just spilled out.

"Yep," she said. "He does. And he's not really my favorite person right now, either. But I'll probably need his help to prove Cora and Karl had Noah killed."

"Did he say where? When?"

She nodded. "He gave me an address. As for when, he told me to tell you the clock was ticking. Said you'd know what that meant."

I sighed. "It means we go now."

Chapter Sixteen

Ash

The place Dylan told us to meet him was an old park on the other side of town. The Wells town board voted to stop dumping money into it six years ago, and the place had fallen into disarray. The rumor was, the park was used by the braver listed to meet with estranged family members because no one else ever came.

It wasn't too far from the house we'd commandeered, a mile or so at the most. We'd been walking for a few minutes, and every so often Noah would glance at me—thinking himself slick—then turn away without saying anything.

What he'd said to me earlier had been harsh, and deep down I knew he was only reacting to the situation. He was worried about his sister and friend and needed an outlet. I hated that I understood, but I did. My Noah had been the same way. He was sweet, but had never mastered dealing with certain emotions. His reactions to fear were much like this Noah.

"Stop squirming." I thrust my hands into my pockets. "Just forget about it."

"I shouldn't have—"

"Probably not," I agreed. "But what's done is done." I tilted my head down so that my hair fell to hide my face. I understood, but that didn't mean what he'd said hadn't cut like a sword straight through to my heart—probably because it was partially true. I had no one.

"It doesn't feel done."

I shrugged. "Sounds like your problem."

He stopped walking, shooting a quick glance over his shoulder before looking back to me. "That's just it. It's *not* my problem. Not usually." He hesitated, then started walking again. I thought that was the end of it, but after a few minutes, he said, "I'm an asshole. I've always been kind of an asshole, but after Kori… I'm mean, abrasive, and pretty damn thoughtless most of the time. I am what I am, though, and I've never really given a shit."

"So you suddenly give a shit?"

"I hate what the Andersons did to you."

It wasn't the words he'd said, but the way he'd said them. Full of anguish. It made my chest hurt.

"I hate what *I* did to you," he added.

"I told you, its fine. You were—"

"I didn't mean what I said. Yeah. That was a dick thing to do, but I'm talking about before that." He spread his arms wide. "Before *this*."

"What are you talking—"

"Nice of you to finally join us," a voice said from the darkness. A moment later, the same tall guy with a crooked nose and sharp features from the Doon emerged from the dark. "Thought you'd never show—but, where's the rest of the crew? My brother isn't planning to try ambushing me?"

Brother?

"Cade isn't here." Noah's jaw was tight and his fists had tightened on either side. "Neither is Kori. They're a little busy with my parents."

"Oh, wow. Sucks to be them! I heard this world's Cora and Karl weren't the most welcoming."

"Moving on… Where's Rabbit?"

"You mean *Phil*?" Dylan rolled his eyes and leaned in close to Noah. I had to give him credit. He didn't back away—or rip the guy's throat out. "This one is a drag! He's got the stick wedged so far up his ass, it's about ready to shoot out his nose!"

"Where is he?" Noah repeated, this time with menace.

Dylan looked like he was having too much fun pushing his buttons, though. "Did you know he was wearing loafers when I found him? *Loafers*? Our Rabbit would die!"

"Dylan…"

"All right. All right. Cool the hell down. He's fine."

"What is it you want?" I told myself I'd keep quiet and let Noah do all the talking. I mean, he knew this whacko and all. But I was losing my patience.

"Well, well. I see you finally found the right brother, huh?"

I grabbed Noah's wrist and tugged him away. "Come on. I'm betting this jackass doesn't even have Phil. He's—"

"Oh, I have him. And since we have a very real problem—" He glared at me, the smile disappearing from his lips. "You'd better listen up."

"Listening." Noah folded his arms.

"The cuffs are busted, but I think you already knew that. Since I already checked and it doesn't appear that Ava is here, I decided it was time to bring the old thing in for repair."

"Meaning Rabbit."

"He *is* a genius. Maybe even smarter than your mom

here. Who knows?"

"Lemme guess." I couldn't help snickering. "He refused to help you?"

Dylan laughed. "Oh. She's *cute*, Noah."

"I don't get it." He'd said it like it was some kind of insult.

Noah made a low growling sound, then said, "Dylan wouldn't have given him a choice."

"Of course not. No, good old Phil is going to fix the cuff. Says he can upgrade and improve it—and disconnect me from you two asshats—well, it's three now, isn't it?"

"Could you get to the point? I'm dying of old age."

"He needs the rest of the cuffs to do it."

It didn't sound funny to me, but something he'd said made Noah snort, then double over with laugher. Maybe the world they'd come from, laughter meant something different. Maybe it was a sign of aggression. I had an ill-timed vision of two gun-toting bad guys, faced off and cackling hysterically, while they blew each other away.

"Well, then you're fucked."

Dylan lost his grin. "'Scuse me?"

"Cade and Kori? Unreachable at the moment."

"We can wait," Dylan said cautiously. He folded his arms and leaned back against the nearest tree.

"Gonna be waiting a long time. *Mom* and *Dad*? They've kind of got them locked up."

Dylan was quiet for a moment, gaze alternating between Noah and me. "What the hell does that mean, locked up?"

Noah grinned. "As in, taken prisoner. Held against their will. Tossed in the pokey—"

"I get it." Dylan lifted his hand, irritated frown changing to match Noah's smile. "But we both know you'd never leave Cade behind. And what about your sister?" He shook his head. "Nope. I suggest you get creative and plan a jailbreak."

"Why? When we skip, they'll get pulled right along with us." He was posturing. I knew he never intended to leave Cade and Kori in the Andersons' dungeon. He might not know the full extent of Cora's insanity, but he'd seen enough to be worried. "All I gotta do is sit back and wait for you to get bored."

Dylan laughed. "That so?"

"Eventually you'll move on. We'll all move on with you. End of story."

"No," he said with a grin. "I won't. Can't. I've tried to skip four times. We're all dead in the water and stuck here unless Phil can fix our ride."

Noah's smile faded and I could tell he was trying to decide whether or not to believe the guy. I didn't know them, had no idea about the dynamic between them, but it was obvious to anyone with a pair of eyes and half a brain that there'd been a lot of lies tossed around. Still… something about his expression, about the way he held himself, screamed of truth.

"I swear on your dead sister," Dylan prodded, grin growing even bigger. "You know, the *real* one."

Noah lunged for him, but I threw myself between them. "Need to keep your head," I reminded him.

He ignored me, eyes full of fury and entire body rigid, but at least he didn't move any closer.

Dylan gave a satisfied snort and took a small step back. "As I was saying… Phil can fix the cuffs, but he needs all of them to do it. Unless you want to spend the rest of your days in this twisted place, you'll find a way to get to Cade and Kori. I think you've got my number, right? Call me when you get your act together. Until then, I think *Phil* and I will do a little chilling."

Chapter Seventeen

Noah

We left the park empty handed and with no path in mind. "I never thought I'd say this, but I miss Cade's *we need a plan* attitude. I got nothing. You?"

Ash kept pace beside me. "Well, for starters, we know Phil is lying to Dylan."

"Lying? How?" Obviously I'd missed something.

"Don't you remember? He told us at the cabin—he doesn't need all the cuffs. You asked him and he said he just needed the main cuff. The one Dylan is wearing—the one he *already has.*"

How the hell had I forgotten that?

"Assuming that was his way of calling for help when Dylan nabbed him. Unfortunately it kind of backfired," Ash added.

"Cora has the other cuffs and we have no hope of sneaking in to get them without Rabbit—unless you have another ace up your sleeve?"

"I got nothing," she repeated. "But maybe there's a way

around it all. Maybe we don't have to sneak in."

I snorted. I could see it now. The girl she wanted to blame for her son's death accompanied by the guy wearing his face. That would go over real well. "You wanna try skipping right through the front door?"

"Yes."

I stopped walking and stared at her.

"If the truth about what really happened to Noah comes out, not only will Infinity be ruined, but Cora and Karl will go to jail. I know them. They'll do anything to prevent it."

"So your suggestion is…?"

"Offer her something she wants. Something she needs. Cade and Kori for me. You're an annoying thorn in her side, but I'm a time bomb looking for the right place to detonate. They want to pin Noah's death on me, but they know I'm not going to go quietly. I can still kick up enough dust to put the spotlight on them. I probably wouldn't win, but no matter what, Infinity would get dragged around. Cora is going to want to deal with me herself. Out of the public eye."

In the back of my mind I knew we shouldn't be standing here discussing this. Yeah, it was nighttime and we weren't exactly loitering in a well-lit area, but we were too exposed for two people wanted for various reasons. But my survival instinct was overwritten by the fact that Ash had obviously lost her goddamned mind. "Are you insane?"

I could just make out the narrowing of her eyes and the twist of her lips. "I don't matter, though, remember? I have nothing. No one. Who'll miss me?"

I opened my mouth, then slammed it shut. No matter what I said here I was screwed. If I said *good point*, then I was a heartless bastard willing to sacrifice an innocent girl to save his friends—and a liar. If I spoke the truth, that I would rather hack each of my toes off with a machete then tap dance through a vat of salt before letting her hand herself over to those bastards, then I was insane. One of those freaks who believed in love at first sight. Which I wasn't. I was…what the hell was I?

Obsessed. Obsessed and feeling guilty for acting like an ass. As usual.

Instead I settled for a neutral response. "If you do that, best case scenario, they lock you in the basement along with their failed experiments. Worst care—or best depending on how you wanna look at it—they kill you."

"And I ask again, why does it matter?"

"It doesn't."

"Then what's the problem?"

She was testing me. Christ. A little over twenty-four hours and she already knew how to push my buttons and make me crazy. Never in my life had any girl—any person—gotten under my skin like this.

"I just think it's a stupid idea." Yeah. Great response. Very convincing. This was the best I could do? The guy with the genius level IQ, MCAT scores the highest our state had ever seen, couldn't just tell this girl he had a thing for her?

"Look." She glanced around, then stepped off the sidewalk into the shadows, pulling me with her. I could no longer make out the specifics of her features, but I had them memorized. Every line of her face, each curve of her body. The way her right eyebrow sat just a fraction of an inch higher than the left, and how she gnawed on her bottom lip when thinking too hard. "You were right, okay?"

My resolve crumbled a little. I grabbed her arms and gave a slight shake. "I'm right about a lot of things, but that wasn't one of them." I snorted. "*You* aren't one of them.

Seems like with you, I'm always saying the wrong thing." The scent of mint filled my nose, intoxicating and distracting. I found myself leaning closer. "I'm always doing the wrong things…"

She leaned in, too, and I could feel the heat of her breath as her lips lingered, just shy of touching mine. My heart kicked up and every nerve ending lit like the Fourth of July. But the ember never caught fire. Instead of delivering another mind-blowing kiss, she pulled away. "I have nothing," she said, her voice just barely a whisper. "Even if we manage to clear my name and wipe my listed status away, I'll *still* have nothing. I will always be a Bottom Tier citizen. Noah was all I had here. He was my lifeline and now he's gone. I think I confused things for a second. I felt this insane pull toward him and even though in the deepest parts of my heart and soul I never felt *that way* about him, I kissed him. I made a mistake and will never have a chance to explain myself. To fix things. But at least I understand. I talked to Kori and I get it now."

"Get it?"

She stepped back into the moonlight and gestured between us as she started to walk. "All the versions of us have this crazy connection. He wasn't in love with me—I was never in love with him—but it's like we couldn't help ourselves. That's why he was so vehemently against anything ever happening between us. We were drawn to each other— like we are. But you didn't have an Ashlyn where you come from, and I had a Noah. He might not have been my perfect Noah, but he was all I got and for as long as I live, I will be thankful for him. Your perfect Ash might be out there somewhere. If you don't let me help you get your friends back, you'll never have the chance to find her."

The part of me that'd watched his sister die over and over again agreed with her. He was logical. He knew the score. Then there was the other part. The guy whose icy heart cracked just a little every time she looked at him. The person who grew ravenous at the thought of just one more kiss.

"What's to say you aren't her?" There. I'd said it. Out loud, even. "How do you know that you aren't the right Ashlyn?"

She laughed, a soft sound so full of pain. I knew that tone. The forced amusement mustered up to mask the dead parts inside. "Me? Be serious, Noah. We can't occupy the same space for more than ten minutes without bickering."

"And that's a bad thing?"

She snorted. "I wouldn't classify it as a *good* thing."

"I would. See, we've proven that there's an attraction between us." I reached out and ran the tip of my thumb across her bottom lip. The warm, smooth skin was inviting, just begging for a taste, but I revisited. I had a point here and was determined to make it. "I've seen it before. I've *met* you before. It's always there. It's always been the *only* thing that's there."

"So?"

"So?" I repeated. "So this time it's *not* the only thing. You drive me absolutely insane."

"Thanks. The feeling is—"

"That's my point. I'm an asshole. I don't normally give a shit about other people. What they say, what they do—no one affects me. No one until I landed here and met you."

"So you're, what? Professing your eternal love for me? You think we were destined to be together?"

"I told you, I don't believe in that crap. I don't love you—I don't *know* you. What I'm saying is that I feel *something* for you. I want to *get* to know you."

She thought about it for a minute. "Before Dylan showed up, you were apologizing for something…"

"I was." Would she understand? Did I still have the guts to come clean? Was there even a need to come clean? I technically hadn't done anything wrong. Despite my fucked-up motives, everything I'd done had been with eager consent. "You have to understand something about me. When I saw us, together and happy, I felt, I dunno, hopeful? Like maybe one day I'd get my chance."

"Okay…"

"And that wasn't okay for a whole slew of reasons that I'm not even going to go into. I decided to prove to myself that the thing between us was nothing more than chemical. Flimsy attraction that went no deeper than a scratch on the surface. I slept with you to prove to myself I could walk away."

"You slept with me," she repeated.

"Four times."

"Four—why are you even telling me this?"

"Does it bother you?" It did. The not-so-subtle rise in her tone gave it away.

"A little," she admitted. "Which doesn't even make sense."

"I *am* sorry, Ash. What I did wasn't exactly the same as what the Andersons did to you. I think it was worse in some ways, though. They paraded you around to make themselves look better. I used you to essentially punish myself, and in the process, hurt—"

Her expression clouded over. "Them? Did you promise them forever? Did you swear to call?"

"Never. I made sure they understood it was nothing more than two people—"

"Then why apologize to me?"

"You said it bothered you."

"It does, but not for the reasons you're thinking. I get it, Noah. Of all the people out there, and as screwed up as it all is, I get it. I mean, I kind of did the same thing. There were guys… Not you, but Freddy… Sure, they were using me, but I was using them, too. They were a way to feel something other than loneliness."

"It is *not* the same thing."

She shrugged. "Maybe not exactly, but I get it. And since you share a lot of the same traits as my Noah, then I'm going to assume that I share traits with those other Ashlyns. If they're like me, they weren't hurt. They understood. You were trying to get through to the other side."

"Maybe." I bristled and squared my shoulders, suddenly uncomfortable with the turn the conversation had taken. I'd never been the *discuss your feelings* kind of guy. "Anyway, the reason I told you was because I'm not wanting to walk away this time. I don't know exactly what I want, but I'm not feeling the need to bail."

"This has to be one of the most surreal conversations I've ever had." She ran her hands through her hair and sighed.

I had no idea what to say, so I settled for something general—and safe. "Let's just think about things. Maybe we can come up with an alternative to, you know, just walking into the lion's den and giving up. Wait until morning to do anything stupid. Agreed?" I held out my hand to her.

She hesitated, but after a moment, took it and offered a small smile. "Agreed."

Chapter Eighteen

Ash

My life had a rocky start. I didn't remember my parents. Sometimes, as a child in my bedroom at the Andersons', I would swear I heard voices whispering in my ear, my parents showing me that they were still here. Guardian angels looking over me from wherever it was they were. Some days it was the only thing that made my life tolerable.

Other days, it was Noah.

I hadn't loved him. Not in the way a girl hopes to fall in love with a guy. I loved him as a sense of comfort and home and safety. He was the embodiment of everything I'd been missing, of the things I'd never had. Connection, love, family… I fooled myself into thinking he could be those things for me. But not long before his death, I woke up. I realized that only I could be those things for me.

This new Noah was so different. Rough compared to the smooth demeanor mine had. He was refreshingly abrasive where my best friend had been plastically polite. He was warm in ways that my Noah never had been, and like ice in areas that mine had been fiery. The same person, yet someone else entirely.

So why was I standing on the corner, a block away from the Infinity Division, ready—if not eager—to throw my life away? *Because* he was an entirely different Noah. This new Noah was the polar opposite. He kept telling me what a bastard he was, yet everything he'd done had proven the reverse. I felt something for him. I had no idea what it was. Slapping a label on something so new, so alien, was impossible. What I did know, though, was that he was right. It *was* more than attraction. I could see the light where previously I'd only seen dark. If I could do something that would help him? Then it went without saying that I would.

I'd called Cora once I was far enough away from the abandoned house. Cade and Kori for me. That was the deal. Was there a chance she'd double cross me? Possibly, though I doubted it. She didn't need them, but she needed me. I would never stop. Until my last breath, I would work to prove her evil. I would stop at nothing to take her company down. I was a loose end she needed to tie up fast.

The agreement was to meet in the first-level parking garage on the Infinity complex. I headed up the last stretch of sidewalk and pulled the sleeves of my hoodie down over my fingers to stave off the chill. I tilted my head up and took a good long look at the sky. I didn't know when—if ever—I'd see it again.

When I arrived at the gate, I found it open, an almost eerie invitation that had never before been extended to me. It was still early and the lot was mostly empty. Well, empty except for the black limo on the far side. I took a deep breath and started forward. When I was almost to the car, the back door on the passenger's side opened.

"I was skeptical that you'd actually show," Cora said. She motioned to someone inside the car, and a few moments later, Kori appeared, followed by Cade. Both seemed relatively unharmed with their hands bound behind their backs. "I despise everything about you, but I commend your valor."

"Just what I always wanted." I rolled my eyes. "Your approval."

"Where's Noah?" Cade's gaze was heavy and I had to look away. "I can't imagine him letting you do this."

"He doesn't know." Kori shook her head. There was sadness in her eyes, but also understanding. It was that look that made me realize she and I were a lot alike. In my position, I had a feeling she would have made the same choice. "She didn't tell him."

"How very romantic," Cora snapped. "So you've seduced the skip as well? I suppose any version of my son will suffice?"

"It's not like that." Defending my actions was pointless and would change nothing, but I couldn't help it. "I'm just doing what's right for everyone."

Cora gave Cade a push forward, but held tight to Kori's arm. She quirked her finger at me and I started forward as Cade crossed the lot. "I want you out of here by nightfall," she warned him.

"Don't worry," Kori said. Her eyes were narrow and her posture stiff. Cora was still holding her arm. "You are the worst possible version of Cora Anderson I could imagine. The faster we leave, the sooner I can forget you exist."

"Oh, my dear, sweet Kori…" Cora gave her a look of mock pity. "I've met multiple versions of myself—and of you." She leaned in a little closer and winked. "You ain't seen nothing yet."

Kori's eyes widened, and I realized she hadn't told Cora who she was.

Cora laughed. "Did you really think I didn't recognize my own child? Male or female, I would know you anywhere."

"Then why let us go? I mean, you've got the entire planet out looking for Noah—"

"You aren't—*weren't*—on the same level with my Noah. I imagine you are just like my other son. Worthless, spineless, and wholly disappointing in a way I find hard to fathom." Her lips twisted into an ugly scowl and her fingers, still wrapped around Kori's upper arm, tightened to a point that made Kori cringe. "Your version of my Noah is vile and crude and I will not have him walking around here to sully my son's memory. Besides..." She smiled. "I'm not letting *you* go."

"We had a deal," I shouted, while at the same time, Cade let out a snarl and started back toward them.

He made it halfway across the lot before Cora pulled Kori against her and grabbed her by the neck. Fingers digging into her flesh, she said, "Please stop where you are, Mr. Granger."

Cade stopped so suddenly that he almost tripped. He glared like he wanted to rip her to shreds, but didn't move another step.

"Yes, I know who you are, as well. Did you honestly think I'd created a device that allowed travel to other dimensions and not used it myself?" She snorted and waggled a finger between us. "I've seen dozens of variations of this little group dynamic—always sad and pathetic and, quite frankly, annoyingly tragic. I would assume Dylan is here as well?

Looking for that silly Fielding girl? Following her? It's the same song played out in slightly different chords. You and Kori and Ashlyn and Noah. I suppose in some ways I find it utterly fascinating." She let out a small laugh. "It's made for some…interesting…times. Now, if you don't mind, I have things to do."

And with that, two men exited the car, positioning themselves on either side of me. With a snap of Cora's fingers, I was stuffed into the backseat of the limo while Kori was crammed in on the other side. From out my window I saw Cade, standing a few yards from the car. He hadn't moved a single step, staring with the barely contained fury of a man teetering on the edge.

"Now…" Cora slipped in and took the seat across from me as the driver closed the door. She smiled as the car jerked into motion and acid bubbled up in the pit of my stomach.

I knew that look. Had seen it a thousand times over the years. Cora wasn't going to kill me. That'd be too easy. She was going to make me pay. Over and over. For that kiss with Noah, for trying to take her down—for simply existing. I was in for a world of hurt and I knew it.

She folded her hands neatly in her lap and crossed her legs at the ankles. A truly deceptive picture of beauty and grace. "I think it's time we had a nice, long chat. Don't you?"

Chapter Nineteen

Noah

I hadn't realized how tired I was until I leaned back and closed my eyes. I must have dropped off immediately, because I'd intended to talk to Ash about that stupid decision of hers before it was too late.

Swiping the crust from my eyes, I sat up. We'd gotten used to sleeping in weird places over the last year. Out in the grass, on rocks and hard floors—once we'd even camped out in a trench in the middle of a war zone. The United States was at war with Canada and Wells—of all places— was ground zero.

My back had adjusted and I was able to move with little to no kinks. Using the edge of the ruined couch, I dragged myself up and scanned the room. There was no sign of her and a knot of worry formed in my gut. "Ash?"

No answer.

Fine. Okay. There was no reason to freak, right? It was a big house. She could be anywhere. The bathroom, or maybe scrounging for something to eat? I checked the kitchen, the bathroom—which, considering the state of the rest of the house, had been a mistake—the rooms upstairs. Hell, I even checked the closet. She wasn't here. I poked my head out the back door. A small, overgrown lawn with a rusting swing set and rotted wooden table were all I saw.

I gave up and made my way back down to the living room, passing the other end of the couch on my way in. That's when I saw it. A small slip of dirty white paper propped up against one of the torn cushions. I wanted to kick my own ass all the way to the moon.

I unfolded it, already knowing what it would say.

I went to meet Cora. Cade and Kori should contact you soon. This is whats best for everyone.

Then, at the bottom, in scrunched writing—the slip of paper was small—there was more.

You were a better, brighter version of him. He made me laugh, but you...you made me smile. Please, for me, find your Ashlyn. Let yourself be happy.

My fingers tightened, crumpling the paper into a tiny ball. I threw it down and reached for my jacket just as my cell started going off. I fished it out and without looking at it, swiped to answer. "What?"

A few seconds of silence, then, "Noah?"

Cade. I took a deep breath, counted to five, then blew out slowly. "Yeah. You okay? Kori?"

"Ash—"

"I just found the note." How the hell could she do this? What was she thinking? After all that shit I'd said last night? "Cora has her?"

"Took her away. Kori too. They let me go. We'll get her back, though, Noah. Her and Ash."

He was right. We'd get them back. Regardless of what feelings I did—or didn't—have for this Ashlyn Calvert, I refused to let someone sacrifice so much for me. I gave Cade the address of the house we'd hunkered down in, then went to work on a plan.

*B*y the time Cade arrived, I was no closer to coming up with a brilliant plan than I had been when I'd hung up with him. He had a black eye, but other than that, he was fine. Apparently Cora had both he and Kori in a cell—because Mom had *jail cells* of her very own in this crazy reality—and left them alone. No questions. No scare tactics. Apparently she'd reserved those for me.

Wasn't I the lucky one?

"Since I'm dead here and everyone knows it, that rules out the obvious." We'd posed as ourselves a few times to get where we'd needed to go. It usually didn't end well, but there had been a few wins. "You didn't learn anything about the security setup or layout? Patrols—anything?"

"They dragged us from the car and brought us into the building through a door in the parking garage. I know they took us to a sublevel. Seven it was, I think?"

"Okay. That's something. At least we have a floor."

"Other than that, we were put in a cell at the end of a hallway just left of the elevator. We weren't alone, either. There were other people there." Cade stood and started to pace. An annoying habit, but I'd learned to deal with it years ago. "At least two other cells were occupied."

"You don't know by who? Think one of them was the guy Brewster was talking about?"

Cade shrugged. "Possible. I yelled, but no one answered." He frowned. "We have to get them out."

"That goes without saying."

"All of them."

"*All*—whoa," I said, jumping to my feet. I wasn't sure why I was even surprised. This was so *Cade*. "Do you think it's the best time to play superhero?"

"Have you met that woman?" He rolled his eyes.

"Um, yeah. I have, in fact, met her. She's fucking certifiable—which is why I'd like to get my shit, pack my bags, and get the hell off this rock as soon as possible."

He stopped pacing and leaned against the wall by the door. "What about Ash?"

"What about her?" Did I want to leave her? No. Did I intend to leave her? *Hell, no.* "Obviously we'll get her out. I won't leave her with Cora, but that's all I can do."

"There's no way you're going to get me to believe you'd just leave her here to rot. She's got no future if she stays in this world. And what prompted her to do something so stupid?"

"Yeah. See, that's another problem we have."

"Why do I not like the sound of that…"

"Dylan is to blame for this." Just one more thing I owed the bastard for. "He contacted me last night. Has Rabbit."

Cade cursed. "Why didn't I see that coming?" He kicked the side of the couch. The worn material tore and the frame inside groaned and caved. "Of course he'd go after Rabbit. Aside from Cora, he'd be the only other person with any chance of fixing the cuff."

"Rabbit told Dylan he could fix the cuffs, but in order to do it, he needed the entire set."

"So Ash sacrificed herself for nothing then. She's perfect for you, man. Acts before putting any thought to it." He let his head fall back and groaned. "She got me out, but Kori is still in there. We're still at square one."

"Except that it's a lie."

"Huh?"

"Rabbit doesn't need the whole set. He just needs Dylan's—which he's already got. He was saying that to buy time."

"I assume Dylan instructed you to contact him once we were all back together?" There was a hopeful gleam in his eyes.

"That was the plan."

He let out a breath and some of the tension drained away. He was acting like I'd just told him he'd won the damn lottery—which, if you understood Cade, I had. The guy was all about hope and determination. Give him the smallest sliver and he ran with it. When he set his mind to something, he saw it through. No matter what. It was admirable—but it had cost him. "Then at least we have a little time. We'll figure out a way to bust in there and get them out, then call—"

I hated to burst his bubble, but he wasn't getting it. "Yeah. See, that's the *other* problem."

He ran his hands through his hair, pausing to tug at the roots. "You're killing me here."

"I don't know how true it is, but Rabbit also told Dylan that unless the core in the cuffs is repaired, recharged—whatever—within the next fifty or so hours, then they'll be useless and we'll be stranded."

"Stranded? He told you the cuffs stopped working completely?"

"That's what he says. Tried to skip off this rock four times. We're all still here…"

He cursed again. A bad habit he'd picked up from me in the fourth grade. It was funny. I was raised in the perfect environment. A loving family, a great home, and had every advantage a guy could have. Schools, clothing, food… We weren't rich like we were here, but we were comfortable and happy. Cade's family was horrible. He'd been abused and neglected, and only knew what it was like to have a real family after we'd unofficially adopted him. Yet I was the one who ended up in trouble. I was the one who became the bad influence. How many nights had my mother sat us down and tried to explain to Cade that he didn't have to go along with every crazy thing I did? He had gotten into his own fair share of trouble, but for the most part, I was the one with the morally gray compass.

"How much time has it been? How much do we have?"

I fished out my cell and checked the time. "We probably have a little over four hours."

Cade nodded. "Okay. Then I think I have a plan."

Chapter Twenty

Ash

"You look worried, Ash." Cora sat in the chair across from me wearing a grin that clearly screamed *I won*. Her hair was styled in artful waves, secured by pins decorated in what I had no doubt were real diamonds. Everything from her shock-red lipstick to her snow-white pantsuit was designed to stand out. To intimidate. "Why is that?"

I had no idea where we were exactly. I'd been to the Infinity building a million times over the years, but I'd never been in the basement. The elevator had taken us down to sublevel seven and I'd been deposited in a small room with pristine white walls and a strong chemical scent that made my eyes water. Like disinfectant—which made me wonder what they'd had to clean up with something so strong. What evidence had they needed to wipe away?

There were a couple of chairs and a small television in the corner and nothing else. We'd taken so many different hallways that I'd lost track of things. Even if I managed to get free somehow, I'd never find my way out. Then again, that was unlikely. If there were even the smallest chance of escape, Cora would have blindfolded me. The fact that she'd marched me in, view unobstructed? That was her way of saying I was out of luck.

"Oh, I dunno." I wiggled my fingers to stave off the growing pins and needles sensation. After being *delicately* placed in the chair, my hands had been cuffed behind my back, uncomfortably tight. "Maybe because I know exactly how unhinged you are."

"It doesn't have to be that way." She plastered on a sickly sweet smile and leaned forward. The material of her shirt wrinkled and she frowned, immediately smoothing it back down. When it was perfect again, she refocused on me. "After all, you are my foster daughter. Do you really think I take pleasure in causing you pain?"

"Is that, um, a trick question?"

She laughed. To an unknowing person, the sound might come across as delicate. The soft amusement of a refined lady. Me? It was the hiss of a viper. I knew the poison that lay beneath. The true ugliness it hid. "I wonder if that dull sense of humor is what my son found so amusing."

Actually, Noah had never truly appreciated my sense of humor. He always found it a bit too dark and sarcastic. "So what happens now?"

"Now you tell me what it is you know."

"I know a lot of things." I flashed her my most innocent grin. "Is there a topic in particular you're interested in? I just read this great article about the panda population and how it's overrunning Central Park. Did you know that they're only here because of an agreement signed with China in the forties? We traded pandas for red squirrels. I think they got the better end of the deal. Have you ever seen panda shit?"

"What do you know about Omega?"

"That it's a symbol in the Greek alphabet?"

"You're trying my patience, Ash."

"I wasn't aware you had any, Cora." The best defense against Cora Anderson was to keep your cool. She lived to rattle and it drove her nuts when she didn't have that effect. The woman thrived on intimidation, and one of the things that had enraged her over the years was that I'd always come across as indifferent. I just had to focus on that. Channel that air of aloofness and hoped to hell it hid the terror squirming just beneath my skin.

"Let's switch gears for a moment, shall we? Let's talk about Noah. Did you think you were being sly?" She stood, and I didn't miss the way her fingers flexed, tightening and stretching like she was just itching to take me apart. This was the Cora people didn't get to see. The one hidden just beneath the surface. The snapping, screaming woman who I'd watched go from smiling to destructive rampage in half a second more times than I could count. "You poisoned his mind—turned him against his own family. Then you had the nerve to try seducing him to boost your standing?"

"We've never liked each other," I said as calmly as I could. "But you know damn well that wasn't what happened. First, I didn't *poison Noah's mind*. I didn't do anything to turn him against you. You and Karl did a bang-up job of that all on your own. As for the other thing… What you saw—that kiss—was a moment of stupidity on my part. Our relationship wasn't like that. Not at all."

"Of course it wasn't. How could it be? You and my Noah…" She snorted. "You know, I tried pushing you toward Corey in the beginning. He was so simple and in need of a distraction. Something to keep his small mind entertained instead of those stupid little paints and pencils he was so fond of. You were mildly pretty. I felt it was a good match. He could do as he pleased, then we could be rid of you."

"Classy," I said.

"I spoke to Noah about it. Multiple times." She stopped in front of my chair and bent down so we were eye to eye. "In those early years I encouraged him to push you toward his brother. To stop spending so much time with you because it was beneath him. Do you know what his reply was?"

"Can't say that I do."

"He asked if it bothered me. He said that you were interesting, but if it angered me, then that made it all the more fun." The corner of her lip twitched with a grin. "Even as a young child my Noah had a rebellious streak."

My chest tightened.

"And you know what? I decided to let it go for the time being. I'd always found you utterly useless. A waste of space inside my home that could have been better spent on a coat rack. But if finding amusement with you pleased him for a short time, then I felt like taking you in hadn't been such a waste."

"I don't believe you."

"No? I think you do. See, I believe if you think long and hard about your time with him, you'll be able to see it for what it really was. My son used you. You were a tool of rebellion. A way for him to show his father and me that we couldn't control every aspect of his life." Her smile widened. "If you think I'm lying, then how about I let Noah tell you himself."

I didn't understand what she was talking about. Not

until she straightened and crossed the small space to the television in the corner. Fingers gliding across the remote, the thing came to life with a small pop. On the screen, she and a much younger Noah were having an animated conversation in the middle of his bedroom.

"Oh, excuse me. This works so much better with sound."

"Mother, you never learn," the on-screen Noah said. The sound was slightly tinny and low, but I could still make out every single word with painful clarity. He was fourteen or fifteen judging by the clothes and the posters on his wall. My heart gave a violent squeeze as he ran a hand through his hair—nearly shoulder length right before he caved to his mother's thrashing and cut it all off. "The more you protest, the farther I'm going to go."

"You—you had a camera in your son's room?" All the things I'd said to him in confidence behind those walls, the times I'd let my guard down and confessed my deepest fears… Cora had seen and heard it all. White-hot embarrassment mingled with fury. She'd always known just how to get into my head. Now I understood why. "How could you—"

"Shut up!" she screamed. With a deep breath, she regained her composure and jabbed a perfectly polished finger at the screen. "Best part is coming up."

"I will not tolerate this, Noah," her on-screen version said. "That girl is beneath you. You will end this sickening experiment immediately."

"Sickening?" A slow, devastating grin spread across his face. "Hell, if you think my being nice to her is *sickening*, Mother, then what would you say if I married her one day? Paraded her around to all your clubs and high society friends? Would our children have the signature Anderson charm? Or would they be born with her gutter class humor?"

Gutter class humor? The tightness in my chest formed a bubble that threatened to explode. To hear him talking about me like I was some *thing* to be used to manipulate his parents, to hear him speaking about my worth like someone who believed in the tier system, was devastating. I fought back the tears gathering in the corners of my eyes. She'd chipped a piece of my soul away, but I refused to let her see me break.

Cora turned the television off and set down the remote. "He used you to anger us, but unfortunately, after a while, he developed a...*fondness*...for you." She waved her hand in a circle. "Kind of like one would with a *pet*. He began feeling guilty and trying to do things that might please you in order to make up for his actions. He'd always been resistant to what we do here, but when you voiced your disapproval of our company's dealings, well, my son started digging. And, being the brilliant boy that he was, found some things he shouldn't have."

"So you killed him," I spat.

"He was never comfortable with what we did, but you... you pushed him. You made him curious. What happened to him was *your* fault."

"It's *my* fault you decided to kill your own son?" I couldn't hold in my snort. "Sorry. That's all on you."

She made a sound low in her throat then grabbed the arms of my chair, jerking it forward a few inches. "I had to make a choice. An impossible choice. You put me in a position where I had to pick between a great advancement in science for the good of an entire world, and my own son!"

I lifted my head so that I could look her in the eye. For the first time in my life, there was no fear. Cora Anderson didn't intimidate me. She wasn't the larger-than-life demon casting a shadow over my life. She was simply a woman. A crazy, insane woman who had chosen greed over her own child. "You made the choice you did for money. It had nothing to do with science. You're disgusting."

For a second I thought she'd finally lose it. Slip over the edge of sanity and take me right along with her. But to my surprise, she took a deep breath and let go of the chair, pulling away. She straightened and fixed her blouse, then tugged the sleeves of her jacket back into place. "Well, yes. There was quite a bit of money involved."

I shook my head. "I don't get it. What could have been so important that you would kill your own son to hide it?" I wiggled my fingers again. My hands were starting to go numb. "You already dump our criminals on other societies. He found proof of that, didn't he? He found proof that you don't research the worlds?"

She frowned, but it wasn't sincere. "He did. He confronted me with it, too. But I took care of it. Convinced him that as hard as it was to swallow, we were doing what was best for *our world*. We had to worry about ourselves."

"There's no way he would go for that. It's not something he would have sat on." Though after seeing that video, I wasn't so sure. Noah had always insisted he hated the tier system. He felt it was archaic and cruel to treat people differently depending on the family they were born into. But that was a lie. Or, at least partially a lie. Cora said he grew fond of me after a while. As sick as it was, a small part of me couldn't help clinging to that sentiment. It was currently the only thing connecting me to the friend I thought I knew, and if I lost that...

"A little bribery goes a long way—especially with someone as materialistic as my son. Noah was not quite as eager to leave his wealth behind as he would have you believe." Her expression darkened, lips pulling back in a snarl. "But he stumbled onto something else. Something to do with a project called Omega."

I shook my head. He'd been willing to keep the Guardian project's true nature a secret but was going to blow the whistle on Omega? How bad could it have been? "I can't imagine Omega being worse than dumping the worst of our society in someone else's backyard."

Her smile widened. "My dear, when we launch the Omega project, when people see what they can gain from my company, no one will care about where we're dumping our criminals."

"What could you possibly have to offer that will make people forget what you're doing to innocent communities?"

"What could I offer? How about giving people back the ones they've lost?"

Chapter Twenty-One

Noah

"I dunno if this can work. And even if it could—I'm not okay with it." We were waiting just inside the gate of the park where Ash and I had previously met Dylan.

Cade sighed. He looked tired, and who could blame him. This was his plan and here I was bitching, but this had to be just as hard on him as it would be on me. The fact that he'd suggested it just proved how much Kori meant to him. "You can do this. *I* can do this. What other choice do we have?"

I wasn't sold on that, but I nodded anyway. Why take that away from him? He'd need something to get him through the next few hours. I knew I would. Dylan had what he needed to fix the cuffs, even though he didn't know it yet. Unfortunately, we needed to get Kori—and Ash—out of Infinity. For that we needed Rabbit.

To get to Rabbit, we needed Dylan.

"Math might not be my strong suit, but I've got the basics down," Dylan's voice rang out from the shadows. A moment later, he came into the light beaming from the dirty street lamp above us. "Seems like you're missing someone."

I'd called him and said we were ready to meet. Except I'd left out one small detail. "Where's Rabbit?"

Dylan shrugged. "Safe. Where's Kori?"

"Not safe," Cade replied. "There's a small hitch in your plan."

"Oh?" His tone was casual, but I didn't miss the slight twitch in the corner of his lip. "And what would that be?"

"I got Cade out." I folded my arms and leaned back against the rusted monkey bars. "But Kori was impossible. She was in a different part of the building. One I couldn't get to."

"If you want to skip out of here, if you want Rabbit to fix the cuffs, you're going to have to make some concessions." Cade grinned.

"Such as?"

"You're going to have to let him go."

Dylan snorted. "Just how stupid do I look, little brother?"

"Do you or do you not need all the cuffs?" I still wasn't sure he'd fall for it. "This is your shot—and time is running out. We have no hope of getting in to save Kori without Rabbit's help."

He watched me for a moment, then turned and did the same to Cade, searching for the lie. I was the bullshit king, but Cade…the guy couldn't lie to save his life. "You're bluffing."

Cade shrugged. "Maybe. Maybe not. Can you really afford to take a chance? You said Ava isn't here. If the cuff doesn't work, you're stuck here without her."

He cursed. "No. I'm not letting the geek out of my sight. But I will go *with* him."

"You're going to help us save Kori?" This was what Cade had gambled on. With Ava absent, Rabbit was his only leverage now.

"Of course not." The sneer on his lips made it hard to stay where I was. No way. I couldn't do this. I couldn't work with my sister's killer. "I'm going to help save *myself.*"

*W*e'd followed Dylan back to the road where he'd led us to an old, parked van. When he'd pulled it open, Rabbit was there, zip tied and duct taped in the back. After he'd been untied and threats had been made—if we tried to grab Rabbit and run, his family would get the nasty surprise he'd left for them—we hunkered down to come up with a plan of attack.

"This is going to work out well." Rabbit rubbed his wrists while glaring at Dylan out of the corner of his eye. His Dockers were stained and he was missing his right shoe. "I could probably scrounge up what I needed to fix the cuffs on the outside, but getting into my office will make it easier— and faster. We're gonna be cutting it close."

"How close?" Dylan hadn't taken his eyes off Rabbit since untying him—which was a little unsettling, considering he was driving the van.

"Hard to say. Really depends on when the core in your chip stopped working."

"Wonderful." I groaned. The inside of the vehicle smelled like rotting fish and the floor in the back right-hand corner was rusted out. Every time we hit a bump, little bits of debris would pop through and I wondered how long before the entire floor fell out.

"So how do we get in?" Cade kept his focus on Rabbit

the entire time, not daring to glance in his brother's direction. He could hardly look at the guy. Me? I could stare. I could stare, and as each second ticked by, imagine the things I'd do to him the moment this was all over. This was our last stop. End of the line. He was going down this time.

"I can walk right in through the front door—not that I ever would. I have my own lab entrance." He stopped rubbing his wrists and had moved on to retying his remaining shoe. Over and over. Tied. Untied. Tied. Untied. It was starting to drive me nuts. Our Rabbit did it, too, though. Serious OCD issues. Cade and I would rib him as he checked a hundred times to make sure he'd turned his heater off—in the middle of July.

"Good. We'll go with you," Dylan said from behind the wheel.

"No." Rabbit shook his head. "You won't. Everything is surveyed by camera. You follow me in and they'll be on us before you can blink."

"Then how do *we* get in?" Cade and I were in the back with him. I'd contemplated flinging the door open and having us all jump when the van slowed, but Cade would never go for it. Not with Rabbit's mom at risk.

"I'm going to have to get inside and scope things out. Make sure I haven't fallen under suspicion. If everything looks good, I can disable the cameras."

"Won't someone notice?"

"Nope. I can loop the feed on all the cameras except for the main one in Cora's office."

"What are we supposed to do about that one, then?" Dylan asked. The van slowed, then let out a horrible squeal as it stopped completely.

"Pray she's busy."

...

I had no idea how long we'd been waiting for Rabbit to come back. He'd left us huddled in the woods, not far from the Infinity building and about a mile from where he'd parked the van. He promised that once the coast was clear, he'd come back to get us, assuring the group that no one—even Cora—ever came into his lab. It was one of the deals he made when coming to work for them. His paranoia was epic and I wondered what our Rabbit would have to say if he could see himself this way.

"So this is a kick, eh?" Dylan had settled against a thick pine tree and had been picking at the edge of his boot for the last few minutes. He glanced up and winked at Cade. "Never thought we'd be hanging again."

"Shut up," Cade mumbled. He had his back to his brother, pretending to keep watch on the building beyond the trees. Every once in a while I'd see his jaw clench. His fists would tighten and he'd close his eyes tightly for a moment before opening them and breathing in deeply. Inner calm. Meditation. Calling on all that stoic soldier bullshit. Before meeting this new Kori, that stuff had been the only thing getting him through some days. I hadn't made it easier on him in those early weeks, sometimes going days without saying a word to him. Not because I blamed him, but because I blamed myself. But I was his best friend and we'd both lost her. He'd needed me and I hadn't always been there.

"Is that any way to talk to the guy trying to save you?"

"Said it yourself," I interjected. Cade looked like he was ready to start swinging. "You're here to save yourself."

"True. True. But you get to come along for the ride. Don't

worry, though. We'll be back to trying to kill one another soon, I'm sure." He snickered. "Though I technically never tried to kill either one of you. I just want Kori dea—"

That was all I could listen to. I launched myself at him, hauling him off the ground and slamming him back against the tree as hard as I could. "Not another fucking word. The only reason I haven't torn your throat out is—" I glanced over my shoulder at Cade. "Remind me, man. *Why* haven't I torn his throat out?"

He came up beside me and set a hand down on my shoulder. "Enough people have died because of him. There's no reason to drag Rabbit's mom into it."

Right. Rabbit's mom. Anyone else would have heard a chivalrous sacrifice. A wronged man willing to shelf his bloody vendetta for the safety of others. I heard the barely bridled rage. I had a nasty temper and highly questionable morals, but Cade…Cade had a dark side that blotted out my own at times. I'd seen him lose it. Had pulled him back from the brink many times. He'd gotten a proper hold on it as we grew up, but being here, having to deal with Dylan while Kori's condition was unknown, might just be enough to snap him.

I kept my eyes trained on Dylan and gave him a good shake. "Yeah, but if you remember correctly, my moral compass doesn't point North. Isn't that right?"

Dylan didn't look overly impressed, but there was a hint of concern in his eyes. "Posture all you want, Noah. My brother would never risk it. That poor innocent woman…"

Most days I would agree with him. But looking at Cade in that moment, I wasn't so sure. *Screw Rabbit and his family. To hell with Ash and her issues. So what if we're stuck here…* I saw it all in his eyes as strongly as I felt it in my bones. "If you think—"

"Guys?" Rabbit poked his head through the brush and Dylan smirked. "Hurry. We don't have a lot of time."

Reluctantly, I released Dylan and stepped away from the tree. Kori. Ash. Rabbit's mom. All decent people whose lives would be ruined if we couldn't keep our shit together—at least for a little while longer. I nodded to Cade. "You good?"

He didn't answer right away, breathing in, holding it, then blowing out slowly. He nodded. "I am."

We followed Rabbit back to the building and slipped in through a thick metal door marked Phil MaKaden. Once inside, Cade let out a whistle. "Our Rabbit would be crapping himself if he could see this."

He wasn't kidding. There were at least seven computers, all lined up against the farthest wall, the wraparound marble countertop stacked with papers between each monitor. The room itself was huge. It had to be forty by forty, the other three walls lined with an assortment of file cabinets, locked cabinets, and a workstation. The thing that made me jealous, though? In the far corner was a huge vending machine. Candy, chips, cookies—there was fruit, too, but yuck. I gave it one more longing once-over, then turned my back.

"I found the girls," he said, bending over his desk and pulling what seemed like random things from the top drawer. "They're on sublevel seven."

"Girls?" Dylan crossed the room and jabbed a finger at him, then turned back to Cade and me. "We're here for *Kori*. No one else. We find her, fix the cuffs, and get the hell out. End of story, end of deal."

"Not quite," I said. "Ash is here. We'll be getting her out, too."

"Nonnegotiable," Rabbit mumbled. I didn't miss the

bitterness in his tone. "I need her to take down Cora." He looked up from his desk drawer. "You want the cuffs fixed, we get Kori *and* Ash."

Dylan's face reddened and the muscles in his neck twitched. His fists curled, knuckles turning white, as his jaw flexed several times. He had no choice and he knew it. Finally, he gave a short nod. "Previous statement still stands. If I don't get what I want, your mother is a goner."

"I heard you—and I believe it. No one here is going to screw you over. I said I'd fix the cuff and I will—as soon as the girls get here."

"And just how do we go about doing that?" Cade asked. He kept glancing at the door.

Rabbit noticed and waved a hand in its general direction. "No fear. No one can get in unless I let him or her in."

"Cora doesn't have a key?" I found it hard to believe my mom—on any earth—would allow herself to be locked out of the lab where her tech was being tinkered with.

"She did. Does, actually." He walked to the door and tapped the metal above the knob. There was a small keypad with bright blue numbers. "But if she tried to use it, it wouldn't work. I've made some improvements to the lock. Trust me. This baby is impossible to bypass."

Dylan snorted. "What about breaking down the door? You think a lock will deter them?"

Rabbit rolled his eyes. "I imagine they could eventually break it down. It's reinforced steel, not titanium—but it would take forever. I'd have more than enough time to get out."

"Good." I stuffed my hands into my pockets and fought back an involuntary shudder of anticipation. "Then let's get this show on the road. How do we break out the girls?"

Chapter Twenty-Two

Ash

We'd been going back and forth for the better part of two hours now. Cora was sure I knew something more about the Omega project than I was admitting to, convinced I'd hidden proof of her wrongdoing somewhere out in the world or told someone something that would implicate her in Noah's death. But really, all I knew was that she intended to *give people back what they'd lost*—whatever the hell that meant.

She stopped pacing the room and settled in the chair across from me. This was the fifth time she'd done it, the first four times having said nothing before standing to resume her pacing again. I didn't like the slow smile that spread across her face now. "Did you know that I personally oversaw Andrew and Rebecca's skipping?"

Andrew and Rebecca. *My parents?*

The air in the room stilled and the temperature plummeted. "What?" She was wrong. Was saying these things to play with me. No one knew how to manipulate better than

Cora Anderson. No trick was too dirty. No tactic too low. I'd seen it firsthand a hundred times. "My parents are dead. An accident several months after I was born."

She covered her mouth and gasped. It was a totally manufactured response. "Oh, did I forget to tell you that wasn't true? There was no accident. They were very much alive when I had them skipped. Rebecca worked for me. She was my assistant."

"Your—" I couldn't believe what I was hearing.

"Rebecca Calvert was a brilliant woman—despite being Bottom Tier trash. I saw her potential, and even though I received quite a bit of flack, I took her on as my assistant."

"No…"

"It's true." Cora frowned. She sat back in the chair and shot me a look of regret so real that another person might have eaten it up with a spoon and asked for seconds. Me? I knew it was pure fabrication. "And after everything I did for her, *everything I gave*, she betrayed me and I gave her exactly what she deserved."

I tried to focus on her words and not on the fact that I wanted to punch her. I wanted to open my mouth and scream until my voice was gone and my chest ached. "No. This is a trick. Some ploy to get me to tell you what I know— which is nothing. *I know nothing!*"

Cora ignored me and kept going. "In the early days of Infinity, I, shall we say, broke a few eggs? After switching from the cuffs to the chips while trying to get the Guardian program off the ground, we had a bit of an issue making things to work as they should. The first-and second-generation models had a nasty little habit of causing heart failure within the first forty-eight hours of insertion. Your mother discovered that I was using listed individuals to test the product."

"You knew it was killing people and you still kept trying?"

"That's how science advances, Ash. Besides, I paid the house for each and every one. Bought fair and square."

"You can't *buy* people," I shouted. "You can't purchase them to experiment on!"

"I think you'll find that I can do whatever I like—or I could until she started kicking the dust around." She sighed. "Of course the universe repaid her for biting the hand that fed her. There was a horrible accident and she lost her first child."

I opened my mouth—then closed it, stunned. "*First* child?"

Cora narrowed her eyes and drew back her hand. The blow came, causing my vision to swim as the resounding slap echoed in my ears. "Still talking…" She took a deep breath, composing herself. "I did something very special for her. I helped her through it in a way that no one else on earth could have. It should have bought her loyalty. My actions should have ensured her compliance!"

"But it didn't." I couldn't help grinning. Some people just couldn't be bought. "She tried turning you in anyway, didn't she?"

She bared her teeth. "Two years later Rebecca went behind my back. She met with reporters and heads of government. She supplied notes and documentation that she'd stolen from my office. She'd almost gotten to the president when I uncovered her betrayal. It was quite a mess for me to clean up—and I wasn't happy."

"So you had her skipped."

"Obviously—but that wasn't enough. I trusted her. With my secrets, with my work. Punishing her wasn't enough—especially after what I'd done for her. I skipped her and your father, assuring them not to worry about their poor, sweet little girl. I promised that I would take you in. That I would feed and clothe you and keep a roof over your head. I would strive every day to make sure you truly understood how *unloved* and *unwanted* you were. Then, when I couldn't stand the sight of you any longer, I would make sure you ended up listed."

My head spun. My entire life, every wicked exchange, every dirty glare, was Cora's way of hurting my mom. I'd suffered my entire life for something someone else had done.

"Every day, the older you got, the more you looked like her... I do believe I hate you more than I did Rebecca." She smiled. Like she'd just told me the funniest joke in her arsenal. "When you think about it, it's all very funny, considering."

"Considering what?" A funny feeling bubbled up in my stomach. She was looking at me. Smiling in a way that made me think the worst was yet to come. Cora had this grin she reserved for special occasions. The secret smile she held back for her truly awful actions. That smile was on her face and it was making the air in the room frigid.

She stopped in front of my chair and grabbed my chin, nails digging into sensitive skin. "Quiet now. Grown-ups are talking." She cleared her throat and resumed her path. "Rebecca was going to tell everyone and that would have ruined our public image. The president would have pulled our permits and closed us down before we really even got started. Think of all the revenue we would have lost!"

She gave one final squeeze and let go, stepping away and folding her arms. I flexed my jaw and glared. "So, again. It was all about money."

"Do you have any idea how much money we make per

inmate skipped? Three hundred thousand dollars. Small change, though, when you think about it. For each individual Omega deal we broker, we will get seventeen million."

My mouth fell open. What the hell could they be doing for seventeen million a pop? And who had that kind of green?

She studied me for a moment before folding her arms with a *humpf*. "Huh. Maybe you didn't know."

"That's what I've been telling you."

"Really, I owe it all to Rebecca. The heart of what Omega is was born of her misery. She was devastated when she lost her child. A small girl of only six years old. Utterly useless— and I needed her mind. I had to act."

A chill crept up my spine. "What did you do, Cora?"

"My first attempt was such a success that I was eager to try again to see if I could replicate the outcome. At first I tried using Skips. If someone was foolish to venture here from another dimension, they were fair game. Unfortunately it happened so rarely. Apparently most other realms aren't as advanced as we are here. The best answer was to simply take what I needed from other earths." She snickered. "It made sense, I suppose. It's what I did in the first place."

"In the first place?" I was sure I'd heard her wrong. Things were starting to take shape in my head and I *didn't* like how they were forming. "Cora, tell me what you did. To help my mother. What was it?"

She snorted. "You went to see Markus Brewster. Didn't you wonder what I wanted with someone who dealt in such crude chemical substances?"

"Obviously."

"I needed a way to wipe someone's mind. To present them to the world as a blank slate, a sponge ready to soak up life. Brewster was impressive in the beginning. The first couple of times he did it was a success with only minor issues—of course the subject was the same. But it got me thinking... The idea for Omega was born and I insisted he come work for me. Unfortunately, his later attempts failed multiple times with varying degrees of disaster. The subjects ranged from deep hysteria and madness to violence. Some had a partial wipe, but still retained unwanted memories. It's been a long road, but I think we finally found the winning recipe."

"Tell me what you did." I still didn't understand fully. She was saying a lot—yet nothing at all. It was just gibberish without specifics, with just enough bait sprinkled in to induce madness.

She bent down and narrowed her eyes. "I replaced Rebecca's dead child." She straightened, looking pleased with herself. "With you."

"With—" I couldn't breathe. My arms, my legs—my entire body—everything was numb. I had a feeling I was biting down hard on the inside of my cheek, but I didn't feel it. The only thing I was aware of was the erratic beat of my heart as it hammered, thunderously loud, in my ears. The thumping banged against my chest and my vision swam in and out of focus. Acid rumbled in my stomach, burning bile singing its way up my throat.

"You're not from here, Ashlyn. I stole you. Plucked you from another world. I stole you and gave you to Rebecca so she could focus again. I wiped your six-year-old memory, then wiped you again at eight when I got rid of Rebecca." She laughed. "The most ironic part? I brought you here to live as a lowly Bottom Tier, when where you're from, your family is actually richer and more powerful than mine."

Her words snapped me back to the here and now. They brought rage and fury and focus. So much focus. "I'm going to kill you, Cora."

"When we present the first *official* working trials of the project to the public, along with the case study I've been doing on you for years, people will be in awe. A multiple wipe and still functioning... The president will have no other choice than to allow us to proceed with the venture. He stands to make billions." She laughed. A deep, dark sound that sent a ripple of fury through me. "Once the project launches, Infinity will not only be in the business of ridding our world of its unwanted criminal element, but thanks to you and Rebecca, we will also be reuniting people with their lost loved ones." Her grin widened. "Well, versions of them, at least."

*A*fter Cora dropped her bombshell, she had me escorted to a cell. I had no idea how long I'd been here. My head was spinning. They were stealing people. Kidnapping alternate versions of loved ones and bringing them here. They were stealing their lives away, wiping their memories, and selling them off to the highest bidders. A big wig politician lost his son in a tragic car wreck? No problem. For the right amount of money, he could have him back again. Some rich guy lost his trophy wife to an *argument*? Why get a new one? He could keep up appearances by having Infinity hijack the one he'd had.

Just like me.

I leaned back against the wall and pulled my feet onto

the cot. I wasn't born in this world. That idea alone was enough to send my mind into a crazy tailspin of *what if*. Add to it the fact that I'd lived as an orphan while my real family was out there somewhere and you treaded into the deep end of insanity. This whole time I'd been alone and feeling hopeless there was someplace better out there for me. A place I actually belonged. "This is seven different kinds of sick."

"...hello?"

That voice. I knew that voice. "Kori?"

"Ash?"

"It's me. You okay?" I didn't know her well, but I found that I was overwhelmingly relieved to hear her voice. I slid off the cot and pushed myself up against the bars. A few cells over, across the hall, she was doing the same.

"I'm okay," she replied. "You?"

"Same."

She let her head fall forward against the bars. The small thud it made echoed down the hall. "Thank God."

I snorted. "Yeah. For now." We had to get out of here—I just had no idea how we were going to do it. There was little doubt in my mind the boys would try coming for Kori, but I couldn't find it in my heart to believe they'd actually make it. "Anyone else here?"

A few moments ticked by. Finally someone coughed. "Me. I'm here."

A girl's voice. "What's your name?" I called out.

There was a short pause before she let out an agonized growl. "I'm—I—I don't know. I can't remember."

"They did something to you." God. Cora had stolen this poor girl's life, too. Her family, her home, her friends... I couldn't decide what was worse. Knowing or living in not-so-blissful ignorance. "Are you alone? Is there anyone else here?"

"I'm here," a guy's voice said.

"I think that's it," the girl called. "Until you two got here, it was just us. There have been others, but…"

"But these freaks took them and they never came back," the guy shouted. Metal clanged and he let out a string of curses, ending in an echoing thud.

"Shh," the girl urged. "We talked about this. Keep your voice down. If they come for you—"

"I know." His tone was softer. "I know."

"Did they take you together?" I pulled against the bars to test them. Solid.

"No," she said. "We've just been here the longest. G and I—"

"Is that your name?" Kori called to the guy. "G?"

"No clue." He grumbled something I couldn't quite hear. "Had to call each other something. She calls me G, I call her Sera."

"Okay then." I pushed off the bars and spun in a slow circle. Three solid walls. No way out. "There's four of us now. Let's put our heads together and get the hell out of here."

"Guard schedule," Kori said. "Do they come down to bring food? Random security checks? Surveillance? Surely they're watching you somehow."

"They bring food once a day," Sera said. "G is on the very end, the first cell in the row. He can usually see the elevator light up just before they get here. As for random checks, no. They do come down once a day in the morning, though. No cameras that we know of." She let out a snort. "Cora once said there was no need because a chance at escape was impossible."

"Every few days they drag us from the cell and bring us up a few floors." There was fury in G's tone. "They run tests. It happened this morning, though."

"Most of the time it's just simple blood tests. Sometimes an EKG," Sera whispered.

"Sometimes it's not. They hurt Sera this morning. They've hurt her before."

The rage in his voice made me think of Noah. Both of them. Mine had been so protective—or so I'd thought. But, thinking back, he'd really only been like that in recent years. Since Cora's big reveal, I'd been picking apart every aspect of our relationship. Some things made me numb, while others reinforced the belief that yes, he had cared about me. Maybe it hadn't started out that way. But Noah Anderson had loved me. Then of course there was this new Noah. He tried to hide it, but it was there. He felt something for me that he—and maybe I—was afraid to acknowledge. That unmistakable, protective tremor in G's voice? He had it, too, and I hadn't realized until that moment how comforting it was.

"I'm okay," she insisted, though not in a very convincing way. "It wasn't bad. It's been worse. And it's nothing compared to what they do to you…"

There was an angry sound from G and mumbling, followed by another metallic thud.

"Well, it's over." I moved to the bars again and pressed myself against them, craning to see down to the other end. I could make out Kori leaning against the bars of her cell, as well as a dark form a few cells down. Sera. "We—"

"Shut up!" G whispered, then let out a string of colorful curses. "The elevator. Someone's coming down!"

A few moments of silence ticked by, but then I heard

it. The faint squeal of the elevator doors, followed by an assortment of footsteps—one of which I knew all too well.

"How are you doing, Ash?" Cora stopped in front of my cell. "Comfy?"

"Snug as a bug in a rug." I flashed her my sweetest smile. "So what's the deal here? You keep us all locked away forever?"

She laughed. "Of course not. It wouldn't be cost effective to simply house and feed you until you died of old age, would it?"

"So...?"

"So you're going to fulfill your role in all this. You're going to help us secure permission from the government to make Omega official. You're living proof that our procedure can be done safely with no major side effects. I have a meeting and presentation set up for two weeks from tomorrow."

"You're insane." If she thought for even one second that I'd do anything to help her in any way, she was hitting the happy juice.

"We're still perfecting the formula we got from Markus Brewster. We're also trying to figure out why there are some from other earths who seem resistant to the drug. Take your female roommate—I'm sure you've all *met*?" She winked. "The girl has been treated twelve times and we only had success after several implants—we're trying something a little different with her. The boy is part of another exciting project. But you... You're special. You're proof that it *can* work."

What she was saying sank in and I felt like I'd swallowed a rock. "Can—but *doesn't*. You said so yourself. You present me as proof and it's a lie." No. This wasn't going to happen. She wouldn't get away with it. Not while I was still alive.

"You might as well just kill me now, Cora. You try to present me to anyone as proof and I'll tell them the truth! The serum doesn't work. Not on everyone. If you push forward with this, how many people's brains are you going to fry?"

"Science is messy. To advance we must be willing to sacrifice." She narrowed her eyes, smile growing wide and wicked. "After we have this all buttoned up, though, perhaps I'll start my own private house. You seem to like to play with boys above your stature. Maybe I'll wipe you again and rent you out—"

I spat at her through the bars. She flinched, jumping away as she wiped her face with horrified vigor. When she recovered, she made a motion to the three men standing behind her. They came forward, and instead of opening my cell door, they went to Kori's.

"I think today we'll start with the unknown element. My *daughter* is from an entirely new earth. We've never come across her frequency. Maybe she'll wipe easily—maybe she won't."

"If you touch me I'll—" Commotion from Kori's cell and the sounds of melee filled the hall. One of the men cursed. There was shuffling and the scrape of rubber against the tile floor.

Kori gave them one hell of a fight, and despite the situation, I found myself impressed. She was a tough one. Then again, she was Noah's sister. I should have expected as much.

They dragged her from the cell and down the hall. She fought them the entire way.

Chapter Twenty-Three

Noah

"You ready? This is going to hurt."

I glared at him. "Do it." Pain wasn't normally an issue for me, but I didn't like the look of the needle-like thing he had dangling above my forearm. Instead of a point, it had a flat, razor edge about the width of a dime and flashing red and white lights. Like something out of some cheesy science fiction flick.

"Just get it over with," Dylan snapped. He'd been in a bad—okay, worse—mood since Rabbit informed us that our cuffs were D.O.A.

There was nothing he could do to save the core because we'd waited too long. Luckily, this world's Infinity was years ahead of ours and could simply tune their own chips to an individual. No fast prep method needed. No clunky, unwanted jewelry. Just a small, implanted chip. After some *persuading* from Dylan, he'd agreed to give us the small stash he'd stolen just yesterday from Cora's office. My theory was that he didn't want Dylan here any more than we wanted him on our earth.

In the beginning it was hard to look at him without seeing the guy who'd once been a friend. I'd never been as close to him as I was Cade, but we were tight. Still family. But that was gone now. The only thing I saw when I looked at him now was red. Betrayal and rage. For myself, for Kori—for Cade. Even for Ava. She never would have wanted this. She'd been a lot like him. Wild and short tempered—but she'd had a good heart. She would be disgusted if she could see the monster he'd turned into in her name.

Rabbit's right eyebrow twitched and he pressed the needle against my forearm. "One, two, three." There was a loud snap and an intense sting, accompanied by a volcanic burning sensation that leeched down to my fingers, making the tips numb for a moment before subsiding entirely.

Dylan and Cade had already been implanted, but Rabbit refused to activate them until we recovered Ash and Kori—which was smart. He'd stood up to Dylan like a pro, and my Rabbit would have been proud. There'd been a brief moment that he'd refused to put the chip in at all, but after Dylan not-so-gently reminded him that his lack of compliance would assure that his mother had a *bad day*, Rabbit gave in. That threat was the only thing keeping him safe. I think he knew that, which was why he didn't push activation. This wasn't like holding Kori over our heads.

He held out his forearm and splayed his fingers. "Watch closely because there's not going to be time for me to explain this all again. After a few moments of inactivity, the chip will go to sleep. To wake it up…" He tapped the area below his wrist twice and his skin began to glow. A muted blue light grew darker with each passing second until a thin box appeared as an image on his skin.

"That is amazing," Cade said with a whistle. He reached out to poke it but Rabbit smacked his hand away.

"Cora invented the tech. I improved on it," Rabbit said proudly. He tapped the first blue button on the top row, the one that was labeled HOME. "When I activate the chip, the first thing you're going to want to do is tune it to your own personal frequency. This button will link the chip to you, and when pressed, will skip you back to your home world."

"So it's like the emergency button on our cuffs?"

"Um, I guess? This isn't a one-time use thing if that's what you mean."

I swallowed, positive I hadn't heard him correctly. "You're saying we can go home and leave again? That we wouldn't be stuck?"

He was looking at me like I had a half dozen heads. "Of course. Why would it—oh. Yeah. Your cuffs were way primitive." He shook his head. "I can't believe you haven't been home in almost a year."

"Moving on," Dylan snapped. "Make sure my chip isn't part of their set. I don't want them following me." He glared at Cade. "Feel free to skip home and leave me the fuck alone."

"Our chips aren't manufactured in sets like your cuffs were," Rabbit said. His gaze darted from Dylan to Cade, then back again. "Each one is their own individual entity with its own programmable memory."

Dylan flashed me a smug smile.

Rabbit tapped the button next to HOME labeled PATH. "This one records all the frequencies a chip visits. There's an option here to make notations so you can remember which was which." He pressed a small button within the PATH section, marked by a small F. "By pressing the F-button you can manually add a frequency by touching your forearm to an object or person. The chip will record their frequency and store it. After that, you can skip to them directly no matter what world they're on."

"Before you get any ideas, don't." Dylan backed away from the small table. "My location is off limits."

Rabbit rolled his eyes and refocused on the blue box illuminating his skin. "To follow a specific PATH—meaning, visit a certain frequency— be it a person or world, all you need to do is tap the line and *boom*. You skip instantly. You can leave and return to any place in your list, or hit this button…" His finger hovered over an even smaller button within the panel labeled with just an R. " —you will skip to a random frequency."

"It's that simple?" Cade's eyes were wide as he stared, mesmerized by the light on Rabbit's skin. I agreed. This made skipping seem as blasé as driving a car.

"It will be as soon as I activate them." He let his arm fall slack and leveled his gaze at Dylan. "Which only happens when Kori and Ash are safe. Be careful what you're touching when you skip, though. The chip will change the frequency of your body to move you from one place to another, and by extension, anything you're touching. If you want to skip inconspicuously, I'd avoid leaning against cars or buildings when you activate it. If you want to skip and stay together, I suggest you all hold hands or something because there's no guarantee you'll end up in the same place as someone else with a chip."

"Okay. Lesson over." Dylan hitched a thumb toward the door. "Let's do what we need to do."

Rabbit nodded and bent over a small computer. His fingers scurried across the keyboard, lines of code flashing on the screen.

I peered over his shoulder. "What are you doing?"

"We have to get down to sublevel seven. It won't be as simple as walking into the hall and hopping in an elevator."

"I figured." I inclined my head toward the screen. "So you're, what, creating a diversion?"

He glanced up at me, brows knitting together to form a deep V. "Diversion? What do you think this is, the movies? That never actually works."

"Um, okay. So you're…?"

"Opening up an alternative route." As if on cue, a loud creak filled the room and all the crap on the desk in front of us shimmied and shook. A few feet away, on the floor next to one of the computers, a large door in the floor opened. "Cora was desperate to gain me as an employee. I have *a lot* of quirks. Anything I requested she fell all over herself to supply."

Cade peered over the edge of the newly opened hole in the floor. "You requested a *trap door*?"

I snorted. "Rabbit has a *rabbit hole*!"

"I requested a way to move around the facility without having to interact with anyone." He glared, then waved me away. The guy had no sense of humor. "I have personal space issues."

"Yeah, but Cora must know about this. She'd be keeping an eye out."

"Cora would never think I was working with you." The conviction with which he said it made me a little curious. I studied him, searching his expression for something—a small hint that he'd betray us. He caught me staring and shuffled, adjusting his shirt and clearing his throat. "I'm a good little worker bee. They leave me alone and I don't interfere. Besides, like the main lab entrance, Cora believes she has access—but doesn't."

"Even so." Cade pulled the door up the rest of the way to reveal a narrow set of stairs. He hadn't noticed the weird exchange between us. "It can't possibly give you access to every room in the building."

"No, but I can get us close to where we need to be. It's completely soundproof and no one has access to it but me, so you three will be safe while I make sure the coast is clear."

"Cameras?"

"Still off. But we don't have a lot of time. As stupid as Cora's security is, someone is going to notice eventually."

"Good point." Cade was the first one into the hole. "Let's move."

We followed Rabbit down his hole. When we got to the bottom of the stairs, a long hallway stretched out in front of us. "Where does it go?"

"The better question would be, where doesn't it go?" Rabbit flicked a switch on the wall and light flooded the tunnel. "I have access to every floor except sublevel seven and eight from here."

"Seven? Isn't that where we *need* to go?" Dylan stomped his foot. "What the hell is the point of this if we can't get there from here?"

"I told you, I can get us close. We just need to get to sub-six. I can hack the elevator code from there to take us down one more floor."

And that was it. No one else said a word as we followed Rabbit down more stairs and around twists and turns. The whole thing was insane. Knowing this world's Cora, she'd just about shit a moose if she found out that Rabbit had changed all the locks and essentially barred her from his lab. Then there was the tunnel. When you thought secret passageway, it was darkness and cobwebs with dusty air and stench. Rabbit's little slice of heaven had what looked suspiciously like marbled floors, oak wood trim, and really tacky red wallpaper.

By the time we made it to a blue door marked S-6, Dylan was beyond antsy. "If you're trying to stall, remember what I said about your—"

"Just wait here. The door will lock the moment I close it and no one else has access. Cora thinks she has the code…" A sly smile spread across his face, similar to the *I've been up to no good* expression our Rabbit usually wore.

"That's the plan?" Normally I would never agree with anything Dylan said, but hurry up and wait? Not a game I played well. And aside from that, the last time the three of us had been left together, it hadn't gone well. Pushing our limits, especially when everyone's nerves were just about frayed, seemed like a disaster waiting to happen. "Stand around until you come back to get us?"

Rabbit rolled his eyes and pushed me away from the door. Then, without another word, he slipped through and closed it with an echoing snap.

Dylan huffed and slumped dramatically against the wall. "What shall we do while he's gone? Rock, paper, scissors? Maybe truth or dare?"

"Do you really think it's a good idea to poke us?" I said through clenched teeth. "You're in an enclosed area with two people who already want to tear out your spleen."

"There'll be no spleen tearing and we all know it. You wouldn't risk Rabbit's dear, sweet mother—which is exactly why you failed to save all those other versions of Kori."

Cade stiffened. "What did you say?"

"Come on now, Cade." Dylan jabbed a finger in my

direction. "If you were just a touch more like your buddy over there, you might have managed to save a few more of your girls. Hell, if you hadn't gone all Boy Scout and turned me in in the first place, none of us would be here right now."

"Dylan," Cade warned. Every visible muscle was taut. If Dylan kept poking, I wouldn't be able to keep him locked down—and I wouldn't want to.

Dylan threw up his hands and inclined his head in my direction. "Just sayin'! Take a page from the doc's book. Be a little selfish. Like, for example, if you really wanted to take me down, you'd just do it. Here and now and be done with it. Screw Rabbit's mom. To hell with the innocent lives I've threatened." He leaned forward and waggled his brows. "Unless, of course, she wasn't that important to you. I mean, you've both replaced her with that new, improved model and I gotta say—I approve."

The little voice in my head told me this was stupid. Counterproductive. If we were discovered, none of us was getting out of here alive. But just like Dylan and his running mouth—an issue he'd always had—I was unable to stop myself.

I couldn't be sure which one of us lunged first. Could have been that we went at the same time. I reached him first, swinging hard. The blow connected with the underside of his chin and sent him sprawling back—right into Cade.

He let out a grunt of satisfaction and brought his knee up, square in the center of Dylan's back. Dylan let out an anguished howl and doubled over just within my reach. I kicked out, the corner of my boot catching him in the side of the head.

In the back of my mind a little voice told me this wasn't a fair fight. The little voice in the *front* of my mind laughed like a drunken asshole. Fair fight? I'd never given a shit about those. Use what you had to gain the upper hand.

With each injury we inflicted, another part of my brain wondered if I was really meant to be a doctor. Healing the sick and tending to the injured. That was the shtick. Lately though, I'd been too invested in creating injury. What did that say about my future? But I wasn't a med student right now. I was a guy facing off against the bastard who tore apart his life and family.

"That all you got?" Dylan stumbled to his feet between Cade and me. His voice was a little slurred, lip split and already swelling. I couldn't be sure, but I had a feeling we'd knocked a tooth or two out.

Cade had his back to the wall while I stood with mine to the door Rabbit had gone through. Call it karma for starting the fight, or simply bad timing, but just seconds after Dylan lunged for me, Rabbit opened the door. We toppled out, the three of us landing in a heap in the main hallway, a few feet from an elevator.

Of course, the shitstorm didn't end there. A woman came around the corner, nose in a thick book. When she saw us, she dropped the thing and scrambled for a small blue panel on the wall. A second later, the lights were flashing and a siren wailed like a damn banshee…

Chapter Twenty-Four

Ash

"What's going on?" The sound was horrible and the lights flashed from ordinary white to red and blinking, pulsing with dizzying speed. I closed my eyes and pressed my fingers into my temples. "And how long until it stops?"

"That's the security alarm," G said. There was a note of excitement in his voice. "Something's going down somewhere in the building."

"It's them. My—Kori's friends. They're here. They came to get her."

"The elevator," he exclaimed. "Someone's coming down again."

I couldn't hear the elevator over the wail of the siren, but I heard the footsteps. "Hurry up and get her back in the cell," a gruff voice snapped. There was a dragging sound, and a moment later, two men walked past my cell, Kori listless and limp between them.

"What did you do?" I threw myself against the bars and

stuck my arm through in an attempt to grab them. "What did you do to her?"

They ignored me as though I didn't exist and continued on until they got to the cell she'd been in before. I heard the door squeal, and the shuffle of them dragging her inside — and then a string of curses.

A black and gray blur flew past my cell, launching itself at the men. It was followed closely by another blur, this one I'd know anywhere. Cade and Noah took down the guards with ease, and even though I couldn't quite see the throw down, from the sounds of it, there hadn't been much of a fight. Then again, they'd both fight like demons for her. Those guards never stood a chance.

A few moments later, Noah appeared in front of my cell. "You okay?" He gripped the bars on either side of my hands and let his head fall forward. "Tell me you're okay."

I did the same, taking comfort in his nearness, and nodded. "They're stealing people, Noah. That's what Omega is." I'd meant to reply simply with I'm fine, but seeing him just brought it all pouring out. "Taking people who don't exist here anymore and skipping them in to take their place." I wanted to say more, to tell him that *I* was one of those people, but the words wouldn't come for some reason.

His eyes widened and his skin paled. "Brewster…"

"They're wiping memories. Giving the new people a clean slate. They took Kori. I don't know if they — "

"I'm…okay." From the hallway there was more shuffling and a soft groan. Cade helped her from the cell and they stopped in front of my door. His face was ashen as she stumbled forward. "They were prepping me but the alarm went off." Cade didn't look like he was buying it and she rolled her eyes. "I swear I'm fine."

Noah opened his mouth, then closed it again. He looked from his sister to me. "We have to get you out of here." He glanced back down the hall and motioned for someone. A moment later, Phil appeared. "Get her out of there."

"I—"

"Now," Noah growled. He looked truly ferocious and it made my heart beat a little faster knowing that it was for me.

They'd come for Kori, but they'd also come for *me*.

Phil groaned and mumbled something, then pushed him aside. He fiddled with the keypad for a moment before exclaiming. "Gotcha!" With a wave of his hand, he added, "Might wanna stand back, Ash."

I did as I was told as sparks erupted in a small fountain from the lock. They fizzled and spit for a few seconds before the lock disengaged with a soft *pop*. Noah flung the door open and reached inside. He grabbed my arm and tugged me from the cell, starting for the elevator.

"Wait!" I dug my heels in and pulled against his grip. God only knew what sadistic plans Cora had for G and Sera on top of what she'd already done. "We can't leave them."

"Them who?"

Kori's eyes went wide, like she'd totally forgotten about them. It was also that moment that her gaze fell to Dylan, standing off to the side. She opened her mouth, face pale. For an instant they simply stared at each other. Hate in her expression, amusement in his. The tension in the small space was palpable, but like a champ, Kori shook it off. "Sera and G. They're locked up here, too," she said finally. "We can't leave them."

"Phil." I jabbed a finger down the hallway. I was just as thrilled to see Dylan—he'd killed Corey right in front of me, then threatened to do the same to me—but now wasn't the time to lose my shit. With a nod, I said, "There are two more cells. Please."

He groaned, but thankfully took off without argument. At the other end of the hall, I heard him grumbling as he messed with the lock. "I can't believe it. Of all the things I thought Cora might be doing—" He wasn't listening. Noah was staring at something over my shoulder. In fact, everyone else's attention seemed to be suddenly riveted to something on the far end of the hall as well.

I spun to see what they were all looking at, terrified that Cora's security had us blocked in from the other end. However, when I turned, all I saw was my first glimpse of Sera—a beautiful girl with dark eyes and hair that framed a pixie-like face, and G, who aside from his scruffier face and longer, darker hair, was a carbon copy of Cade's brother, Dylan.

"I can't believe it," Dylan whispered. He pushed past Cade and Noah and crossed to his double. Except it wasn't his double that had him entranced. It was Sera. "You're here."

"He knows her?"

Noah shook his head and took my hand. There was a hint of sadness in his eyes. "We all know her. That's *Ava*."

Ava. The girl who essentially started a war. The person whose absence from a world had inadvertently caused so much pain and suffering. The one he'd been skipping from place to place to find. He'd said she wasn't here, but Sera wasn't from *here*. Cora's team had dragged her here. Experimented on her.

Dylan reached for her, but Sera jerked away. G stepped up and moved between them instantly. "Lose something?"

"Matter of fact, yeah." The venom in Dylan's voice was acidic. "Her. So if you'll kindly get the fuck out of my way…"

G rolled up his dirty flannel sleeves and flashed Dylan a wicked grin. "Go for it, man. I might not know much about my past, but I'm pretty sure people used to tell me I was my own worst enemy. Seems like kicking your ass is a good chance to prove them right."

Cade recovered from his shock and ran to wedge himself between them. "We don't have time for this," he snapped. He gestured between them, the hint of a grin shadowing his lips. "Any second now security is going to be on top—"

The door at the other end of the hall exploded inward and a group of Cora's security detail flooded the narrow hall.

"—of us," he finished.

"I blame you for this." Noah let go of my hand and jabbed a finger at Cade. "Every damn time you say that…" He launched himself into the fray without hesitation. Cade was next, followed by G. Dylan lingered, unwilling—or unable—to take his eyes off Sera, while Phil inched toward the edge of the melee, trying to stay clear from flying fists. I wondered if there was a version out there that didn't avoid confrontation.

Cade kicked, sending his opponent flying in my direction. I was able to move out of the way as he harmlessly sailed by, crashing into the wall. Unfortunately, the impact didn't deter him. He picked himself up and recouped almost immediately. And this time his sights weren't set on Cade.

He made a swipe for me but I danced clear, which only made him scowl. "You've got no way out. Just surrender."

"Oh. Well if you're asking nicely…" I awkwardly ducked his next attempt and pivoted. As the move sent him slightly off center, I brought my arm up and punched out blindly. Luckily the blow caught him in the gut. He doubled over and I braced my foot against the small of his back and shoved out as hard as I could. This time when he hit the wall, it was head first. There was a muted thud. He didn't get up to try again.

Noah and G were back to back, dealing with the last two. When they were down, everyone regrouped in the center of the hallway. "We're out of time." Cade shot a pointed look at Phil. "Assuming we need to get back to the lab to get Kori and Ash chips?"

Phil glared at him. "I'm not carrying any on me."

"Me? What do I need a chip for?"

Noah stepped in front of me, standing so close that I could almost hear his heartbeat. "You have any reason to stay?"

"You want me to go with you?" Sure, anyplace was better than here, but I'd been raised to fear skipping. No one left and went to a *better* place. It was a punishment, used to tame crime and clean up cities. But Noah and his friends had been doing it for a while now. It didn't sound like it'd been all fun and games, but it didn't sound like it'd been all horrible, either.

Then again, maybe there was a chance to go home. To see, to *meet*, my real family.

"I'm not gonna twist your arm or anything, but it doesn't seem to me like you'd be walking away from much here."

"This can wait," Phil said with an irritated snort. "Yes. We have to get back to my lab. Problem is, I can't access my hallway from this floor. We need to go up one."

"Then what are we waiting for?" Dylan snapped. He was still staring at Sera, who was trying to avoid noticing. She kept inching closer and closer to G, who was shooting Dylan challenging glares.

"Can't use the elevator. Once security leaves it, it's

disabled to prevent any intruders from traveling through the building easily."

"Stairs?" Kori said.

"Doors automatically close and lock once the alarms go off."

"Then it looks like we're climbing." There was a mischievous gleam in Noah's eyes as he tugged me toward the elevator. The doors were frozen open and all the lights on the control panel were flashing red. "Cade?"

Cade followed him, then dropped to his knee in the car. Cupping his hands, he boosted Noah up to where he pushed out the ceiling panel and hauled himself through the opening. One by one Cade hoisted and Noah hefted. Once everyone was safely on top, he replaced the ceiling panel.

"There." Cade turned Kori toward the small foothold that led to a narrow metal ladder. "Follow me up. Quick but careful." One by one we climbed to the floor above, Cade in the lead with Phil directly behind him and Noah bringing up the rear.

It took a minute, but Cade managed to pry the doors apart. He hoisted himself onto the floor and ushered Phil up. "Hurry. Get the door open before—"

"Don't move," someone shouted as I pulled myself over the edge.

"Before that happens?" Noah finished with a snort. He pushed past me and lunged at the guard while Phil dove for a door a few feet away.

It was a single guard, but more would be flooding the hallways soon. Phil insisted the cameras were off and I didn't doubt him, but by now Cora would realize the only person in the building who had the skill to dupe her was him and they'd be coming, full force.

"Hurry! Get inside." Phil stood aside and waved his arms frantically as we filed through the doorway. Once it was secured, we sprinted for his lab. He had the door opened and was ushering us all inside. All except for Noah, who he grabbed and held back. I saw him lean in and whisper something. He reached into his pocket and pulled a small sheet of paper out, gripping it tightly in his fist.

Now wasn't the time to hang out and chat! "Are you—"

"Ash!" Cade shouted from the lab. I ducked inside to find him waving a nasty looking needle in the air. "Hurry. We don't have a lot of time."

"I—"

I went to turn back to the door, but Phil was there, pushing me aside and snatching the needle from Cade's hands. He motioned for Kori to come forward. She didn't look thrilled, but complied.

"So what do you say?" Noah leaned in close, warm breath fanning against my cheek. I caught a flash of white as he slipped something into his pocket. "Want to ride with us?"

I did—but only long enough to ride off this rock. There was someplace I wanted to be. People I *needed* to see. "I— Cora told me—"

Phil tapped the edge of his weird needle-like instrument against the desk, then snapped the fingers of his free hand in front of my face. "If you're gonna do this, it's gotta be *now*."

"Doing it," I said without hesitation. We could hash out the specifics later. I stepped up to the table and held out my arm. "Go for—"

"No," Dylan roared. We all whirled around and found that he had G in a choke hold with a long screwdriver poised at his throat.

"Don't!" Sera started forward but Kori grabbed her

before she made it two steps.

"Easy," G said. He didn't look concerned. "I'm okay."

"This is how it's gonna work. Ava and I are going to leave. Whatever the hell you idiots do after that is fine with me. Once we're gone, you won't be able to follow—I'll finally be free of you. You don't have to go home, but you can't come with me."

"Not going to happen," Cade said. He moved to stand beside Noah, who'd stepped up to the front of the small group.

In response to their move, Dylan pushed the screwdriver into G's skin. It didn't break through, but it wouldn't take much more pressure to make that happen. His gaze fell to Sera. "Your choice, Ava. I know it seems harsh, but trust me. You'll realize this was right. *We* are right."

There wasn't any doubt in my mind that Dylan believed every single word he was saying—or that he was insane. And it should have been obvious from the way Sera kept looking at G what her choice would be.

"Okay," she said, slowly moving toward the table. "You have to promise we'll leave without hurting them. Leave G and Ash and her friends alone and I'll go with you. Deal?"

Dylan seemed to relax a little. "Deal." He turned to Phil and said, "Now activate my chip."

Phil didn't move.

"I swear," Dylan said. He pressed the screwdriver harder into G's throat. He hissed as a small trickle of blood rolled down his neck. "If you don't move your ass to that computer and activate my chip, I'll kill him. And then, I'll kill your mother."

He hesitated a moment longer before his shoulders slumped. He moved slowly, making his way to the computer across the room and punching in a series of codes. His fingers flew across the keyboard, frantic, as numbers and symbols flashed on the screen.

"Well?"

"It's not as simple as pushing a button," Phil snapped. "This is complex technology."

I could hear voices outside. Right on the other side of the lab door. They'd started banging. "How long before they get in?"

"We have some time. They'll get through eventually, though, so let's not take all day. Done," he said, turning back to us. "*All* the chips are now activated."

Dylan released G and shoved him away, then grabbed Sera and dragged her close. He fumbled with the inside of his forearm, then threaded his fingers through hers. With several jabs at his left forearm, he flashed Noah one last, smug grin, and disappeared.

But not before lunging forward and plunging the screwdriver into Phil's chest.

Chapter Twenty-Five

Noah

G let out a horrible wail and fell forward, swiping furiously at the air where Ava and Dylan had just been. Cade cursed and dropped to the floor beside Rabbit, shrugging out of his hoodie and pressing it into the wound to try to stop the bleeding.

"How bad is it?" Kori glanced at me, then fell her knees beside him and gingerly lifted Rabbit's head into her lap.

"I dunno," Cade said, panicked. "I dunno. If I pull it out... Noah?"

I ignored him and tapped the inside of my forearm twice to wake up the chip. The others were huddled over a bleeding Rabbit. I didn't need a decade of med school to tell me how it would end. I knew Cade was waiting for me to help—but there was nothing I could do. At least not for Rabbit. I could, however, go after Dylan. It had to be now, though. Any longer and I risked losing him—and that wasn't something that could happen. Not again.

Cade and Kori were still trying to stop the bleeding

while G just stood there, staring at the place Sera had been. I fished into my pocket and yanked out the paper Rabbit had given me before coming into the lab. I skimmed the section I needed—the one detailing that he'd programmed Dylan's frequency into all of the cuffs without his knowledge, then stuffed the paper back into my pocket for safekeeping.

I put his frequency in the chips. No time to go over everything. It's all in here...

Rabbit coughed and sputtered and Kori gasped. "Noah!"

Rabbit had told Dylan the truth. The chips weren't linked together. But even he'd seen the danger in letting a guy like Cade's brother roam free through the multiverse. "I'm going after him. Come find me when you can."

Cade looked up, eyes wide. He opened his mouth and I saw his lips moving frantically—no doubt to call me something colorful and tell me what an ass I was being— but I couldn't hear him. His outline grew blurry, then disappeared. One minute I was standing in the lab, the next I was standing in a cafeteria.

I scanned the room. The place was packed, but no Dylan. Maybe the damn thing wasn't working? Or maybe I'd missed something...

I tucked myself into a corner and skimmed the note again.

—programmed all chips with list of safe PATHS from Infinity database.

—coded their home frequency. Since Cade, Dylan, and Noah share the same home world, that frequency acts like a magnet. Every earth has their own base frequency, tinted with each person's own, subtle frequency. That small difference makes it possible for you to skip to Dylan specifically.

—it could land you anywhere from one foot to half a mile away.

Well, shit. That was going to be more than mildly inconfuckingvenient. I stared down at Rabbit's rushed scribble again.

—only be used four times in the span of twenty-four hours. Any more than that and they fry

Good. Once they were forced to skip because of Cora's guards, they could find me by going to my PATH line— hopefully landing closer to a foot than half a mile. I took one last look at the note.

—Tinkered with the chip so that whenever Dylan activates a PATH, there will be a quick, electrical pulse through the others.

I wadded the paper up and deposited it in my pocket, then woke the chip and scrolled to Dylan's line once again and crossed my fingers. The cafeteria faded, and a moment later I was standing in the center of a snow-covered street. A horn blared and behind me a chorus of angry barks filled the air. I jumped and stumbled backward as a bright blue… sled…pulled by a handful of huskies nearly plowed me over.

I wrapped my arms around myself and tried not to shiver. We'd never skipped into a place where the weather was so drastically different. The day, the year—the season—had always been in line.

I scanned the horizon for Dylan, but it was impossible to see. The snow was falling too heavily, making visibility cripplingly limited. I gave up trying to pick him out and started walking. My best guess was that he'd try to find someplace quiet to take Ava in order to convince her that he wasn't one of the bad guys. He was the victim in all this. The wronged party. He'd sit her down and try to justify all the crappy things he'd done.

We'd seen it before. He'd find an Ava, tell her everything, and inform her that he was the great love of her life and that she needed to come with him. It didn't matter if she already had a Dylan. It made no difference if she'd never met any version of him before that moment. One of the Avas a few months back, right before we found Kori, had even been in a relationship with a girl named Claire and still Dylan insisted. He'd only given up when drowning Claire hadn't made Ava run to him, instead destroying her completely.

She was his weak spot. The thing that tripped him up on each and every world. And on the ones she didn't exist? Those were the ones where he was most dangerous. Lashing out at random and creating chaos wherever he went.

Speaking of chaos—had I done the right thing? Leaving Ash and the others behind? Cade had been chipped. Rabbit was a goner. Could Cade grab Kori and still skip out. Sure, he'd try to take Ash, too, but Cora wouldn't let her go so easily. If they got into that lab…

"Hey!" a familiar voice called. I froze, not quite sure how he'd managed to backtrack to jump me. I turned and found not Dylan like I'd thought, but the darker haired, flannel-wearing, scruffier version of him trotting through the snow. G wore the same scowl I'd seen for years on Dylan, and moved with the same kind of world-is-ending determination. "Where is she?"

"What are you doing here?"

"That science guy crammed a chip under my skin as he was coughing up his insides. Your friend told me to come find you."

"And you obeyed?" I didn't dare ask how Rabbit was. There was a huge pocket of guilt waiting for me for leaving him—even though I knew there was nothing I could do. It would come back to bite me in the ass later. I'd obsess over it and do something stupid to drown the memory, but right now there were other things to deal with.

The scowl grew bigger. "I don't *obey* anyone. I came to find Sera."

"Ava."

"What?"

"Her name is Ava, not Sera. Your name is Dylan—not the letter G."

"I don't care if one of us is named Frick and the other Frack. Where did that asshole take her?"

I inclined my head in the direction I'd hoped they'd gone. Really, there was no damn way to tell. The best solution would have been to skip to his PATH line again and hope it dropped me closer, but with a limited amount of skips available, I decided against it. "Let's see if we can find them."

We walked in silence for a while. Well, silence if you excluded the sound of our chattering teeth. When this was done and over with, we were going home. I was going to see my family and reclaim my life. I'd enroll in med school—but not before taking Ash and skipping off someplace warm. Whatever there was between us, I wanted the chance to explore it. To figure it—and her—out. I wanted to learn all the things that made her tick, and uncover her secrets, little by little. I was looking forward to showing her how the world *could* be. Places that had no class system or evil Anderson family. After that, I would bring her home to meet the real Cora Anderson.

We passed a long row of stores, all closed despite the early afternoon hour, and had ventured into the park. "You don't remember anything? From before you landed in Cora's cell?"

"Nope."

One word answer. Such an annoyingly *Dylan* thing. "What about Ava—*Sera*? You guys from the same world? Is that why you're so crazy to find her?"

"We're not from the same world. I don't remember anything, but I know I'd never met her before being thrown into that…place. And I'm not crazy to find her. We went through a lot together. Just wanna make sure she gets someplace safe. That an issue for you, man?"

I threw up my hands in surrender. It was more than that but I wasn't interested in arguing. As it was, it was taking every ounce of control I had not to pummel him. He might not personally be a murderer, but he was wearing the face of one. The one that took my sister. Kind of a hard thing to work around. Cade had made a mistake sending him of all people. "Cool it, jackass. Just trying to figure this thing out. You and her—all of us—have a pretty twisted up history. Looking at you right now is kind of making me sick."

"You're no prize, either," he grumbled. A moment later he perked up. "There!"

I grabbed out to try and stop him but all I got was air. "G— Shit. Wait!"

He slipped in the slick snow as he took off at a dead run, completely oblivious to my shouts. I followed. Hoping to reach him in time—but it was too late. He called out and Dylan turned. He saw G first, then our eyes met. The satisfaction of his shock, his rage, was short lived, though, because he grabbed Ava and disappeared.

I didn't slow. In fact, my feet pumped faster. I jabbed at my forearm, woke the chip, and followed him off the tundra world. If G figured it out, then great for him. If not, he wasn't my priority. Truthfully, the more distance between us the better I could think. Simply looking at him made me want to start swinging. I wasn't letting Dylan get away to babysit some newbie.

The scenery changed. My feet kept going, only now instead of slipping and sliding in a fruitless attempt to find purchase in the slush and snow, they slopped and squished in wet grass. We'd skipped into the middle of a downpour. Except it wasn't like any rain I'd seen. The puddles on the ground and the drops hitting my face weren't clear—they were translucent red.

"Yeah. That's not fucked up or anything," I huffed to myself. I didn't see Dylan, but I felt another zap and woke the chip. Off I went again, this time landing a few feet away from them. It would have been perfect. All I would have had to do was swing once, floor the bastard, and drag him back.

Not that it really mattered. At least not to the four massive wolves snarling in front of us. "Don't move," I said to them in my calmest voice. A quick scan of my surroundings and I realized we were in an alternate version of Clifton Park. There were *wild wolves* in Clifton Park. That was a first—and hopefully a last.

"You kidnapped me and now you're going to get me eaten by wolves?" Ava let out a nervous laugh. "Have I mentioned just how much I hate you?"

"Several times," came Dylan's response. He was slowly lifting his arm.

"You know I won't stop following you, right?"

"And how exactly *are* you doing that?" He spoke a little too loudly and one of the wolves, the biggest of the bunch, snapped at the air in his direction. He froze for a moment, then continued to lift his arm slowly. "The chips aren't linked—unless Rabbit lied."

"He didn't lie. He *was* nice enough to program your frequency in though." I snickered. "There's no place you can go on any world, in any universe, that Cade and I won't find you. You know that, right?"

He smiled. "I know that. But if you're not physically able to follow me..." With several careful jabs at his arm, hand linked with Ava, he skipped. Or, at least he tried. Nothing happened. He poked at his forearm again, more violently this time. "What—what the hell did you do?"

"Me?" I kept my voice low and my posture relaxed. He'd run out his allotted number of skips. He was stranded here for twenty-four hours. "I'm standing right in front of you. What could I have done?"

"You—"

A shot rang out and one of the wolves to my left yelped. It convulsed and hit the ground, followed by another shot, and another dog down. Dylan used the distraction and bolted for the trees, dragging Ava behind as the third went down.

The remaining wolf didn't take it well. It let out a series of snarls, then lunged. I threw up my arms to protect my face and collapsed beneath the weight of it, biting back a roar as its teeth sank into my arm. I managed to hold the beast at bay, but with every passing second, its teeth got closer and closer to my throat...

Chapter Twenty-Six

Ash

"So the only guy with actual medical knowledge went off to chase the screw driver-happy lunatic?" Phil sputtered and a spray of blood spattered across Cade's shirt. "That doesn't bode well for me."

He'd been able to walk us through doing the rest of the chips, explaining how they worked and how to tune them to our individual frequencies. I didn't miss the way he watched as I followed his instructions, and wondered if he knew his time was running out. After we'd all attuned the chips, he explained how they worked to G, who'd promptly gone after Noah and Sera. The moment he left, things took a turn for the worse.

"They'll be in soon." Cade glanced at the door. The insistent pounding had stopped a few minutes ago. Now it sounded like they were using a machine to cut through the metal. He sank to his knees beside Phil. "We'll skip and get you medical attention on the next earth."

Phil laughed. It was a broken sound full of pain and

regret. "Can't." His breathing was more labored now. His eyes more hooded. There wasn't anything we could do to stop this. I'd known that right away. Noah had, too. That's why he'd left. Cade, though, he was a demon. Obsessed with getting us *all* out of that lab in one piece no matter what. "Have to…give…you some…something," Phil said. His body shook as he let out a rattling cough. "Safe in the…the hall. Combin—three forty-two. Go."

When no one else made a move to stand, I wobbled to my feet and went into his secret hall. I don't know how we didn't notice it before, but on the wall to the right, just inside, was a small metal wall safe. I punched in the combination and opened the door. All that was inside was a single blue envelope.

I grabbed it and hurried back. "Okay. What is it?"

"Proof."

"Proof of what?" He couldn't mean proof of Omega. That's what he'd bargained with us to get.

"Noah… The reporter, Wagner."

A rush of excitement rolled over me, quickly followed by fury. "You had proof she'd been right about them skipping people to un-researched worlds? And you said nothing?" How could he have kept quiet? "None of this would have happened! Noah would still be alive."

Tears gathered in the corners of his eyes and another series of coughs rattled his entire body as he tried to shake his head. "Never meant for it to… He was my friend. She made…me…give him bad…bad chip. Heart failure. I didn't want to hurt—"

An icy chill crept into the room. Surely I was hearing things. He couldn't possibly mean… "Are you saying *you* killed Noah?" The words were as surreal as they were devastating.

"She knew…we were friends. Made…made me steal the Wagner…files and steer him…him away from Om…Omega. But he found out…about…about you."

"That's what he'd wanted to tell me. The night he died…" He'd found out Cora had taken me. The revelation brought a fresh wave of razor sharp guilt to my chest. "How could you do this to him?" And even as the words left my mouth, I still couldn't believe it. That's why Cora hadn't been watching him, why he'd been unafraid to help us. He'd been working with her the entire time so she never would have suspected him. "You told us you wanted out!"

"Did want…out. Was…hoping to find…that you'd find…" An all-over spasm rocked his body and he went limp. Eyes glazing, he lay motionless on the ground.

I looked from him to the envelope in my hands. There were papers inside, as well as a bright blue flash drive. A lump formed in my throat. He'd been playing both sides against the middle. Working for Cora while hoping we found enough evidence to set him free. *He'd* been responsible for Noah's death. Not some clandestine hit squad or one of Cora's top-notch go-to boys? Phil—his *friend*. He'd known what Cora did to me…

Kori got to her feet and tried to reach out to me. "Ash."

I stumbled away, sickened by the idea of contact. Of concern. This place was insane. A twisted world where people were treated like trash if not born under the right name and mothers killed their children all in the name of the almighty dollar.

"What did he mean?" Cade asked softly. "That Noah found out about you?"

"Doesn't matter." My voice cracked and I cleared my throat. I refused to cry. I refused to let this cut take me down. There'd been so many over the years. Most delivered by Cora, with her expert precision and insider knowledge. She'd known just how to wound me, yet I survived. It must have driven her insane when I didn't crumble. That wasn't about to change. She'd stolen me from my home, my family, but I'd have the last laugh. She wasn't going to use me to prove that Omega worked. I was getting the hell off this rock. "They'll break through soon. We have to go."

I folded the envelope and jammed it into my back pocket, then went in search of a pen. I was leaving, but I wasn't forgetting. Cora wouldn't get away with what she'd done. I'd be back and I *would* watch her fall. I found a red marker on Phil's desk, then grabbed a notebook from a small pile. Flipping to an empty page, I wrote in large letters,

I have proof now. See you soon.

Cade held up his arm and tapped it twice to wake up his chip. "Everyone understands how to use these, right? We need to be touching if we all want to land in the same place. Ready?"

We all joined hands. A second later, the same freaky, translucent blue box appeared on Cade's skin. He touched the option labeled PATH, and scrolled down to the third line, the one noted as Noah. Hopefully, wherever he was, he was okay. Phil somehow managed to program all our frequencies into the chip's memory. With G and Noah in pursuit, Dylan must have figured this out by now. Our best bet was to skip to where Noah was and join the search—or fight.

A part of me was hoping for the latter, because right now? I needed to work off some serious anger.

"On three?"

Kori nodded and Cade said, "One, two…three."

I held my breath as he pressed Noah's PATH line. One second I was standing in Phil's lab, the next I was on a street corner in downtown Wells. "That was surprisingly easy." I hadn't known what to expect and there hadn't been time to quiz Cade or Kori. I didn't know if skipping was painful, or if there were side effects I'd have to contend with.

"You okay?" Kori came up beside me.

"Yeah." I turned and scanned the area and miraculously caught sight of Noah. He was sitting on the grass not far from where we were. "There he is!"

"Noah," Cade shouted and took off. He reached him first.

He was hurt. That much was obvious from the amount of blood—and he wasn't alone. Two women, dressed in beige jumpers, stood on either side of him. Both had an odd-looking gun slung over their backs, while a third, kneeling on the ground beside him, wore all yellow. Oh. And scattered around them were four gigantic wolves. I'd never seen one before. On my earth they were extinct. Killed off in the early eighteen hundreds and reduced to textbooks and museum exhibits. For a second I thought these were dead, shot by the strange women in beige, but then I saw the nearest one's chest rise and fall. Asleep. Probably tranquilized.

Cade stepped over one of the fallen animals. "What happened?"

The woman in beige on his right had brunette hair pulled back into a severe bun and pinched face. She wore no makeup and narrowed her eyes at us. "Are you all insane? What is in the water today?" She took a step toward us. "Back up!"

"How many times do you people have to be told?" the other one said with a snap. "You can't cross the fences! Your stupid friend here just got used as a chew toy. We had to tranq them. Now they'll be useless for days."

"Something bit him?" Kori tried to move around the woman blocking us, but she stood her ground.

The woman on the ground with Noah, the one in yellow, looked at Kori, then turned to each of us one at a time. Finally, she turned back to Noah. "You're up to date on your shots, right?"

"Right," he confirmed without hesitation.

She stood and helped him up, then finished taping his arm. "You're lucky there was a patrol nearby." With a nod in our direction, she added, "Best get moving. If you're out after dark, you know what happens."

"Yeah," he said. "Wouldn't want that." He met us on the sidewalk, where the woman had herded the group.

The moment he stepped onto the concrete, Kori threw her arms around him.

He rolled his eyes, but I didn't miss how he returned the hug, almost relaxing a bit. Another few seconds passed and he disengaged himself and took a step back, eyes finding me. He didn't say anything, but I could see the relief in his eyes.

There was no longer any comparison between him and the other Noah. I couldn't bring myself to think of him as my Noah anymore. Partially because of what I'd learned, and partially because I was beginning to believe what Kori said. Technically they were *all* my Noah. This one, though… this one was different. He fit in a way that was comfortable, yet exciting. Both easy and intricately complicated. This thing between us set my nerve endings on fire, but at the same time, made my head spin—in both good and bad ways. No matter how perfectly we fit, though, it wasn't ever going to become something. Now that I knew there was a place for me—a real home and possibly a family who missed me—I had to go there. I had to see what Cora had taken from me.

"Dylan has Ava. She's okay, but he knows we can follow him now. That's going to lead him to do something desperate." Noah was still looking at me.

Cade nodded, oblivious to our stare-down. "This is bad. He finally has her. He won't let go without a fight. We need to be careful. The collateral damage could be huge on this."

"What about G?" I swallowed and tried to look away. I had to tell him I was leaving, but for some reason, the words wouldn't come. "He came to find you. Have you seen him?"

"I saw him one skip back. We got separated. He—"

"I have to leave," I blurted before I lost my nerve.

"Huh?" Cade said, while Kori cried, "You can't!" Noah remained silent, still standing there. Still watching me like he was trying to see straight through to my skull.

"For several reasons, I have to leave," I tried again. "I need to go home."

That got a reaction out of him. He grabbed me by the shoulders, fingers twitching for a moment before his hands slipped upward. Over my upper arms, across my shoulders, then settling on either side of my face. For an insane minute I forgot about everything else. Everything but the feel of his touch. Warm, soft, fierce…

Then he opened his mouth.

"Don't be stupid. If you go back there, Cora will kill you."

I reached up and gently pried his hands free. "First, she won't kill me. She needs me. I'm the only actual proof she has, the only leverage she's got to get Omega off and running. But I wasn't talking about going back there. I was talking about going *home*."

Noah's brow quirked. He didn't get it right away—but

Cade did. "She took you, didn't she? You weren't born on that earth."

"I was the first." I shook my head and swallowed the lump in my throat that seemed to be getting bigger and bigger by the second. "It's a really long story—and it doesn't matter. The point is, I was never meant to be there. I was never meant to live like—" I sucked in a breath and held it for a minute before continuing. "I want to see my family. I want to know what it *could* have been like."

Noah was quiet for a minute before nodding just once. "Okay."

"I'll help you find Sera first, though. Then I'll leave." I didn't know if it was the look in his eyes—sadness mixed with defeated acceptance—or an odd feeling of responsibility. Sera, G...all the others that came and went before them. They were in this situation because of me. I was the one who truly inspired the Omega project. It was my body's acceptance of the serum that made them think it was possible. How many lives had she destroyed? How many people had she irrevocably altered? I owed Sera at least this.

"Shouldn't be too hard," Cade said. He started walking and we fell in step. "The way Rabbit explained these new chips, we really can't lose each other."

Noah flinched. He tore his gaze from mine and turned to Cade. "Speaking of—is he—"

"Dead." My reply came too fast and far too enthusiastic. Everyone turned to stare. "He's dead and got what he deserved."

"Ash—" Cade started.

I cut him off. Their Phil—their *Rabbit*—might have been a standup guy, but this one was a bastard. I focused on Noah. "He did it. He's the one who killed you. *Him.*"

He didn't respond, but he didn't really look surprised,

either. I wondered if he'd had suspicions, which would really make me feel like an idiot for not seeing it sooner. All the dodging. The squirming...

"Well, we have to sit on our thumbs for a while. Dylan doesn't know it yet, but he's not getting off this rock for another twenty-four hours." I patted my right front pocket. "Rabbit slipped me a note with all the things we'd need to know about these new chips. Apparently one of the main things is that you can only skip four times within a twenty-four-hour time frame. It's how they deal with overheating."

"That gives us some time to process and settle on a plan of action," Cade said. I could already see the wheels inside his head churning away. "We should get off the street, though. That woman made it sound like there's some kind of curfew here."

We wandered for a bit, scoping things out. The sun was setting and there was very little activity on the streets. The people we did see scurried about like mice with their heads down and their pace increased. They wore drab colors—more shades of beige, yellow, and brown—and sullen expressions. Wherever it was we'd landed, it didn't seem like the friendliest place in the world.

Kori slowed and pointed to a large brick building ahead. "There's a motel."

"I'm almost afraid to go in." We stopped a few feet from the door. "This place is weird."

Noah smiled, but it was forced. "They all feel weird. It's not the Wells that you're used to. It'll get better."

After I was home, he meant.

"Just take it slow," Cade said. "Do a lot of watching. See how people talk, act, how they dress. React accordingly."

I glanced down at my bright red hoodie. So far, it'd stuck

out like a neon sign. "If that's the case, then I need to get out of this thing."

It was the perfect opportunity. Hand delivered ammo for something flirty with a dash of snark. Yet Noah didn't bite. He stepped up to the desk and said, "We'd like a room. Suite if you have it."

The girl behind the counter, a short blond with bright blue eyes, nodded. She shot me a confused look, gaze traveling from head to toe—she even leaned over the counter to get a better view—before turning her attention to the computer in front of her.

As soon as she was distracted, Cade tugged Noah away from the counter. "A suite? Have you become a multi-dimensional millionaire while I was away? We've got no cash for this place."

Noah grinned and pulled a generic looking black wallet from his back pocket. "Swiped it from that medic chick in the park."

The girl returned and slid an oddly shaped key toward us. Square and silver, with intricate looking groves in the center. "The deposit is seventy-five dollars. The remainder is due upon checkout."

Seventy-five dollars? That seemed cheap. Then again, maybe money was different here. On my world—Cora's world—seventy-five dollars got you a decent lunch. Here, maybe the value of a dollar was tripled or something.

Noah paid her and took the key, and we were directed to the staircase at the end of the hall. The motel was only three floors, our suite on the top. By the time we'd climbed three flights of stairs, I was ready to drop. I hadn't gotten a good night's rest in days. Weeks, actually. Ever since Noah's death. Some time to recharge, as much as I hated the idea, sounded good.

Noah unlocked the door and stepped aside, and the four of us filed through. The entryway spilled out into a large room with a wall mounted television, huge wraparound couch, and a fireplace on the other end. On the wall beside the door was a large sign trimmed in silver that said, *Your needs are our highest priority. You have but to ask. No request is too big—or too small.*

"That's accommodating," Kori said with a snicker.

"And creepy." Cade closed the door behind us. "Given some of the things we've seen along the way, a statement like that could mean a million things."

"Snazzy digs," Kori slumped back into one end of the couch, while Noah did the exact same thing on the opposite end. They both kicked their feet onto the end table at the same moment. When she realized what she'd done, she quickly removed them and sat forward.

I smiled. They really were a lot alike and that meant she was good people, because as hard as he tried to get me to believe otherwise, this Noah Anderson was a rare find. It made leaving all that much harder.

"So now what?" I joined them in the sitting room, claiming an oversized lounge chair. Thinking about Noah wasn't going to make this any easier. The best thing I could do for my sanity was to focus on Sera. "We have to get to Sera. What's the plan?"

"He won't hurt her," Noah said. He grabbed the room service menu and pretended to study it. He wasn't reading it, though. I could tell because his eyes never moved. "This is the first time he's ever skipped with her. He'll do and say anything to win her over."

"I think this downtime might be to our advantage," Kori

said. "He's stuck here at the moment. We have almost a full twenty-four hours that we don't have to chase him. We know exactly where he'll be."

"Not *exactly* where he'll be." I tucked my feet up under me and curled against the couch. "I mean, he's in the *area*, but that's all we know. And what's to say he'll stay here? Couldn't he leave the city? Start driving to, I dunno, Canada and skip when the cooldown is up?"

"He could," Cade said, standing. "But he won't. He'll use this opportunity to try showing her he can be good for her. Normal. He won't drag her around. Plus, he doesn't know about the cooldown. All he knows is that the chip isn't working."

"We hope." Noah snorted. "The guy isn't exactly operating on a full set of cylinders you know."

Cade rolled his eyes and leaned against the wall next to the TV. He inclined his head toward the two rooms off the main. "My vote is that we get a few hours' sleep—we're all beat—then pick this up and hammer out a solid plan. We're no good to Ava if we can't think straight."

"I second that." Kori stood and stretched. She hitched her thumb toward the bedroom on the right, then said, "One on the left is all yours, Ash."

As she and Cade shuffled toward the other room, I heard them arguing about who got to sleep on the floor this time— which I thought was weird. Then again, Kori had said the relationship was complicated...

The door to their room closed softly, leaving Noah and me alone. I didn't look over at him but could feel his gaze on me. It was heavy but not unwanted, and when I finally worked up the courage to lift my head, I found that he wasn't sitting on the couch anymore. He'd stood.

He'd stood and taken a step toward me.

Chapter Twenty-Seven

Noah

What the fuck was I doing?

Cade and Kori left and I hadn't given it a second thought. I'd stood and started walking over to the other side of the room where Ash sat on the couch, purposefully looking anywhere but at me.

Probably because she already told me she was leaving, and here I was—what? What the hell *was* I doing?

She looked up and pointed toward the empty room. There was a slight shake in her hand. "You can take it if you want. I'm just kind of tagging along until we find Sera."

"I'm better off on the couch. That's what I usually take." I sat down a few cushions away from her. "This way I can come and go without waking Cade up. Kori now, too. That girl is an obnoxiously light sleeper…"

"Where do you go?"

"Out," I said. What was the point of not telling her the truth, though? I'd already admitted it. She knew the score. "Looking for you mostly."

"Oh," was all she said. "Yeah. That's right. You—um—yeah."

"Listen, I'm sorry about that."

She shrugged. "You already apologized, remember? It's not a big deal."

"It is. That's not who I am. I swear to you. I can be a dick, and I know I'm moody as hell. But my mother raised me better than that."

"I believe you," she said softly.

I searched her face for the lie but couldn't find it. There was nothing but sincerity there and it was baffling considering the Cora Anderson she'd had to deal with. "You do, don't you?"

"Was there ever anyone? Serious, I mean?"

I leaned back and stretched out my legs. "Nah. I mean, even before all this, before we left home, I dated. A lot. But I never let it get far."

"No one caught your eye?"

"Plenty caught my eye," I said with a grin. "But you've spent some time with me." I couldn't help laughing when I realized that aside from Kori, Ash had actually spent more time with me than anyone I'd ever *dated*. "I'm kind of hard to swallow after a while. Like I said, I am who I am. That's not going to change. I've never played by the rules and I was always in trouble for something—usually dragging Cade along for the ride."

"See," she said with a shake of her head. "There you go again. Trying to build yourself up as this huge asshole. And I'm sorry. I just don't see it."

"No?" A chill crept into my tone. "I *am* an asshole. This whole thing happened because of me."

I tried to close my mouth. I desperately wanted to stop

the shit that was about the come oozing out. But I couldn't. A part of me didn't want to. I'd been walking around with a two-ton brick of guilt strapped to my back. One that not even Cade was aware of. I knew what he thought. That I was grieving and self-destructing because I'd lost my sister—one of my best friends. And he was right—but he was also wrong.

"I blew her off. We'd made plans that morning, Kori and me. We were supposed to go climbing. Our favorite place just outside of town. She went to get ready and I ran down the road for coffee." Every night I relived that day. Over and over. "Deena Sands. I blew her off for that bimbo, Deena Sands. She caught me in the parking lot. I'd been chasing her for a while." My voice cracked and I swallowed what felt like a mouthful of rocks. "Kori was so pissed at me. She said she was going herself and hung up on me. I felt bad, but I went with Deena anyway."

"You couldn't possibly—"

"Afterward I met up with Cade. We grabbed lunch and he said Kori texted him. Told him to meet her at home. We went. I figured I'd just apologize and we'd be good. We found her—I was pre-med. My sister died, she bled out in front of me, and I wasn't able to do anything to stop it."

I had no idea when it'd happened, but at some point, Ash must have moved, because when I looked up, she was sitting next to me. Her pointer finger, the thing so damn small compared to my own, poked me lightly in the chest. "Seems to me like you're carrying a hell of a lot of poison in there."

"Just what I deserve." I grabbed her hand, but instead of swatting it away like I'd intended, I threaded my fingers through hers and held on like she was the only thing keeping me tethered to the earth. It I let go, then I'd be gone. Drift into the oblivion I'd been so damn intent on drowning myself in and never find a way back. "My sister died furious at me. She died because, as usual, I was being selfish."

"When I was in the basement at Infinity, Cora and I had a little chat. She told me the truth. This world's Rebecca Calvert worked for her. She lost her daughter—I died here—and couldn't function. Cora stole me from my world and gave me to her Rebecca, but that wasn't enough to win her loyalty. Cora had her skipped because Rebecca was going to betray her. Before she got rid of her and my father, she made sure she told them not to worry about me. She told them she intended to take me in and make my life a living hell."

"Jesus."

"And she did. My life was seven different kinds of hell. But I survived, and now that I know the truth? That every horrible thing Cora did to me was because she was trying to get back at my mom? I don't blame her, Noah. It wasn't my mom's fault that Cora was unstable. She had no way of knowing what effect her actions would have on me. She might not have been my mother, but I know she must have loved me. For Cora to have made that threat…" She took a deep breath, then blew out slowly. "There is no way that you could have known Dylan would attack her that day. There is no way that, if she could be here right now, she would blame you for what happened."

It was a nice thought. Fluffy and warm and meant to soothe. And maybe it did—a little bit. But the guilt was still there. I had a feeling it would always be there. This wasn't the kind of thing you could just wipe away with platitudes or time. Still, it felt oddly freeing to tell someone the truth. To talk. "Tell me what it was like. Growing up in that house."

She sagged against the cushion, hand still in mine, and

let her head fall back. "It was kind of like having whiplash," she said with a soft snicker. "We would go out to all these parties and functions. She would parade me around in these ridiculous dresses and do my hair in obnoxious curls with these sparkling pink bows... To anyone looking on, she was a doting foster mother, completely taken with the kid she yanked off the streets. Utterly adoring. But if anyone had looked, really opened their eyes, they would have seen the truth. Every day she would start the morning by telling me how worthless I was. How useless. Every night she would cap it off by telling me how lucky I was that she'd felt sorry for me and taken me in. I was no one. Unlovable and without merit."

"That's ridiculous."

"Sure it is," she said. "Now. But try imagining those things being said to a kid. Try imagining the damage that did. You beat that into a kid's head and it's going to stick. I think maybe that's why things happened the way they did. With him, I mean." She waggled a finger between us, then gave my hand a quick squeeze. "We—all of us—have this thing, and I guess I misread it. I was so desperate to find something that was my own, to find someplace I fit, that I just forced it even though in my heart I knew it wasn't what I wanted it to be."

She yawned and I realized how tired she must be. We'd all been going nonstop for days. I was used to it. Cade, too. Kori was still getting used to it, but Ash was probably thrown way off. I readjusted and wrapped my free arm around her shoulder, pulling her closer.

She followed without hesitation, like it was the most natural thing in the world, and rested her head against my shoulder. "We're a pair, aren't we?" she said through another yawn.

My eyelids were getting heavy, too. "Sure are."

This was the point where I'd get up and get gone. In some ways, that conversation had been the most intimate thing I'd shared with a girl. I should have been feeling twitchy and raw. Instead, I found that I was content and comfortable. Ash's breathing evened as she drifted closer and closer toward sleep. She made a soft sound as she snuggled in, the warmth of her washing over me in soothing waves. I didn't have the energy—or inclination—to move her. Or myself.

"This'll be a first," I mumbled. "Never actually *slept* with a girl before…"

God. I was going to miss her when she was gone.

There's that eerie feeling when you're just waking up. The one where you know, in no uncertain terms, that you're not alone. I wasn't. I'd fallen asleep with Ash on my shoulder. Before I even opened my eyes, I knew she was still here, still asleep and breathing softly, curled up against my chest as though she'd been made to fit there. No, the eerie feeling was from something else.

Someone else.

I kept my eyes closed and carefully shifted so that Ash was clear, then I opened them. The lights were off—Kori no doubt. She hated when I left them on and always followed behind me and flipped them off after I'd passed out. It took a second for my vision to adjust, but the second they did, I was in motion.

I let go of a growl and launched myself off the couch at the figure standing over us. We collided and he grunted, blocking my first blow and rallying with one of his own. He landed it, but ended up only clipping my shoulder. I twisted on impact, but recovered and swung hard for his face. It was right about that time that Ash jumped up and turned on the lights.

"Noah, stop!"

The sudden brightness was blinding, but when everything mellowed, I saw that I'd been attempting to pummel G, not Dylan. I shoved him away and hauled myself off the floor using the corner of the coffee table. "What the hell are you doing standing over me in the dark, jackass?"

G climbed to his feet and stumbled back a few feet, glaring. "Wanted to make sure I had the right room. It's dark, *jackass*."

"Yeah? Well, skulking around us wearing that face is like sporting a suicide wish, man. How the hell did you even get in here? The place is supposed to be locked down."

G glared at him. I followed your PATH. It skipped me into the room."

"Noah," Kori said from the doorway. "Easy, okay? He has no idea what's going on. He doesn't know anything about Dylan or why you guys hate him."

She had a point. Another annoying point.

"Since everyone's up, we might as well get this rolling," Cade said. He appeared in the doorway behind Kori, rubbing his eyes and yawning. "G, we're trying to formulate a plan of action to take down Dylan and get Ava back."

"Sera," Ash supplied when G's brow lifted in confusion. "Sorry. This must be really disorienting for you."

He shrugged, but said nothing, taking a spot on the other end of the couch, as far away from me as possible. Perfect. He might not be our Dylan, but like I'd told him, simply walking around with that face was a dangerous thing to do.

"Ideas?" Cade said.

"Not like we can try bargaining with him. He's got what he wants now. There's nothing to trade. No way to draw him out."

"What about telling him there's something wrong with the chip?" Ash suggested. "I mean, it's technically *not* working right now."

Kori came around to the front of the couch and shook her head. "He'd never buy it. Not unless Rabbit himself was there to confirm it, and since he's dead…"

"*Ash's* Rabbit is dead," I said.

"But maybe the one on this earth is still around." Cade grinned. Great minds and all. "We'd have to hustle. There's not a lot of time and he might not even be here."

"He's here." Rabbit was the one thing we'd found on *every* single earth. "All we have to do is find him and ask. He's always down for *shenanigans*."

"Unless he's like Ash's Rabbit."

"Yeah. Let's hope he's more like ours…" I went to the phone and dialed the front desk. "Yeah, hi. This is suite three forty-two. I was wondering if you could look up a name and address for me. An old friend I'd like to visit with while staying in town. Yes. His name is Phillip MaKaden."

"Hold please," the receptionist said. There was a soft beep as she placed me on hold. When she returned, she gave me the information and said, "Will there be anything else for this evening?"

"Yeah. Could you possibly call me a cab or something? I think I'll drop in on him now."

"A cab, sir?"

Huh. Maybe they weren't called that here. "Or, like any

kind of car service? A ride?"

"I'm sorry I'm unable to do that at this time. It's after nine p.m. The lockdown has already been initiated. I will have a car waiting at sunrise, though."

"Oh. Okay, yeah. Thanks. I hung up and turned back to find everyone staring. I stood and went to the door to find that it wouldn't open. "So apparently we're locked in.""

Chapter Twenty-Eight

Ash

"Locked in?" Kori jumped from the couch and pushed Noah out of the way to try the door herself. She had the same result he had. "Why the hell would they lock us in?" She glared at him. "You just had to steal someone's wallet, didn't you?"

"The whole place is locked down from what the clerk said. I guess it's a thing, here." He winked at her. "I promise the po-pos aren't coming to drag you away. I'm not adding to your budding criminal record."

"Criminal record?" I found it hard to believe Kori had a criminal record. Noah on the other hand…

"Oh yeah," he said with a snicker. "She'd a hardened criminal."

"*I* got in trouble with the police once. For vandalism." She jabbed a finger in Noah's direction. "All the other times were his fault."

"You got her arrested?" That *was* something I could believe. I wished I could have seen him in his element.

"Only a few times." He was fighting a grin.

"*A few times*?" Kori shrieked. "Try eleven. He's gotten me arrested *eleven* times."

"Minor infractions." He waved his hand and rolled his eyes. There was a definite gleam of mischief there. "Chump stuff. Though the kangaroo thing was funny as hell."

Cade snickered and Kori glared at him. He cleared his throat and quickly looked away, but I could tell he was still laughing.

"Kangaroo thing?"

Noah didn't try to hide his grin, which was something he should definitely do more often. The guy had the most amazing smile. "I might have convinced her to break a kangaroo out of a zoo."

I glanced at Kori, who had turned a pretty awesome shade of red. "What could he possibly have said to convince you to steal a kangaroo?"

"Technically I was liberating the kangaroo, not stealing." She narrowed her eyes at her brother. "As for what he said—"

"I'd just come back from a walk and Kori was still up. We'd just gotten to that world so everything was pretty much an unknown. I might have convinced her that I found our mother and that she needed our help."

"…By freeing a kangaroo?"

"He had me convinced Mom *was* the kangaroo," Kori said sheepishly. "He insisted that this world had the ability to change people into animals."

I tried not to laugh. "Still….that's a huge pill to swallow."

"It is," she agreed. "What he's not telling you is that I was still drunk from the previous world and new to skipping. I had no idea what was out there—and what wasn't."

Noah slapped his leg and let out a shrill whistle. "Party

world! Oh my God that place was fucking awesome."

"In my defense, I had no idea what I was drinking. What's next?" She poked him in the chest. "Are you going to have me kidnap a buffalo?" Kori was trying to maintain her anger, but with each exchange, it melted away.

"I was actually thinking of bringing you back to monkey world."

Kori's eyes widened. "You wouldn't dare…"

"Monkey world?" That sounded horrible! "There's a *monkey world*?"

"We landed on a world where they viewed monkeys as sacred. The damn things were everywhere," Cade said. His grin was as big as Noah's.

"One jumped down from a tree and crapped on Kori's shoulder." Noah snorted.

"Yep." Cade tugged a piece of his hair. "Then it tried to pull her hair out."

"I slapped it away—which was apparently equal to going on a murder spree with a chainsaw—then called it some choice words as it ran away."

Noah was laughing now. Grunting and doubled over. "She—listening to her curse at that stupid animal—it—it was—"

He couldn't finish, and Cade was laughing just as hard, so he couldn't add anything to it. Kori was trying to look annoyed at the both of them, but she couldn't hide her grin. I almost felt like I was intruding. They had an amazing dynamic and it was impossible not to feel the synergy. It was exactly the thing I'd always longed for…so why was I choosing to walk away?

Home. Family. Taking back the things Cora stole from me.

"Okay," Cade said, getting himself under control. "Since we're stuck here until morning, let's crash. We have a plan."

Everyone mumbled and scattered. Kori and Cade headed back toward the one room, while G stayed where he was, but closed his eyes. "I'm gonna…"

"Yeah." Noah sank back onto his end of the couch, eyeing G suspiciously. "See ya in the morning."

*D*espite the situation, morning rolled around far too soon. The bed was unbelievably comfortable, and the sheets smelled like lavender. When Kori had knocked on the door, the last thing I'd wanted was to pick my head off the pillow, much less jump into the back of a smelly cab.

The ride to Phil's house had taken close to half an hour, and when the car pulled up in front of the place, Noah paid with the last of his stolen money. "This looks more like Rabbit," he said as we made our way up the concrete walkway.

Weeds grew through the cracks and in the spaces where there were chunks missing—which were a lot. The house itself wasn't much better. In shambles and peeling, the siding was a sickly off-white color with tiny dots of black scattered at random. I couldn't tell if it was mold or bugs.

Cade wedged himself between Noah and the door. "Do we need to go over this again?"

He rolled his eyes and reached around his friend to bang on the door. Three echoing slams and a grin like I'd never seen before.

A few moments later, the door creaked and a bleary-eyed Phil appeared. "Eh?" He had half a Twizzler hanging from his mouth and a beer in his left hand.

"You read my mind." Noah threw open the screen door and pushed past him, grabbing the Twizzler from his mouth as he passed. "I'm starving, man."

Phil grumbled something, then shuffled after him as Cade followed with a look of pure horror.

"What the hell are you doing back here?" Phil jabbed his beer in my direction. "And why the hell are you here? Didn't you swear to never come within ten thousand feet of him again?"

"I—"

"And stop eating my food. Every damn time…" He stalked over to where Noah was leaning against the wall and snatched the Twizzler back. He obviously knew this world's Noah and me, but judging by the less than friendly welcome, it didn't seem like he was a fan. "Babe, get up here. The disaster is back. You deal with it."

"Babe?" Noah waggled his brows, not the least bit offended. "Do you have a *girlfriend*?"

Phil stared at him like he had three heads, then shoved him out of the way. "You down there?"

"Dude!" Noah tried to poke his head around the corner to get a glimpse of Phil's girlfriend. "Her turn to *deal*? Are you dating my sister?"

Phil's stare grew even more confused. "Hurry, please. I think he's on drugs again."

A moment later, the stairs creaked and a woman wearing a crinkled white button-down shirt—and nothing else— poked her head out from around the corner. She had wild blond hair and dark, streaked makeup.

"Oh my God…" Cade made a sound almost like he was

choking, then doubled over in a fit of hysterical laugher.

Noah didn't find it as funny. His skin had paled and I thought he might be trying to speak, but no sound came. The woman let out a squeal when she saw him and ran to throw her arms around his. "My baby!"

I didn't find it funny, either. Every muscle in my body stiffened as I took a long step back. I held my breath, waiting for the explosion even though this was not the woman I'd known most of my life.

Noah's entire body went rigid. "Hands! You all see my hands, right? Not moving. Not moving an inch."

This world's version of Cora Anderson let go of him and laughed. "Always a joker."

"I don't think he's joking," Phil said. He came and rested an arm around her waist. "He thought I might be dating his *sister*."

Cora laughed even harder. "Sister? Oh hun. One of you was more than enough for me."

"I don't get it." Kori stepped forward. She actually looked like she might throw up. "What about Da—Karl? Is he—"

"I haven't spoken to Karl since just after I met my little bunny here." She mussed Phil's hair and hitched her thumb toward the kitchen. "You hungry? I'm done in the lab for now. I could make—"

"Little bunny?" Wow. Now *I* was going to be sick. Both Kori and Noah had insisted their mother was a saint in other worlds, but my bad memories kept me on guard.

"Listen, this is entertaining in a way that you guys will *never* understand, but we have an issue and a tight schedule." Cade shot Noah an amused grin. "We need to talk to you about something important. We need your help."

"Money! He needs money," Phil said. He threw up his

hands and snorted. "What else is new?"

"Dude. This whole thing is beginning to freak me the fuck out." Noah, still pale, was looking everywhere but at Cora. "And could you please put some clothes on, *Mom*?"

She huffed, but ran into the other room. When she came back, she had on a pair of super tight, low rise jeans. "Better?"

"Rabbit—" Cade cringed. "Assuming you go by Rabbit here?"

"Who are you, again?"

"My name is Cade. The other two are Kori and G— but that's not important." He pointed to Noah. "What's important is who he is. Or, who he's not."

Phil didn't say anything, but he and Cora exchanged a look and were suddenly serious.

"We're not from around here," Kori said.

A few moments passed. Neither Cora nor Phil said a word.

"Have you ever heard of the Infinity Division?"

More blank stares.

"Lab," Noah tried. "You mentioned a lab?"

Cora narrowed her eyes. "Hun, you know all about my lab."

"No, he knows about our Mom's lab," Kori said. "Because where we're from, her set up is, um, a lot...bigger."

Another moment passed in silence before Cora let out an earsplitting shriek. "Rabbit! They're from another earth!"

Phil, not nearly as impressed as Cora seemed to be, rolled his eyes. "I got that a few sentences ago, babe."

Cade glanced down at his phone. "The long and short of it is, yes, we're from another dimension, and like I said, we need your help. The Rabbit from our last world was helping us with something. There was an accident and now he's no longer able to help. We were hoping—"

I understood the need for delicacy in certain situations, but Cade was crawling around the bush and we didn't have time. I knew they were sure Dylan wouldn't hurt Sera, but I wasn't. Someone as unhinged as him had no self-control. The first time she denied him something he felt she owed... well...I didn't want to think about it. "We need you to pretend to be the Phil from my world so we can stop the bad guy and save the girl."

Chapter Twenty-Nine

Noah

"Oh my God, you're just as bad as him." Cade groaned and Kori snickered.

Ash didn't look apologetic. In fact, she was kind of smirking and I found it hot as all hell. "There's a girl, her name is...*Ava*. Someone really bad took her."

"And that involves me how?" This version of Phil wasn't as much like mine as I'd hoped. He'd answered the door in a grungy, stained yellowing wife beater and a pair of jeans that barely stayed put. His hair was dirty and disheveled. Oh, and he was doing my *mother*. How the hell that had happened, I didn't even want to know.

"You're Rabbit. A stickier, less eloquent Rabbit, but still him." I looked from him to Cora. I pointed to Kori. "Where I come from, you had two kids. Me and Kori. Dylan, this guy we're tracking, killed Kori. We're—"

"But she's standing right there." Cora's eyes were wide. "Wow. Did we invent a way to raise the dead, too?" She nudged Rabbit. "How amazing would that be, bunny? We need to work harder."

No wonder Infinity didn't exist here…

"I'm from another world," Kori said. "They saved me from this guy, but now another girl needs saving. Dylan has her here and we have a limited window to get her back."

"If you could just pose as the other Rabbit and tell Dylan there's something wrong with his chip—"

"Chip?"

"That's how we skip from one place to another," Cade answered. He had more patience than I did. "Tell him his chip isn't programmed right or something, get him to agree to meet us and we'll take it from there."

"Why do you need me to do it?" Rabbit eyed me suspiciously. "You know him—you tell him."

"We're the ones chasing him," I said, resisting the urge to smack him across the back of the head. "I doubt he'd agree to a sit down."

"Please," Ash chimed in when he didn't respond. "This guy is dangerous, and the girl, Ava? She's already been through enough."

Rabbit thought about it for a minute, then nodded. "I'll help you—but in exchange, you have to give us something that helps with the cuffs. A tip—anything."

"Deal," Cade said. "Don't try using cuffs."

"Why?" Cora asked. "My prototypes are amazing. We made them pink with blue shimmer!"

"You—I—" It took me a minute to recover. Yep. This world would be better off without an Infinity. The universe didn't need the people here traveling to other worlds. "The core overheats. It'll take years to figure out and cost lives. Look into manufacturing a chip." I held up my arm and undid the dressing. It was sore but the wound itself wasn't that bad. It would heal in no time. I tapped the skin just below my wrist twice to wake the thing up.

Nothing happened.

"Uh…" I tapped my forearm again, this time harder. We couldn't skip yet, but the chip should still be active.

"What's supposed to happen?" Cora asked. She craned her neck, curious, while Rabbit stood there irritated.

"The chip must have gotten damaged when the dog bit me." Fucking fantastic. Now what the hell was I supposed to do?

Cade rolled up his own sleeve and woke his chip, showing the control panel on his skin to Rabbit, who looked ready to pass out.

Cora squealed. "That's so much prettier than the pink!"

"Noah, we'll figure it out." Cade must have noticed the look of horror on my face. "Until we do, you just have to stay with someone. Right now, we're running out of time."

Rabbit stared at his arm like he was seeing God. There might have even been drooling. "Okay," he said. "Tell me what I have to do."

It wasn't easy to find Rabbit the things he needed to become Phil at his place. The closest we came before sending Cora out for supplies was one shoe that might have been black at one time—before the mildew set in—and a pair of tan pants that said *stud* across the ass.

This world had some fashion issues…

While she was gone, Cade coached Rabbit on what to say and how to act, and I called Dylan. Since he didn't know about the four skips per twenty-four-hour-rule, getting him

to agree to meet was easy. As we figured, he'd already tried—
and failed—to skip off this world multiple times.

"You can do this, right?" I stood on one side of Rabbit
while Cade took the other. Ash waited off to my left. We'd
tried to get G and Kori to wait with Cora at the house, but
they'd both refused. Kori because, well, she was *Kori*, and
G because nothing was going to keep him from Ava. Sera.
What-the-hell-ever she felt like calling herself. They were
waiting in the woods that bordered Clifton Park.

"How hard could it be to act like a nerd?"

"And you understand that the guy we're meeting looks
just like G?" Cade had covered everything from Phil's
mannerisms—the way he'd tap his pointer when he was
being impatient—to a well thought out script on what to
say about the chip. We'd even dotted his shirt with red food
coloring to simulate the wound Dylan had given the other
version and told him to act injured.

All in all, I felt like we had this locked down. There was
no contingency in place this time to keep us in line. No
innocent person to worry about since we all knew he'd never
hurt Ava. This was it. This was the day we took him down.

"Got it."

Except that Dylan was late. Almost an hour had passed
and just when we were sure he wasn't coming, he ran up
the path, Ava in tow, flying like a demon straight at Rabbit.

"What the hell did you do to my chip?"

Cade stepped between them, bracing a hand against his
brother's chest. "Cool down, man. Being an asshole will get
you nowhere."

For a second I thought Dylan would take a swing at him.
I hoped. That would give me an excuse, not that I should
have needed one. But Cade made me swear to keep this as

civil as we could. He didn't want things turning ugly and someone getting hurt in the commotion. We'd seen it happen too many times.

"I programmed in a failsafe," Rabbit said. He winced and gingerly touched his side. Oh yeah. He was good. "Since you tried to kill me, I'm not exactly sorry."

"I'd apologize, but, yanno, I never really liked you. Any of you." He pulled out a narrow metal tube-like thing and pointed it at Rabbit. "Fix it. Now."

"Are you *insane*?" I had no idea what the thing was, but Rabbit was freaked. He jumped back and stumbled, tripping over his own two feet and landing on his ass in the mud.

Dylan's eyes narrowed. His gaze flickered from Rabbit to the metal thing, then settled on me with unadulterated fury. "Almost had me, boys. But judging by how skittish he is, he knows exactly what this is and that means he's this world's Rabbit—not the one who messed with the chip."

Rabbit picked himself off the ground, eyes wide. Whatever it was, he was terrified of it. "How did you get that? Did you—"

"I looked up an old *friend*." He grinned. "Did you know you can get anything you ask for on this world? Drugs, food—information? Come on out and say hello," he shouted.

A moment later, this world's version of my mother walked through the trees. She moved slowly and looked just as terrified as Rabbit did. As she got closer, I saw why. Whatever the thing Dylan had in his hands, there was another nestled in the ties around her hands.

"What are those things?" Obviously it was some kind of weapon, but the more we knew, the better we could deal.

"Cora's first attempt at interdimensional travel," Rabbit said.

"Okay…" That didn't exactly sound world ending.

"It was a failure. Instead of shifting frequencies, it disrupts particles."

"Huh?" Cade said.

"Basically that thing will scatter us into a trillion pieces," I supplied, glaring at Rabbit. "Why the hell would you keep something like that in your basement?"

"I've made it a habit never to deal with you idiots without a backup plan—no matter what. Time was short so I decided to look up Mommy Dearest." Dylan leaned closer and winked. "Gotta say, not the brightest bulb in the box, this one. Invited me in and just started babbling about all the toys she had in her lab!"

Rabbit looked sick. "It's okay, Cora. He—"

"My chip," Dylan snapped. "What the hell did Phil do to it?"

"We don't know," Cade lied. "We couldn't skip out, either."

"Don't bullshit me," Dylan warned. He grabbed Ava's arm and dragged her closer. "I want out of here. Now."

"Then maybe you and I could work something out," a new voice called.

"You've got to be kidding me…" Ash came up beside me. She was tense and her expression was one of pure irritation, but I could feel the shudder that ran through her.

Crossing the field was her world's version of Cora. Dressed in a white floor-length coat and flanked by three men in black on each side, she strode toward us, eyes locked on Dylan.

"Mr. Granger," she said with a sickly sweet smile. "It's nice to meet you."

"Technically you've already met me," he said with a snarl.

He pulled Ava closer. "You had a version of me locked away in your basement."

"I did," she admitted with a laugh. "But I promise he was a pale shadow of yourself. I can see that already."

"What do you want?"

"The chip you have in your arm, I created it. You don't need Phil MaKaden to fix it. You only need me."

"In exchange for?"

She waved a hand in Rabbit's direction and groaned. "First off, get rid of *that*. I feel like it's leering at me."

There was no hesitation. No thought. Dylan simply shrugged and pointed the metal tube at Rabbit. He jabbed it out, poking him in the chest, and pressed the thin red button at the bottom. There was no sound. No screaming or pleas for mercy. One minute Rabbit was standing there, the next his body exploded into a trillion tiny pieces, scattered in every direction.

His Cora let out a horrible wail and threw herself forward, but she tripped. The second she hit the ground, her body exploded just like Rabbit's.

Cora shrugged, her lips twisting into a wicked grin. "Better. The reason your chip isn't working is because Phil designed it with an overheat failsafe. It can only be used four times within a twenty-four-hour period."

Dylan's lips split with a grin. "Really? Well, if that's the case, then we'll just be on our way. Time should be up by now."

"Now, you may keep the chip, but I want the rest of my property back."

He shrugged. "I couldn't care less what you take. Take all of them with it for all I care."

He thought she was talking about something material.

A piece of tech or information. The truth was, I knew she was talking about Ash. If Ash was her way to get Omega off the ground, she wasn't going to let go without a fight.

Which is exactly what she'd get.

"Like hell." I moved to stand between Ash and Cora, ready to shred anyone who came at us. She thought it'd be that easy? She was in for one hell of a surprise. I spread my legs and readied myself. Cade was beside me in an instant, and from the tree line, Kori and Granger were already bolting forward.

Cora sighed. She waved her hand in the air and said, "Get this over with. I have better things to do.

A second later, the six men were moving forward.

Chapter Thirty

Ash

I backed away as Cora's security started forward. I would die. I would die before letting her drag me back there. They came forward, then split, two coming toward me and two heading toward Ava.

"Whoa." Dylan held up the weapon. "What the hell do you think you're doing?"

Cora sighed. "Taking back my property as per our agreement. Have you forgotten already?"

"Wrong girl." He jabbed the metal thing in my direction and I couldn't help cringing. I'd seen what it'd done to Phil and Cora. My stomach turned over just thinking about it. Now he was waving it around like it was a piece of candy? "If you want anyone, it's *her*."

"They both belong to me. Property of the Infinity Division." She hitched her thumb toward G. "As does he."

G and Kori had joined us. He'd taken his place beside Cade and looked completely rabid while she looked fierce and ready to die defending us. "You're never going to touch her again."

"Look at you." Cora laughed again, but unless I was crazy, there was the smallest hint of fear in her eyes. "The feral dog is foaming at the mouth for his little bitch. I must say, grabbing a copy of the two of you was a test in and of itself. I was curious to see what happened. This little scenario—you six—it never ends well."

He twitched like he was going to lunge for her throat, but Cade grabbed his arm to keep him still.

She pointed to Cade and Kori and snickered. "You two are always in a state of flux. I've seen it a hundred times. Never together, yet never apart. And you two—" She jabbed a blood red tipped finger at Dylan and Ava. "You two are just tragic in every way imaginable." When she turned to me, her grin was truly wicked. Filled with satisfaction and greed. "And you, dear Ash? Do you really think you can skip out of here with him and have a *good* life?"

My fingers flexed, tightening into fists. "I think any life away from you will be a good life."

"I've seen you with him. You destroy each other. Every single time. You're like a tornado and he's like a volcano. You're two forces of a destructive nature that always— without fail—wipe each other out in the end." She snorted. Such an un-Cora like thing to do. "If I didn't need you I would let you go. That alone would be punishment enough." Turning, she jabbed a finger at the group. "Now give me my property and I will leave the rest of you in peace."

"She doesn't belong to you," Dylan said with a growl. He dragged Ava behind him. "She belongs to me."

"I don't belong to either of you," Ava screamed. She jerked her arm from Dylan's grip and took a single step away from the whole group.

Cora laughed. She laughed like it was the funniest thing

she'd ever seen. "Running wouldn't do you any good, Ava." She tapped the side of her head twice, then winked. "You have a chip in your head. One that helps the serum work. Without me—without Infinity—you'll die."

Dylan tensed. He stole a glance over his shoulder at Sera, whose face was pale. "You're lying."

I watched as her face contorted, going from horrified to fearful, then landing on anger. Rage I could relate to. She let out a horrible wail then launched herself at Cora. Cora's security responded immediately. One of the guards closest sprang to her side and latched on, while the other kicked out, knocking the weapon from Dylan's hands. Ava had no intention of going quietly. She let out another howl and began to thrash. The action was like a match to tinder and sent everyone surging into the fray.

Cora stepped away to watch from the sidelines as Dylan and G each went for the one trying to restrain Sera. It was surreal to watch. Two versions of the same person, one twisted and sick, and the other, well, the jury was still out on G. Cora had messed him up, but we really didn't know the extent of it.

Cade launched himself at one of the men making his way toward me, swinging hard right out of the gate. I'd watched both him and Noah fight and they were amazing. Cade graceful and refined, every blow he struck was taken in honor. I couldn't imagine him throwing a dirty punch. Noah on the other hand, he played to win. Nothing was out of bounds. No blow too dirty. He was a street fighter, feral and raw.

I caught sight of him, facing off against the fourth of Cora's elite. They were well trained. The best of her best, known for hand-to-hand combat rather than weaponry.

I watched as the guard grabbed a handful of Noah's jacket, hauling back as hard as he could. He teetered, and while he was off balance, the guard went for a chunk of hair that had slipped free from the rubber band, making for an easy target. Or, it would have if he hadn't been faster.

Noah grabbed his wrist as he came, jerking forward enough to reach just below his elbow with his other hand. Like slinging a garbage bag over your shoulder, I couldn't help thinking. He then pivoted and gave a good, hard twist. The guard howled in pain and Noah followed the move, pulling him close as he brought his right knee up hard. It was poetry to watch—so much so that I didn't see the newcomer stalk up behind me.

"I told Cora to lock you up years ago to prevent exactly this," a voice said as a steel grip encased me, locking both arms at my sides. That voice. I knew that voice. Yancy, the leader of Cora's guards. "Since you were kind enough to simply stand here waiting..."

Oh my God he was right. What an idiot.

I couldn't fight like Cade or Noah, or even like Kori. That girl was pretty damn badass and I was jealous. Dylan could hold his own, and G...he was a monster in his own right, tearing through the guards with fury. Yancy was unstoppable. I'd seen him in action just once. Brutal and seemingly without any speck of human compassion. He would take me in no matter what he had to do. But I had no intention of making this easy.

I threw my head back as hard as I could. It smashed into his face, his nose specifically, I thought, and he cursed. But, his grip didn't loosen. Taking a deep breath, I leaned into him and lifted my feet from the ground. He wobbled, slightly off balance, but still he didn't let go. But help was on the way. It was charging across the field like a prizefighting bull.

Noah launched himself at Yancy, the sheer force behind the tackle taking them both to the ground. I went with them and managed to scoot away as the guy took a swing at his head. The blow landed—he was too busy making sure I'd gotten to a safe place—and his eyes kind of rolled back. Unfortunately, before he could get his bearings and retaliate, Yancy repositioned and locked his arms around Noah's neck. He clawed and dug, fingers gouging at the arm restraining him, but it was no use. This man had the mother of all grips and I knew he wouldn't stop until Noah was dead.

I had to do something.

I stumbled inelegantly to my feet and kicked out as hard as I could. I was aiming for the general area close to his head, so if you considered the intent, I basically scored a home run. The corner of my shoe connected and Yancy let go—which, despite the action, surprised me. Noah gasped and coughed.

"Hurry!" I got behind and helped him off the ground. Sera had joined me. She was limping and had a split lip, but was otherwise in one piece.

Noah recovered and motioned for us to follow, then started for the trees. "We know why Cora wants Ash—what about you and G?"

Sera's face paled. "They did things to us."

"*Things* is a little vague," he snapped.

"Noah!" I tugged her into the trees and around a large pine. God only knew what Cora had put them through, and now she and G were in the middle of some twisted game of tug of war? Sera had to be close to losing it. I knew I was. "Be less of an asshole, okay?"

"It would help to know why Cora is obsessed," he

shouted. "If we know what she wants, then we know how far she'll go to get—"

Sera screamed a half second before another blur, this one dark blue, flew by. It crashed into Noah and took them both to the ground.

"Why?" Dylan roared as his fist slammed into Noah's gut. "Why the hell do you insist on trying to keep us apart?"

Noah wasn't a pushover. He fired back with everything he had. "I'm trying to—" Noah assaulted Dylan's shoulder and mid-section in a lightning fast one-two jab "—reunite you two right now. Hold still—" his next blow landed at the jaw line "—while I kill you!"

Dylan rocked back but didn't go down. "Maybe I'll change my MO," he huffed. His next swing caught Noah in the stomach. When he doubled over, Dylan brought his knee up and smashed it into his forehead. "Maybe I'll go after Ash from now on, too."

Noah let out an enraged howl and flew at him like a demon. Shoulder in Dylan's stomach, his feet left the ground from the force of impact and sent him sprawling backward. Noah followed him down and started swinging without mercy. "Go." It came out more like a grunt than a word.

"Go?" I glanced around. "Where am I—"

"He can't follow you. GO! I *will* find you."

He can't follow you.

Oh my God.

Now I understood. Skip.

He wanted me to take Sera and skip out.

Chapter Thirty-One

Noah

I didn't see her go. I was a little preoccupied with mincing Dylan's head into pudding. But when he finally stilled and I looked up, she and Ava were gone. Someplace safe, I hoped. The fight was winding down. Cade had gotten hold of the weapon and had used it to take out the guard who'd grabbed Kori, and G was repeatedly kicking another. Cora and the big guy who'd tried to take Ash, the one from Brewster's place—Yancy—were notably missing.

Kori came jogging up and held out her hand. "You okay?"

I let her help me up, then tried to swipe some of the mud from my jeans. "Banged up but breathing. You?"

She grinned. "Pretty much the same. Everyone seems to be in one piece." She glanced down at Dylan, unconscious at my feet. "Except him."

I couldn't help myself. I kicked him. "He's still in one piece. It's a messy piece, but it's *one* piece. For now." He was out cold, but I didn't trust it. We'd come too far to leave anything to chance. Dropping to the ground, I untied my left boot and pulled the lace from the eyelets. Wrapping the thick black string around Dylan's wrists, I knotted it so tightly that his skin turned white.

Her grin widened—then faded all together. She turned in a slow circle. "Wait a sec. Ash? Ava? Where are—"

"I had Ash skip Ava out. Just in case Dylan got in a lucky throw."

Cade came up behind and wrapped his arms around her shoulder. "Good thinking. Rabbit didn't program our frequencies into his chip. We can follow him but he can't get to us. She's completely safe now."

"Cora is gone," G announced, rounding out our new little posse. God. Were we all going to skip together? It was going to get crowded.

No. It wouldn't. Ash wouldn't be skipping with us…

But did it matter? We had Dylan. This was over. We could skip to where Ash had Ava, return to evil Cora's world to deliver the proof Rabbit had stashed away, and then we could…. "Holy shit!"

Cade was instantly alert. "What? What is it?"

"We're done, man. We can go home!" The realization was like lifting a ten-thousand-pound weight off my shoulders. My parents, my home—my future. Everything I thought I'd never get back. We had these damn chips imbedded in our skin. I didn't have to lose Ash. I could see her anytime I wanted. She was only a skip away.

Cade's eyes lit—then darkened. "Wow. Yeah. We did what we said we'd do…"

When I saw Kori's expression, I understood. She'd told her father that she'd return home once we made sure Dylan couldn't hurt anyone anymore. As far as I knew, they hadn't discussed the possibilities of what that might mean for the two of them. They hadn't even really decided what their relationship status was.

But really, they didn't have to, did they? He was in the same boat I was in—and that damn boat floated across dimensions.

"We're not using the cuffs anymore, guys." There was no reason she couldn't go home to her world and him to his. I didn't intend to lose either one of them—or Ash. "We can come and go as we please, remember?"

"Could we hash this crap out later?" G snapped his fingers in my face and I had to bite the inside of my cheek to keep from ripping them off. "You said that girl took Sera somewhere. Let's go."

Kori looked over her shoulder. The field was empty now, the remaining guards presumably having skipped back home. "What about Cora?"

"What about her?" Cade lifted his arm and woke the chip.

Kori sighed and did the same. "Seems like she really wanted them. She gave up? Just like that?"

From what I'd seen of this Cora she wouldn't just give up. An icy sense of dread washed through me. G was still with us, but Ash and Ava had skipped out. Cora and Yancy were gone. Here we were celebrating our future when Ash might be in danger.

"This is your call, man," Cade said. "We can detour and take Dylan home and lock his ass up, then go look for Ash. Or we can go for Ash first and chance losing him."

I knew what he would do. Despite wanting—needing— to go home, he would go after them. Regardless of the fact that the end of our mission was within reach, that we could grab Dylan right this very moment and skip him back to our world to pay for his crimes, Cade would go after Ash and Ava first because it was the *right thing* to do. That wasn't me and he knew it—hence the choice. The old me would have put our world—our family—first. He would have skipped home and left the rest of the multiverse to deal with itself. After things were settled, then maybe he would have gone looking for Ash.

If she hadn't been involved, the choice would have been easy. Cut and dry and never thought about again. I would have grabbed Dylan around the throat, locked arms with Kori and Cade, and skipped my ass home where I belonged. Or maybe I wouldn't have. Ash might not have changed me. Like I'd said to her, I was who I was and that was it. But she'd had an effect on me. And that effect included feelings I couldn't walk away from.

"Everybody grab hands." I grabbed Cade's arm, woke his chip and jabbed a finger against Ash's PATH line.

A moment later, the clearing was gone, replaced by a different grassy field that sat close to the edge of a cliff. Aside from the addition to the cliff, the scenery was mostly the same. Some of the foliage was different and there were rocks and bushes in other places. There was one major difference from the last world, though. Two, actually.

Ash—and Cora.

"Don't!" she screamed as the others began to appear. Cora's eyes were wild as she stood beside Yancy who had Ash by the throat. On the ground a few feet from them, Ava lay still. She was alive, though. I could see the steady rise and fall of her chest. "I'll have him toss the little bitch right over the side."

"No one's moving," I said in as even a tone as I could muster. Every impulse in my body was screaming at me to jump forward and rip them apart. But it was too risky. They were too close to the edge. I might manage to knock one of them over — but the action could take Ash right along. She needed Ash alive, but never underestimate the actions of a desperate person.

"Let's work something out, Cora." Cade was beside me, the others on his other side. He let go of Dylan's arm and stepped over his still unconscious form. "Tell us what you want."

She laughed and nodded toward Ava, then pointed to Ash. "I have everything I need at the moment. I'll take them and be on my merry way. I'll even let you go." She glanced at G. "As for him, I can find him any time I want. All my lab rats have trackers. I designed them with a unique frequency — so no matter where they go, I can follow. When I have need of him, I'll simply drop in and take him."

"What the hell makes you think we're going to let *you* go?" G dared to step even closer than Cade and me, fists balled so tight that his entire hand was white.

"Hey." I growled. All it would take was the wrong flinch and Ash could end up over the edge of the cliff. This idiot had tunnel vision and was only concerned about Ava. "Back the fuck up."

But G ignored me. He took another step and Cora smiled. "Testing me, are we, puppy?" She laughed even louder and nodded to Yancy who jerked Ash closer to the edge. "Please be my guest. You're welcome to stay with the other one. Come back willingly and I'll even let you have a cell all to yourselves. If not, do as Cade says and back away. Remember I have *ways* to assure your compliance…"

G let out a growl but didn't come any closer. Whatever methods of coercion Cora had, they must be powerful.

"Just let them go. You have me. You have your damn proof that Omega can work." Ash had been quiet until now. She'd kept her eyes on mine, scared, but brave despite her situation. Now she stared at her foster mother, gaze defiant. "What is so important that you can't just let them go? You've already taken their memories. What more do they have left to give you?"

"The girl is one of a kind. She had anomalous reactions to Brewster's serum, forcing us to take additional measures to make it work. Without me she will die. That makes her my property. As for the boy, let's just say he's going to be a new frontier for Infinity. I own their lives."

We were all so engrossed in her ranting speech, that we never saw Dylan move. He'd come to and managed to crawl to where Ava lay. His chip was awake and he had his bound, bloodied hands resting across her face.

Cora must have seen it the same moment we did. She screamed for Yancy and started forward. In her haste—and probably likely due to the wicked size of her heels—her foot caught. Except instead of falling toward Dylan, she fell sideways. Toward the cliff. Toward Ash and Yancy. The momentum had her teetering, and she hovered for an insanely drawn out moment, before slipping over. Yancy dropped Ash and lunged for Cora.

"No!" I dove for her, but I was too far away. I missed the edge of the cliff—and Ash—by a foot, maybe more.

Luckily G had been closer. He caught her wrist as she slipped over the side. But the ground was muddy and he had no traction. A second after latching on, he was being pulled right along with her.

I scrambled up and grabbed his feet while Cade joined him, leaning over the side to help haul Ash to safety. It took some maneuvering but a few moments later she was on solid ground and in my arms. "You're okay."

"None of you are okay," Cora roared. Yancy had hauled her over the edge and stood beside her with a gun trained on the group.

Cade's gaze flickered to mine and I shook my head slowly. There were five of us, but it wasn't worth the risk. The chances of us all making it without injury — or worse — was slim.

"I might not have all your frequencies logged, but they're both chipped," Cora continued. "The bitch and the feral dog. Even if you managed to get away, there'd be no place I couldn't follow."

"Maybe," I said. "But despite what you might think, you're not the biggest bad out there. My world? We might not be as advanced when it comes to Infinity, but we have you beat a thousand times over in the military department." I didn't know if that was true, but she didn't have to know that. "Like I said when we first met, my father is a general. You wouldn't get within fifty feet of any of us."

She smiled, but it wasn't quite as confidant as it'd been. "Is that where Dylan took my little pet? Back home to Mommy and Daddy?" With a shrug, she came a single step closer. "No. He wouldn't do that, would he? I suppose that means I can find the other one. I don't want to kill Ash. I need her. But if it's a choice between letting her get away and spilling her blood…"

Yancy flipped the safety and trained the gun directly at Ash.

There was no point in fighting it now. I supposed there'd never really been any point fighting it. Ashlyn Calvert was a part of me. Maybe she always had been. Maybe Cade's stupid theory that we're born with holes in our souls, but able to fill them with the right person was true. Maybe we simply had to find that person…

I had no idea what my future would bring. I didn't know if I was in love or not. All I knew, all I was sure of, was that this was *my* Ashlyn Calvert. What that meant was unclear, but it didn't matter because for once in my life I was going to do the unselfish thing. I was going to let her go.

In order to do that, she had to live…

Chapter Thirty-Two

Ash

Up until now I'd been going on the theory that Cora wouldn't kill me. *Couldn't.* She needed me — not that I'd had any intention of helping her.

Unfortunately, things had changed.

I took in the scenery and inhaled deeply. The air here was the freshest thing I'd ever smelled. The grass was lush and bright despite the lateness of the season, and close to the edge of the cliff, several patches of deep purple flowers were in full bloom.

Yancy had his weapon trained on me. His aim wouldn't waver, his shot wouldn't miss. The problem was, Noah and the others, they wouldn't let it go. They'd attack. Trying to save me, trying to avenge me. Either way, the body count would surpass just me and I couldn't have that. It left me with a single choice.

"Fine." I stepped around Noah and squared my shoulders. "I'll go back with you."

Noah let out a horrible roar and was in front of me

immediately. Apparently, he'd forgotten about the gun. "No. You're not going back there."

I didn't want to. Not when I'd finally made it *home*.

As he'd fought Dylan on the previous earth, I'd grabbed Sera and woken my chip. I hadn't really given it much thought at the time. I'd simply pulled up the PATH list and poked. It wasn't until we landed here that I realized I'd taken us to my own personal frequency.

My real home.

I lifted my hand to touch his face, to tell him that this was my choice and he had no say in it, but he never gave me a chance. He whirled on Yancy and launched himself forward.

The group circled Yancy. He was ready, and though they got what looked like some good blows in, he was a machine and dealt with each as they came, scattering them like bowling pins across the field. Even G, who appeared to be the fiercest of the bunch, was no match.

"I've put up with too much from you to lose it all now," Cora said from behind me. "Dead or alive, I am bringing you home."

I turned to face her. This was the woman responsible for making me miserable. This person stole me from my home and family, then raised me as though I was the stain she couldn't wipe away. I'd never been a violent person, but in that moment, looking at her and thinking about all she'd done, the only thing I wanted was to make her bleed. I let out a roar of my own and launched myself at her.

The action surprised her. I saw her eyes go wide and noted how she attempted to scamper out of my path. She was too slow, though. We collided and I took her down, fists tight and swinging before we even hit the grass.

Over and over my blows struck. Tears streaming down my face and making it impossible to see. The only reason I knew I was actually hitting her was the growing numbness in my fingers.

I was vaguely aware of a thundering pop followed by an unearthly wail. There were several moments of silence and then I was being hauled backward. Soaring through the air for a second, weightless, before the oxygen rushed from my lungs and everything swam at warp speed.

It hurt to breathe, but I managed to suck in a lungful and open my eyes. When my vision cleared, Yancy was bent over Cora. I struggled to my feet as Noah rushed over to me. He was covered in blood and bruises, but still standing. Still breathing.

Yancy looked up and our eyes met. He was too far away so I couldn't hear him when he spoke, but I could see his lips moving. The message was clear as the sky. "See you soon." A moment later their forms shimmered and disappeared.

I swallowed and scanned the area to take stock of the damage. On the grass a few yards away, Kori and G were huddled around a form lying still on the ground. I turned back to Noah. I took note of his blood-stained shirt and hands. Saw the anguished expression in his eyes. "No," I said and started forward. "No. Cade—"

Noah grabbed my arm, then jumped ahead of me. "Is going to be fine. The shot went straight through. We'll need to get him to a hospital. I don't have anything to clean and properly dress the wound, but he's okay."

I sighed with relief and let him lead me over to the group. Kori was helping Cade sit up. They'd bound the wound with one of the sleeves from G's flannel.

"Looks like we're not going home after all," Cade said.

He leaned back against Kori and tried to flex his injured arm, wincing. "Dylan's gone."

"And he took Ava," Kori said. She wrapped her arm around his waist and leaned close. "We'll get there, though. Eventually."

"Yeah." He nodded. "Eventually."

"So where do you think we landed?" Noah turned in a slow circle. "Seems nice enough."

"I hope so," I said softly. "This is home. My home."

He stiffened and turned, but refused to meet my gaze. "You skipped back to your PATH line."

"Not on purpose. Not really. I just woke the chip and—"

"No. That's good. Saves us a trip I guess. I know you got back here safe, so, yanno, less shit for me to worry about."

He was right. I was here—but I wasn't technically safe. Cora said Sera and G and I were chipped. She might not have realized this was my home world, but she could find me no matter where I went. If I stayed, would I be putting the people here—my family—at risk? And aside from that, did I want to let Noah go? Could I?

We'd been through a lot together in the short time since we'd met. He had the same face and voice as the Noah I'd grown up with, but he wasn't him. I'd loved the other Noah. I still loved him despite learning the truth. He'd had my back in the end, and really, that's what mattered. The rest would probably always be a dark cloud over our relationship, but it couldn't blot it out.

This Noah, though, the way I felt about him was different. It was fire and ice and pleasure and pain, and even though in the back of my mind I feared what Cora said—that we would destroy each other—I knew I couldn't walk away.

I couldn't let him walk away.

"I'm not staying."

Something like hope flashed in his eyes and he lifted his gaze to meet mine. "Not staying?"

"Don't get cocky." I tried to fix him with an annoyed stare, but I was pretty sure I failed at epic levels. "Cora can come back and nab me any time. I'm safer on the move. Besides, I feel responsible for Sera. I need to make sure she's okay."

"Responsible—"

I clamped my hand across his mouth. He didn't know the whole story. The things Cora had divulged. I would tell him, I would fill them all in, but there was something I needed to do first.

"I'm going back there, to Cora's world."

He grabbed my hand and pried it loose, the hope in his eyes fanning into anger. "You can't possibly—"

"My God." I slapped my hand down again and shook my head. "Shut up for five seconds, will you? I'm going back there to make sure the information Phil gave us gets to the right people. It probably won't stop her from chasing us, but it will kill Omega. After that, I'm going with you—if you'll take me."

He was still for a few minutes before gently peeling my hand away. "If we'll—" His arms encircled my waist and he hefted me into the air, spinning us around several times. "I considered taking you whether you wanted to come along or not." He laughed. "I'm not willing to let go, Ash. Not anymore."

I rose onto my toes and kissed him. Nothing too steamy. We had an audience, after all. But it held the promise of tomorrow. Of many tomorrows.

"What will he do? To Sera?" G had been quiet, watching the exchange with a mildly irritated expression. I felt bad for the guy. It wasn't really his fault he'd been born a Dylan. He had some issues, that much was clear, but at least he seemed stable.

Or, more stable than Noah's Dylan.

"We'll find her," I said. I meant it. It'd been Cade and Noah in the beginning. They'd left behind their home and everything they knew. They'd had to deal with this alone. Then they found Kori. Now they had me and G. Surreal when you stopped to consider that we were a group again. Different versions of an original family that had once stood strong. A family that not all of us knew, but one we'd surely all come to depend on.

For the first time in a long time, I had hope. Hope for a future. Hope for love. Hope to belong…

"Do you want to see them first?" Noah set me down, but didn't let go. "Before we go, do you want to look in on them?"

Did I? More than anything. But it was a bad idea. If I saw them, came face-to-face, would I be able to leave again? Or would I beg Noah to stay here with me so I could get to know them. Get to know *him*.

"Not now. I'll be back," I said, resolved. I tapped my forearm and woke the chip, then went to take Noah's hand. He, in turn, took Cade's, who was still threaded with Kori's. She rounded it out by grabbing G. Then, as a team, I scrolled down to Dylan's PATH line and skipped us to our next location.

Acknowledgments

As always, the biggest thank-you to my husband. You make me laugh *and* smile, and I would be lost without you. And, of course, my parents, who would support me no matter what (though I'm fairly certain they're happy I decided on writing rather than goat herding as my five-year-old self declared that one time).

Thanks to my first readers and sounding boards on this one, Gia Mallory, Sue Jens, and Baker Hartford—who I owe two pounds of M&Ms after that four a.m. plot hole freak-out.

Big hugs to Nicole Resciniti—my agent, my cheerleader, and my friend. Thank you for believing in me even when I don't believe in myself. ❤

A huge thanks to Stacy Abrams, Candace Havens, and Greta Gunselman, for the amazing insight and edits, and L.J. Anderson and Toni Kerr who made this book look so pretty. To everyone in the Entangled family who helped get this baby off the ground—Liz Pelletier, Melissa Montovani, Christine Chhun, and all the people working hard behind the scenes so I could share Noah and Ash's story with the world—thank you! I say this every time—it takes a village to bring a book to life and I'm grateful for each and every one of you.

My unending gratitude goes out to anyone who has ever picked up one of my books. You make it possible to do what I do—the thing I love—and for that, I have no words.

Grab the Entangled Teen releases readers are talking about!

Project Pandora
by Aden Polydoros

Olympus is rising…

Tyler hasn't been feeling like himself lately, his dreams are full of violence and death, and there are days when he can't remember where he's been.

Miles away, Shannon finds herself haunted by similar nightmares. She is afraid that she has done something terrible.

As the daughter of a state senator, Elizabeth has everything she could ever hope for. But when an uninvited guest interrupts a fundraising gala and stirs up painful memories, everything goes downhill fast.

Murder is what Hades is good at. So when two of his comrades go AWOL, he is rewarded with the most exhilarating hunt of his lifetime. For him, the game has just begun.

27 Hours
by Tristina Wright

Rumor Mora fears two things: hellhounds too strong for him to kill, and failure. Jude Welton has two dreams: for humans to stop killing monsters, and for his strange abilities to vanish.

But in no reality should a boy raised to love monsters fall for a boy raised to kill them.

During one twenty-seven-hour night, if they can't stop the war between the colonies and the monsters from becoming a war of extinction, the things they wish for will never come true, and the things they fear will be all that's left.